"I feel like there's something big we don't know about. Something those students were protecting. I mean, really, why are we here?"

I thought it was just me who was confused. "Well…the recruiters said we're creative and focused."

"Yeah, that's what Principal Locke said too."

"And we have the right personality."

Ben looked up at the sky, sighed, then turned toward the forest. "What did he say…something about how it will soon become clear why we're here, and there's some ultimate purpose for our creativity?"

"I know. That whole creativity part was a bit bizarre."

He shrugged. "It seems everyone is going with the flow. But I have so many questions." Then he touched my arm to stop me, so I turned toward him. "I'm thinking they're isolating us for some special reason," he admitted in an embarrassed tone.

I tried not to laugh—he was acting paranoid. But I didn't know Ben well. Maybe he was joking, trying to freak me out. Or was he hitting on me? The flutter in my chest moved to my stomach. I was already anxious about being away from home and whether or not I could hack the academics. I didn't need to obsess about anything else. But I still had to know about Ben's dream.

"So…I also had a dream about Dickensen before I accepted the offer."

Ben's head snapped toward me. "You did?"

Dickensen Academy

by

Christine Grabowski

Dickensen Academy

Cover Art by *Kristian Norris*

The Wild Rose Press, Inc.
PO Box 708
Adams Basin, NY 14410-0708
Visit us at www.thewildrosepress.com

Publishing History
First Mainstream Fantasy Rose Edition, 2018
Print ISBN 978-1-5092-2123-3
Digital ISBN 978-1-5092-2124-0

Published in the United States of America

Dedication

For my family and friends who believed in me from the beginning, especially Rich, Anna, Calvin, Stephanie, Gary, and Laurie

Acknowledgements

This book would never be in your hands (or on your electronic device) if not for so many people who helped me bring this story into the world, many more than I can name on this page.

~*~

My husband, Rich, believed I could write a novel before I typed a single word. My daughter, Anna, was my first reader and fan. My son, Calvin, kept my spirits high and like the rest of my family never complained about my long hours on the laptop. My sister, Stephanie, saw the manuscript's potential. My parents, Gary and Laurie, were my biggest cheerleaders. My sister-in-law, Luz, made the Dominican chapter possible. And our Welsh terrier, Rylie, was my constant companion through it all.

~*~

So many friends read the manuscript and offered needed encouragement, especially Allison, Chuck, Eileen, Evelyn, Georgia, Jacob, Karla, Kelly, Lisa, Lori, Mackenzie, Marie, Marlo, Matthew, McKenzie, Michele, Mike, Rose, Sangeet, Sharon, and Shelley. The members of my long-standing book clubs pushed me to read a wider variety of books.

~*~

My writing community taught me so much about the industry and the craft of writing, particularly Kidcrit members (Adrian, Andrew, Anitha, Ariel, Chrissy, Don, Helen, Ian, Kaye, Mar, Marsha, and Steve), the Ampersands (Claire, Judy, and Sonja), Blessy, Joan, Katherine, Kathleen, Laura, Maureen, and Michelle.

~*~

Finally, thank you to everyone at The Wild Rose Press, especially my editor, Josette Arthur, for falling in love with *Dickensen Academy* and making my dream of getting published a reality.

Chapter: 1

Clues to the secret existed from day one, yet they appeared to belong to separate puzzles. Most students either missed these signs or chose to ignore them. We were busy acclimating—as the faculty called it—to a new environment. Some outsiders might call what they did to us those initial weeks a form of brainwashing or fostering a cult-like mentality.

But not me.

I agreed with Principal Locke. We weren't ready. We needed time to separate from our families and become a cohesive group. And some of us, myself included, even needed a little nudge to accept the invitation. If someone had told us the truth on Day One why they'd brought us to Dickensen Academy, we would have never believed them. We'd think they were crazy. Or worse, we'd turn around and run back home. But if we left, we would have missed out on something extraordinary. Something worth the wait.

My first day was confusing enough. I hopped out of the backseat the moment our SUV stopped. The sun was bright without a cloud in the sky, but the air had a definite chill. Fall must have begun earlier in the mountains.

"Excited?" Dad said as he climbed out, along with Mom and my older brother Josh.

I nodded slightly as I took it all in. The parking lot occupied the edge of a huge clearing surrounded by towering evergreens and distant peaks. Birds sang a welcome and pine scent hung in the air. This place was larger than I'd imagined.

When I turned toward the cream-colored buildings, I gasped. Images of myself on campus flickered through my brain: walking between the dorm and the school, crouching below a huge modern art sculpture, and sitting near a pond reflecting this same wooded backdrop.

I'd been here before.

No. Impossible. The three largest buildings were plastered all over the academy's brochure and website. That's where I'd seen them. I ignored the fine hairs sticking up on the back of my neck. Must've been the breeze.

A young guy trotted toward us with a clipboard and gave us a school-portrait-worthy smile—likely one he'd practiced for the parents. He looked a few years older than me, probably a senior like my brother. "Welcome to Dickensen Academy. Can I get your name?"

As I opened my mouth to answer, Dad beat me to it. "Autumn Mattison."

I forced a smile while my hands bunched into fists at my sides.

He scanned his list and marked something down. "All freshmen are assigned to O'Reilly Hall. That's the dormitory off to the left." He pointed the way. "Follow those people across the quad."

We each grabbed a bag and headed toward the dorm. None of my friends went to boarding school. Most everything I knew about them came from books and movies. But this place might be a lot different. It would be packed with the most creative teens from the western side of the United States, not a bunch of rich kids since tuition was paid by the Dickensen Foundation. I jogged ahead, mentally urging my family to walk faster, but they carried the heavier items.

In the center of the grassy quad where multiple concrete paths intersected, I paused to inspect three life-size statues of students: one painting at an easel, one reading a book, and one writing at a desk.

I turned to Mom when she caught up. "I can't believe this is actually happening."

Her eyes glistened as she gave a tight smile. "Me neither."

Dickensen Academy was *invitation only* to apply. My summer had been filled with testing and interviews, but the chance of acceptance had been slim. I didn't know who was most shocked when two recruiters appeared at our house ten days ago to offer me a spot. But one thing remained clear. Mom was the least confident in my decision to move away from home just shy of my fifteenth birthday. Avoiding further eye contact with her, I continued toward the three-story building ahead.

Once inside, we found a spacious sitting room of dark woods and rich reds where several people milled about. Wide hallways led in opposite directions. A woman with gray hair, thick glasses, and a warm smile introduced herself as Margaret Humphrey, my resident advisor. She handed me a thick manila envelope. "You'll be rooming with another freshman named Aditi Singh on the second floor."

She proceeded to rattle on with some basic information, but my mind drifted. Thoughts of Aditi filled my head. What was she like? Would we get along?

Soon I realized Josh was no longer in our midst. I surveyed the room while pretending to listen to my RA. There he was already chatting with two girls. I couldn't believe it. Well, yes, I could. This had been happening for years. Even though our olive green eyes, pale skin, and light brown hair marked us as siblings, his features came together more perfectly, as evidenced by the stream of girls who trailed him like groupies. I never had this problem with guys.

A change in the tone of voices snapped me back to the conversation.

"What do you mean we can't visit?" Mom asked.

"It's school policy," Mrs. Humphrey explained. "Freshmen are not allowed off-campus, aside from vacations and Dickensen-sponsored outings. Except for emergencies, of course."

She had to be kidding. I'd assumed I would only be gone for a month or two at a time. But I could handle it.

"I'm sorry. The recruiters should have explained all of this."

"Well, they didn't." Dad's tone betrayed his frustration. "I would've remembered it if they had."

Mom placed a hand on his shoulder and addressed my RA. "But we're planning an anniversary party for my parents in October. I thought it'd be a nice break for Autumn."

I stepped away. I couldn't bear to have my parents change their minds and take me home over some stupid misunderstanding. Landscape paintings hung on the walls, so I edged closer to read the descriptions under each piece.

Several minutes later, my parents joined me.

"Are we leaving?" I asked.

Mom shook her head. "Of course not. This school is important to you. Mrs. Humphrey explained it's a bonding thing and assured us it's for the best." She let out a long sigh. "Your grandparents will understand."

But what about you? No way would Mom have ever agreed if she'd known about this two weeks ago. Lucky for me, it would be awkward to back out now.

Dad leaned over. "It's not like they can keep you here against your will. If you're miserable, forget the asinine policy. You can attend school back in Seattle."

I chuckled and returned my attention to the wall. "So…can you believe this stuff was done by students?"

Mom held a finger to her chin as she admired the artwork. "I'm no expert. But I'd say these pieces could be hung in a gallery."

I swallowed hard. "I doubt I'll ever paint this well. The people look so life-like. And check out the leaves on this tree. You can even see the veins."

Mom placed a firm hand on my shoulder. "You'll do fine, honey. You're very talented."

I tugged her away from the paintings. She'd probably only said it to bolster my shaky ego. My fiction writing caught the attention of the recruiters, not any remarkable artistic ability.

"The important thing is to do well in your classes," Dad said. "The academics here are supposed to be as impressive as their fine arts program." He turned to my brother. "Josh, time to go."

Once he excused himself from his admirers, we took the elevator up.

****

Mom surveyed the room. "Looks like your

roommate has moved in." Aside from an open box at the foot of one twin bed, everything seemed to be unpacked.

"Uh-huh." *Please be nice, Aditi.* I held my breath as I opened the pint-sized closet next to the door. Yep. Already three-quarters full…and organized by color. I took a moment to inspect the rest of her belongings. She'd tucked her purple bedspread in with military precision and stacked her books in size order. The only items not impeccably arranged were the picture frames scattered on her dresser. But perhaps even they followed an order she understood. I stepped closer. The largest one showed an Indian family with three children: two girls and a boy. Which girl was Aditi?

A tall, narrow window between the beds drew me to the far side. Our room was on the backside of the building, overlooking several trees with leaves showing the beginnings of the yellows, oranges, and reds they'd soon become. *This sure beats the view of our neighbor's beige siding.* Pressing my face to the glass, I could see a winding path below, which branched into the dense, green forest. It beckoned to me. Maybe later. I smiled. Maybe with Aditi.

"Why don't Josh and I give you two some time to unpack?" Dad suggested. "It's too cramped in here."

I bit my lip. "Hey, Dad. While you're out, um, do you think you could grab the book I was reading? I'm pretty sure I left it in the seatback pocket."

I braced for his response. Although Dad was impressed with the academy, he had hinted multiple times he didn't believe I was responsible enough to succeed without continual parental support.

He let out a long breath. "You need to learn to

focus, Autumn. You're going to be on your own up here."

My eyes fell to his feet, and I mumbled okay. Today of all days I wasn't about to utter an excuse. Besides, he'd just twist my words around and somehow make me feel even worse about myself. He was an expert at it. A few more hours and I'd finally escape his daily scrutiny.

Mom and I got straight to work unpacking. I too had brought photos, but I simply pinned mine to the bulletin board hanging above the built-in wood desk: one of my family, one of our Welsh terrier Zoey, and a couple with my two best friends. Julia and I had been tight since sixth grade. She had insisted I'd miss out on a real high school experience by not attending Haller Lake with her. Drew was more encouraging. He lived across the street, and our families had been friends as long as I could remember. His uncle graduated from Dickensen years ago and was a huge factor in my parents' willingness to allow me to attend.

When Dad and Josh returned, I was far from organized, but at least everything was out of the suitcases, and the room felt a bit like my own.

As we were leaving, a girl whose height barely reached my nose walked in alone. Her wavy, black hair and the smile lighting up her face were familiar, yet I couldn't place where I'd seen her before.

"Hi. I'm Aditi." Her voice flowed like a song with a touch of a lilting accent.

My words came out even softer than usual. "I'm Autumn."

After we exchanged introductions, Mom asked, "Are your parents still here?"

Aditi's smile faded and she looked down. "They couldn't make it. Everything was kind of last minute. Not enough time to arrange childcare and time off work."

"So how did you get here?" I asked.

"I flew in from San Jose, then took the school bus from the airport."

My mouth fell open. "By yourself?"

She nodded.

My roommate had guts. If I were her, I'm not sure I would have chosen to attend. Although the academy was hours away from Seattle, this was still my home state. I'd grown up gazing at the Cascade Mountains. The closest I'd ever come to traveling alone was flying with Josh to upstate New York to visit Grandma Mattison. And that was only for a week's vacation.

"Have we met before?" I finally asked. "Maybe at the testing center in Seattle or something?"

Aditi shook her head. "I've never been in Washington until today."

****

Outside a group had gathered for the tour, and a young woman addressed the crowd. "Welcome. I'm Stephanie Jenson, one of the language arts teachers, but for the next hour, I'll be your guide."

I listened as Ms. Jenson supplied a bit of school history, but then my heart skipped a beat when a student with sandy-blond hair and bright blue eyes stepped into my line of sight. Ben—a guy I'd met at the testing center over the summer when we were both applying to Dickensen. His tousled hair fell into his face like a surfer's. He even had a nice tan. I'd merely spoken with him during the testing breaks but sensed a connection. He also starred in the dream I had last week where I explored the campus through the lens of a camera, taking snapshots along the way. When I'd woken, I not only felt I belonged here, but that Ben was part of my future. The peculiar thing: I remembered the dream clearly for days.

I wasn't sure if I should be relieved to see someone I knew or be weirded out that we had ended up in the same tour group as well. I'd have to come up with some excuse to talk with him later…if I had the guts.

Josh and I stuck together while our parents stayed closer to the guide. Ben hung in the middle of the pack. I couldn't tell if he'd noticed me.

As we walked across the quad from O'Reilly to Rogers Hall—the dormitory on the far side—I said, "This place reminds me of some of the colleges we visited during spring break."

"Definitely." Josh eyed the dorm up and down. "But the ivy and bricks have been replaced by wood and stone. Wonder where I'll be going next year."

I shrugged. "Kind of strange that I'm leaving home first."

"I know." He grinned. "It's going to be great…no makeup and nail polish all over my bathroom. No one to hog the TV. Some peace and quiet for a change."

I laughed. He was going to miss me.

As we climbed the stairs to the second and third floor classrooms, Dad's interrogation began. "So Ms. Jenson, can you tell us more about the science lab experiments in the freshman curriculum? Ms. Jenson, which standardized tests are administered? Ms. Jenson, can you elaborate on the math support available? Ms. Jenson…"

Ugh, shut up, Dad. No one else was asking so many questions. It was bad enough he stood out as the oldest person in our group.

Mom, on the other hand, remained uncharacteristically quiet and wore a polite smile. Only after our group emerged from the school building to tour the outside did she ask a few questions. About student safety, of course. When Ms. Jenson spent close to ten minutes discussing all the rules and precautions in place, Mom's smile finally became real. I reached out and squeezed her hand. This would all be easier if she embraced this opportunity more like Dad.

Sprinkled throughout campus were larger-than-life sculptures made out of random materials. According to our guide, most were student created. Surprisingly, many looked familiar. I must have seen them while researching the academy, but I swore I saw some in my dream too.

As we trailed Ms. Jenson along one of the cement paths, I made a bet with myself that a large, colored piece of art lay ahead. As we rounded the corner, my heart sped up when it came into view. *How did I know that?*

We stopped and our guide spouted off facts about the art classes, so I studied the modern art structure behind her. It was made of metal that glittered in the sun, and colorful rods stuck out at odd angles from its silver cylinder base. The placard said *Donated by the Class of 1972.* In my memory, a group of students posed beneath it.

I leaned over to Josh and whispered, "Was this in the brochure or on the website?"

He raised his eyebrows. "This thing?"

"Yeah. I'm trying to remember where I've seen it."

He stroked his throat and grimaced. "I'd have remembered this."

A shudder passed through me. Josh had gone through the brochure multiple times. The website too. He was my protector *and* my friend. When he'd told me Dickensen sounded perfect for me, I believed him.

After we began moving again, Josh leaned in close. "I don't know if it's just me, but this place is like that online building game we always played when we were younger."

I screwed up my face. "We? You mean the one *you* were addicted to?"

"Seriously, it's like we're in this stone-created world, smack in the middle of a forest. You're just missing the farm animals." He gave me a twisted smile. "And the zombies." I swatted him before I remembered Ben and prayed he hadn't noticed. It was odd to compare a school to a video game, but Josh had a point. Only why did he have to mention zombies?

Overall the campus was impressive, yet I couldn't shake the unsettling feeling deep in the pit of my stomach I'd been here before. Visions of myself on campus kept popping to mind. They had to simply be memories of their marketing brochure getting mixed up with that vivid dream. Besides, if my parents got a negative vibe today, they'd take me home at once. But they were now all smiles, obviously convinced this place was safe enough for their youngest child.

As we wound our way back to O'Reilly, our group spread out and Ben approached. My brother must've noticed because he conveniently disappeared. *Thanks, Josh.*

"Hey, Autumn. Remember me?"

A warm feeling went through my body. He remembered my name. "Ben, right?"

He nodded. "Pretty cool we both made it in."

I bit my lip. "Yeah. It's nice to see a familiar face."

"Uh-huh." He shifted his weight from side to side.

"So…how was your drive up?"

"Not bad. Yours?"

"Good. Good." *Way to be engaging, Autumn.*

Ben stuffed his hands in his pockets. "I had this funny feeling you might be here today."

"Really?"

His head dipped down. "I had a dream about this place, and you were in it."

The blood drained from my face, and I stared at Ben mutely, looking stupid I'm sure. Then worse, my cheeks went hot as the blood rushed back. And if that wasn't enough, out of the corner of my eye I spied my parents approaching. *Could this get any more awkward?*

When I didn't fill the silence, Ben started rambling. "I mean, it's probably because I saw you at the testing center or something. But it's weird, right? I heard only two percent of the applicants were accepted, so what were the odds we're from the same city and all and…?" He trailed off, his eyes flicking over my face. I smoothed my expression, so he wouldn't think my unease had anything to do with him.

I wanted to ask what happened in his dream. But before I could, my parents came up, Mom smiling expectantly like she was waiting for an introduction and Dad scowling ever so slightly at Ben, like he might be lowering my GPA simply by being a boy and breathing the same air as me.

Ben mumbled, "See you around," and sped off toward our dorm. I breathed a sigh of relief. The last thing I wanted right now was to introduce a guy to my family.

"Well," Dad said, "seems like this would be a good time for us to head on home. It's a long drive back, and I have some charting to finish up for tomorrow's patients."

I glanced toward the parking lot then back to my family. This was really happening. They were leaving. Without me. It's what I wanted, but still. "Oh...well, okay. I guess. I'll walk you to the car."

By the time we reached our SUV, tears had formed in the corners of my eyes, but I refused to allow them to fall. Holding a deep breath, I gave everyone a quick hug goodbye.

"I just wish you could come home next month," Mom said.

"Seriously?" Josh asked. "Do you really want to waste twelve hours driving back and forth twice in the same weekend?"

Good point, Josh. But no doubt Mom would be more than happy to make the drive.

"Call tonight." Mom dabbed a tissue to her eyes. "Or at least text."

"I will."

"Remember, Autumn." Dad's focus traveled toward the buildings then back to me. "Your high school education starts Tuesday. Don't get distracted by your new independence. Take advantage of this opportunity."

"Yes, Dad." *Did you have to say that now when*

I'm standing here on the verge of tears? Do you care about anything besides my grades?

But then he surprised me and gave me another hug—a much tighter one. "I'm going to miss you, sweetheart." I held onto him long enough that I hoped nobody was watching, his sweater vest scratchy against my cheek.

Thank goodness for Josh who kept it light. "See ya later, sis." Then he grinned and thrust his face up, pointing to himself. "Chin up!"

I laughed. Josh, always the optimist.

I spun around and walked straight to my dorm so I wouldn't have to see them drive away. I didn't want to burst into tears in public. Only then, for the first time since arriving, did I glance at something other than the camera app on my phone.

There was no signal.

Chapter: 2

When I opened my door, Aditi was facedown on her bed. I tiptoed in. Maybe I could grab my laptop and find someplace quiet to draft the next chapter of my latest story—my online readers were clamoring to find out how Rose escapes from the magical garden. A new idea had come to me during the car ride. Besides, writing would help me relax.

Aditi pulled herself up on her elbows and wiped her eyes with the corner of a pillow, leaving a smear of mascara on the lavender fabric. "It's okay. I'm awake."

Her face mirrored everything I'd tried to erase from my own. The only difference, I'd dried my eyes in the bathroom before creeping back to our room.

I eased onto the edge of my bed. "Do you, um, want to talk about it?"

"It's so quiet here. I've got a little brother and sister, so things are never like this at home." Aditi put on a thin smile. "It'll be nice, right?"

I returned the smile. I might actually miss Josh's irritating sports radio broadcasts penetrating my bedroom walls. "Yeah. I'm sure it will. Hey, why don't I help you unpack your last box?"

"That'd be great."

I pulled out a long orange and purple scarf. "Maybe we can drape this over the window? The colors match our bedspreads."

"You're right. Let's see how it looks."

She nodded her approval when I climbed onto my bed to arrange it.

"Any idea where to put this?" Aditi held up a wooden string instrument, which had to be close to four feet long.

I laughed. "What is that?"

"A sitar. Helps keep my grandparents off my back. They think I'm too Americanized. I've got a flute somewhere around here too."

We found a place to store her instruments. Thankfully Aditi didn't bring any knickknacks, so the stuffed animals I couldn't bear to leave behind had a whole shelf to themselves. Our belongings fit together like we were destined to be roommates. The more we unpacked, the easier the words flowed, though it was a little tough not to be jealous of how supportive Aditi's parents were of her creative activities.

"I write all the time," I said. "But my dad doesn't ever read my stories. He says, 'Do your homework first.' He doesn't even care I have a decent online following."

"You've got to be kidding!"

I shook my head. "He wants me to focus on math and science, so I can go to med school like him and my mom. He's only willing to let me go here because of Dickensen's academic reputation." I snorted. "He thinks the small class size will improve my grades."

"I'm sorry; that sucks. My grandpa was always ragging on my dad to go into a scientific field when he was a kid, so now my parents are all about letting us do our own thing. But why all the pressure? You're only starting high school."

"My dad tells everyone I'm going to be a doctor someday." I lowered my voice. "Honestly, I think he wants me to have a career in medicine so I don't end up like my grandma, raising a child alone on minimum wage."

She gave an understanding nod.

"When I was little, I went with it. Even dressed up in scrubs on career days at school. It made him so happy. But in the last few years, I've come to realize it's my life, and I want to make my own decisions. I just can't seem to tell him."

"Why not?" Her expression changed to one of concern. "Oh, Autumn, is he…violent?"

I laughed, trying to picture Dad hitting me with a belt. "Not at all. He rarely even yells. He's too sophisticated for that. He's used to his word being the law."

She screwed up her nose and cocked her head.

"It's complicated." I picked at a loose thread on my jeans. "Let's just say it's easier to keep the peace."

"So how come *you* wanted to go to Dickensen?"

"The emphasis on creativity. If this was just some ordinary prep school, I wouldn't have come." I shrugged. "But it would be nice to prove I can get good grades like my brother."

Aditi gave a sympathetic smile. "Hey, it's almost six. Want to check out the dining hall?" She grinned. "Maybe the boys too?"

I nodded, relieved to focus on something else. I could already tell it would be fun rooming with Aditi.

****

The dining hall took up one end of the main floor of our dorm. A short line led to a serving bar. Although

17

I was starving, the smells from the kitchen were a mixture of I-don't-know-what and not-exactly-enticing. I selected a grilled chicken breast, some vegetables, and a bread roll, which all appeared safe. Then we found a seat at one of the many round tables. The space buzzed with conversations and clanked with dishes as students emptied their trays into the plastic bins behind us. It'd probably get even noisier over the weekend as more students arrived. Only the freshmen had moved in today.

I perched on the edge of the hard, wooden chair. It was easier when it was just me and Aditi sorting our stuff on the floor, but this room was filled with meandering people sneaking sidelong looks at each other as they chose a group to sit with.

I'd barely taken one bite of my limp broccoli before Ben entered the dining room with a loaded tray and a shorter guy next to him.

"Are these seats taken?" Ben asked.

I looked down for a sec to get a grip on my emotions. Didn't want to appear too excited.

Aditi shook her head as she swallowed. Her wide eyes showed she hadn't expected any boys to join us.

"I'm Ben. This is my roommate, Ryan."

I smoothed my shirt and sat up straighter. Not only did I have my roommate to keep me from sitting alone, but we got to sit with two cute guys. Ryan's looks contrasted Ben's. He had pale brown skin and wore his thick, black hair clipped short.

"Weren't you on the bus this morning from Sea-Tac?" Ryan asked Aditi.

"Yeah. I thought we'd never get here."

"Same."

Aditi shrugged. "But my flight was half the price of one to Wenatchee."

"That's why I flew in there too," Ryan admitted. "And no transfers."

Ben winked at me. "Sounds like we missed out on all the fun."

I smiled, happy to be included in his little joke, not to mention the relief of not having such a long travel day every time I went home.

Partway through dinner, Aditi said, "I saw there's a *Freshman Welcome* on Monday. I wonder what it's all about."

"Maybe they'll tell us why they put a boarding school way out here in the mountains." Ben fiddled with his fork. "We don't even have cell reception. You'd think they would've built this school in Seattle or something."

"I know, man," Ryan said. "Our laptops are practically useless. I actually had to hardwire mine to get internet and download music to my phone. It's like we're in the Dark Ages." Oh, no. I hadn't even booted my computer. "And they've locked down a ton of social media sites. Hardly anything gets through the firewall. Seriously, how am I going to keep in touch with everyone?"

I ran my fingers through my long hair. Julia was going to post a video of her cheerleading routine today. If I didn't comment, she'd assume I was mad at her.

"We can't even text," Aditi added. "You'd think they'd have mentioned that little fact in the brochure."

"Yeah." Ryan chuckled. "That'd be a sure-fire way to guarantee an acceptance rate of zero percent."

I laughed. Ryan was pretty funny. I could use a

friend with a sense of humor—I tended to take life too seriously.

"Maybe some rich graduate from the founding school in Virginia donated some property to build this one?" Aditi ventured.

I shrugged. "My parents believe fewer distractions help students focus."

"Yeah." Aditi sighed. "There aren't any shopping malls or concerts or anything else around here. We'll be forced to study twenty-four seven."

"But isn't it a little creepy being this far into the woods? Like the hotel in *The Shining*," Ben said. "I even had a dream about this place before I showed up."

"Isn't that how Jack Nicholson went crazy?" Ryan asked. "A bunch of dreams of axing his family?"

Ben's gaze darted to me, and he flushed. "I wasn't axing anybody. I was just roaming around, looking at stuff with my family. And Autumn was there too. I mean, if I were going to have some kind of psychic dream about attending an isolated school, shouldn't it be about witchcraft or defeating dragons or something?"

I was about to open my mouth about my dream, but Ryan jumped in. "Ooh, you're Ben's dream girl."

My cheeks turned to fire.

Aditi's mouth fell open. "You dreamed about her before you even met?"

"No. It wasn't like that."

"Sure, man." Ryan nodded and smirked. "I know what you dream about."

I slumped in my seat. *Ugh.* Why couldn't I just disappear?

"Did you guys have any dreams about this

school?" Ben asked hesitantly.

Both Aditi and Ryan shook their heads. I made a concerted effort to chew my rubbery chicken. No way was I going to mention anything now.

"Wait!" Ryan said. "I remember. I did have a dream. I slept through my alarm clock and had to go to school naked."

Ben clamped his mouth shut and closed his eyes. After a few seconds he muttered, "You're so funny, Ryan."

****

I wanted to know about Ben's dream. Why was I in it? Could it have been similar to mine? But I never had an opportunity to find out because he attracted a small crowd as we participated in ice-breaking events throughout the weekend. Ben and Ryan were girl magnets. Every time we were with them, girls materialized from nowhere. It reminded me of someone else I knew. Ben chatted with all the girls, but Ryan seemed oblivious to the attention and focused more on the sports. But even with all the girls flocking around them, the guys still included Aditi and me.

On Labor Day, the school held a scavenger hunt for the freshmen. Normally I didn't enjoy group activities, preferring to hang out with just a friend or two, but getting plucked out of my real life to attend Dickensen gave me a chance to reinvent myself, and I didn't want to screw it up. I'd walked into kindergarten as a child afraid of my own shadow and in middle school became the invisible sidekick of the outspoken Julia. So I forced myself to not only participate but to work with all seven members of my team to try and win. As we ran around campus taking pictures of the items on our list, I played a vital role in solving the riddles. In fact, I was often the first to match the clue with the correct object on campus.

We raced to *A Rainbow Testament to the Class of 1972*. Everyone knew that one since it was on the official tour. We posed under the giant sculpture while Ryan snapped a picture.

He showed me his phone. I barely recognized myself in the group shot, and a surge of joy shot through me. My cheeks were flushed, and I wore a grin as I draped my arms around two classmates. Anyone studying the photo would say this girl belonged.

Then my eyes refocused on the entire frame and my body chilled. The picture was eerily similar to the one in my dream. I hadn't had one of those déjà vu moments since the first day here. I'd assumed all those feelings had passed as real memories replaced the ones from my dream.

A teammate read the next clue, snapping me back to the present: *A Quiet Place to Read on a Throne of Jewels*.

"I know that one!" Aditi said. "Ugh. It's way out past the track."

Aditi and I were the only ones who'd been to the mosaic bench by the pond.

"Why don't we split up since we don't need everyone in the photo?" I suggested. "It's kind of hidden, so it might be best if a couple of us sneak down there to avoid advertising its location. Then the rest of you can work on the last clue, and we can meet up near the finish."

Everyone liked my idea, particularly Aditi—she'd been struggling to keep up with us thanks to the wedges she'd insisted on wearing. Ben volunteered to go with me.

I tried to remain nonchalant, but all I could think was I had Ben to myself at last. As we jogged toward the far end of campus, I thought up ways to ask about his dream. Maybe the rainbow sculpture had felt familiar to him too. Once we got past the sports field, we slowed, and I casually led him to the pond. It was still as glass, reflecting the surrounding forest and mountains. We made our way down a steep dirt path through the cattails to where a few wooden benches and one covered in colorful glass circled the water's edge.

"This place is pretty cool," Ben said. "Didn't know you could get down here."

"Aditi and I discovered it yesterday. It's my favorite spot on campus."

As soon as we took a selfie on the mosaic bench, several voices floated down to us. They were getting closer. Perhaps another scavenger hunt team looking for the path's entrance. We remained silent, hoping they'd pass, so we could sneak away unseen.

"So happy to be back," a guy said. "It's been a long summer."

"You're kidding? Summer's never long enough."

"You know what I mean."

"Thank God we're at Dickensen. Couldn't imagine going to a regular school."

I leaned toward the sounds, straining to hear.

"Had to make up some good stories of why I like it out here. My friends think I'm nuts."

"I hear ya. They don't know what they're missing."

Laughter.

"Wonder when the teachers will send us outside

the fence."

"Probably a lot sooner than last year. I think it's only freshmen who have to wait a month."

Ben looked at me and mouthed, "What?"

"I'm going to send *you* outside the fence this year."

More laughter.

"Good luck with that. Your skills are going to have to improve a lot to reach me. My room is way down the hall from yours."

Someone gasped loudly.

Ben and I turned to the right. Two boys stared at us. Then a third popped into view. His eyes bulged when he spied us.

"Now what do we do?" The second guy's voice was full of panic.

"Robbins is going to kill us," the third boy said.

"Calm down. He'll never find out." Then the first boy turned back to us. "So, what are you *freshmen* doing here?"

I lifted my phone. "Just taking a picture of this bench. For the scavenger hunt."

"Uh-huh. Can I see?"

I showed the boy in front the screen.

He examined it. "Any video?"

I shook my head.

"Come on," Ben said to me. "We have to get back."

The first guy opened his mouth, but words didn't come out.

We squeezed past them to hike up the path. I kept my head down. It was all very awkward, as if I'd mistakenly entered the men's restroom.

"Hey, Gabe," Ben mumbled to the last boy we

passed.

"Hey, Ben."

"You know those freshmen?" the first guy asked.

"Yeah," Gabe said. "Ben's cool. He won't be a problem."

"You make sure of that."

I stiffened. It sounded like a threat. I didn't dare turn back.

When we got away from the pond, I asked, "Who were they?"

"Sophomores. At least Gabe is. Met him playing flag football." Ben hurried toward the field, obviously trying to put more distance between us and them.

I had to jog to keep up with his longer strides. "What do you think got them so worked up?"

"Give me a minute. I'm trying to remember what they said."

We walked in silence as bits and pieces of their conversation replayed in my mind. They'd mentioned a Robbins. I was pretty sure I'd read he was a teacher, but perhaps they were referring to some big shot on campus.

"There you are!" Ryan shouted. "Did you find the jeweled throne?"

Ben winked at me. "Yep."

"Great!" Ryan squished between us to peek at our photo. "Bet we get first place."

So much for my opportunity to ask Ben about his dream. Now I had even more I wished to discuss.

Chapter: 3

Monday evening, I joined Aditi, Ben, and Ryan in the Hayes Auditorium for the Freshman Welcome. The room hummed with conversations. Maybe I'd learn the answer to the question that'd been raging in my head for two weeks: why was I selected for such an elite school? Yes, I could write, but I wasn't much of an artist. And my grades had never been anything to brag about. Everyone I'd met here seemed to have some sort of creative outlet from drama to art to writing, but there were no prodigies as far as I knew. In most respects, everyone appeared to be typical teenagers. So what made the recruiters reach out to us?

And although chances were slim, perhaps the assembly would help me figure out what those students were chatting about near the pond. They'd clearly thought we had overheard something. I still hadn't had a chance to speak to Ben about it, and I wasn't about to mention it to Aditi. No need to stir up trouble with the upperclassmen by involving someone else. It was probably nothing, but it bugged me.

At seven p.m. the lights dimmed, and a middle-aged woman walked onto the stage. She introduced herself as Joan Rothchild, the Dean of Students, and droned on about academics and responsibility while I stole glances at Ben, wondering if he'd come up with any theories about what we'd overheard. I couldn't conceive any reason a group of students would be so worried a couple freshmen had overheard bits of a conversation. And the way they spoke about getting into trouble, presumably by a teacher, made it sound like it wasn't their secret but the school's. But what could a prep school be hiding?

At last, the dean handed the microphone over to Principal Locke as a sigh of relief rippled through the auditorium.

"Good evening, freshmen. Welcome to Dickensen Academy." His voice boomed through the spacious room as if he knew he had to wake us up.

I sat straighter. This guy's animated voice was the opposite of the dean's, and despite looking over fifty, he was in constant motion. When he wasn't prancing across the stage, he was traipsing up and down the aisles like a kid hyped on sugar. I bobbed slightly in my seat as I took it all in. Not only did the school sound impressive, but he made us sound impressive. Still, even with his entertaining antics, my fingers itched to check my phone, maybe search *outside the fence* in case the phrase meant something. But I had to keep reminding myself we had no reception.

When Aditi leaned forward with a slight frown wrinkling the corners of her eyes, I realized the principal's speech was veering away from typical welcome territory. "We have been in contact with your teachers, friends, and family to determine you have a love for children and enjoy the everyday magic in what we call life."

I jerked my head back. Why would they care that we like kids? *Magic*?

"Creativity is woven through the entire curriculum,

and we'll teach you to harness it to learn more from your classes and focus better on school and, um, extracurricular activities. Plus, we will use creativity to do things beyond your imagination."

I frowned. That was a little weird.

At last, he stood still in the center of the stage and gazed out at us. "I promise, before long, you will understand what makes this academy so unique. Please be patient. Study hard. Make friends. Have fun." He winked. "But not too much fun. Best of luck to you. Good night."

The lights flicked on. Everyone began talking at once, making it impossible to have a real conversation. I hadn't learned much except we had a passionate, if a bit eccentric, principal. But as I shuffled behind Ryan, squished between him and Aditi, I couldn't help but grin. Dickensen's program sounded impressive and all, but just as remarkable, I already had my own group of friends—no help from Julia required.

Once outside, the four of us separated from the crowd. "We scored big time on the principal." Ryan pumped his arm. "I bet he makes this place tons of fun. For school that is."

"For sure," Aditi said. "The principal at my last school was soooo boring."

"Imagine, he's been living here for ten years straight," Ben said. "It's a huge campus for only two hundred students, but seriously, I'd go stir crazy. Don't you think?"

Aditi shrugged. "Maybe he has a wife and kids hidden over in Forest Circle."

"Or maybe he's married to his job," I suggested. *Just like Dad.*

Ben opened the door to O'Reilly for us. "Why'd he leave us hanging there at the end and not say what makes this place unique after all the hype?" He sighed.

"Loosen up, man," Ryan said. "He's just trying to get us excited about starting school. Hey, any of you guys want to play foosball?"

"In a while," Ben said. "I'll find you."

Ryan nodded. "Later." Then he took off toward the game room—a large room with a pool table, darts, foosball, and video games. Laughter and electronic bleeps from that direction pulled many of the surrounding kids toward it like a magnet, and Ryan joined their flow.

Aditi motioned toward the elevator. I told her to go on ahead; I wasn't in the mood to go upstairs yet.

Ben turned to me. "Want to take a walk?"

My breath hitched in my throat. *With me*? "Sure."

The sky was still light, although the setting sun cast a golden glow on the trees around us. The air had a slight chill, but I wasn't about to spoil the moment by running off to grab a hoodie.

Something about Ben put me at ease, kind of like my friend Drew, who I'd known forever. But at the same time, Ben made my heart flutter in a way it hadn't before. Now alone with him, I kept my face straight ahead, only stealing a glance or two with my peripheral vision. I loved his big, blue eyes, mysteriously peeking out from under all his hair. I'd never had a boyfriend, only one crush in eighth grade, but the guy had never known I existed, so there was no comparison.

He didn't talk for a while, and an awkward silence developed.

"So," I began, "it sure is pretty up here. They

picked a nice spot for this academy." Everything I said sounded so lame.

He only gave slight grunts in agreement.

After we got to one of the paved paths meandering around campus, he broke his silence. "Sorry about that. I wanted to get away from everyone."

I suppressed a grin. Maybe he did like me.

"I wanted to get your take on this school."

"Oh." I raised my voice to mask my disappointment. *So stupid.* What was I thinking? A popular guy like Ben would never be attracted to me.

"What do you think Gabe and his friends were talking about earlier?"

I shrugged. "Couldn't figure it out. Something about a fence."

"Yeah. They said *outside the fence* a couple of times. Almost like it was a figure of speech."

"It seems like they were trying to hide something. But it didn't sound like much of a secret."

"I wouldn't have thought anything of it except they were so shocked to see us. It could've all been an act."

I nodded. "True. But I've been thinking. They might've known some freshmen would be there. For the scavenger hunt."

He raised his eyebrows. "Ryan says I'm paranoid. And Aditi, well, she's so happy to be here. But you, you were there. You heard."

My jaw dropped. "Did you tell Ryan about them?"

He shook his head. "No way." He leaned in closer. "But I did tell him I feel like we're being watched. Ever since I got here, I keep catching people looking at me. The upperclassmen. And some of the staff too."

I couldn't help but giggle. "I haven't noticed," I

lied. Actually I had but doubted it meant anything like he thought. Because of his height, Ben appeared much older than fourteen, and I'd seen some of the older girls whispering about him. The boys may have simply been checking out the new competition.

"I feel like there's something big we don't know about. Something those students were protecting. I mean, really, why are we here?"

I thought it was just me who was confused. "Well…the recruiters said we're creative and focused."

"Yeah, that's what Principal Locke said too."

"And we have the right personality."

Ben looked up at the sky, sighed, then turned toward the forest. "What did he say…something about how it will soon become clear why we're here, and there's some ultimate purpose for our creativity?"

"I know. That whole creativity part was a bit bizarre."

He shrugged. "It seems everyone is going with the flow. But I have so many questions." Then he touched my arm to stop me, so I turned toward him. "I'm thinking they're isolating us for some special reason," he admitted in an embarrassed tone.

I tried not to laugh—he was acting paranoid. But I didn't know Ben well. Maybe he was joking, trying to freak me out. Or was he hitting on me? The flutter in my chest moved to my stomach. I was already anxious about being away from home and whether or not I could hack the academics. I didn't need to obsess about anything else. But I still had to know about Ben's dream.

"So…I also had a dream about Dickensen before I accepted the offer."

Ben's head snapped toward me. "You did?"

"Yeah. I was taking pictures of students on campus. Then when I went on the tour on Saturday, it all felt familiar. Kind of like déjà vu. I also felt the same way on the scavenger hunt today. Was yours anything like that?"

"Not really. In my dream, I showed my mom, step-dad, and little brother around O'Reilly. But it wasn't at all like the official tour."

So much for my theory. "Did the campus feel familiar when you got here?"

Ben shook his head. "I don't remember many specifics about the school from the dream. I mostly remember my family's faces—they were all excited and happy. When I woke up, I was convinced I should come here. Before I'd been pretty worried, especially about leaving Calvin. He's only five and has a few medical issues." He turned to me. "I know it sounds rather basic. But what's strange is I still remember lots of it."

A tingle went through me. *Just like mine.* "I didn't see a little boy with you on the tour."

"No. Calvin stayed home with his dad. My mom was afraid he might throw a fit with me leaving and all. And there was this birthday party…"

I nodded then bit my lip. "So how did I fit in?"

His tanned skin went pink. Ryan's *dream girl* comment must've gotten to him. "That part's a bit hazy. But pretty sure you were in our car as we drove home, so when I saw you on the tour, I knew I needed to get to know you."

I stared at the ground as I sorted out my thoughts. My palms began to sweat and my heart sped up. The only logical conclusion for the appearance of each other in our dreams was we had made an impression on each other at the testing center like Ryan had assumed. I had to smile. But I wasn't about to add to our shared embarrassment by announcing I'd dreamed about him too.

Chapter: 4

I woke before dawn on the first day of school. The first week was always the best—meeting new teachers, learning their plans for the year, and none of the pressure of homework or tests. My fabulous new commute: a fifty-yard walk across the quad. It sure beat a long bus ride.

Homeroom was first. A pudgy man welcomed me at the door with an enthusiastic greeting. I chose a desk near the window and doodled in my notebook while waiting for the bell. I willed it to be a good day. My parents, and even Josh, had instilled in me for as long as I could remember the importance of high school. From this point forward, my grades would count. Even if med school wasn't at the top of my priority list, I wanted to get into a decent college.

Once the bell rang, it was a whirlwind of introductions, announcements, and locker assignments followed by history, science, and PE. After lunch, I had Spanish, algebra, language arts, and Creative Core. Seven classes. They weren't kidding. This school was going to be tough.

All day I kept my eyes and ears open for something out of the ordinary. But no one seemed to pay extra attention to me or any other freshman. And nothing about the day strayed far from normal. Yes, the classes were small—most had fifteen to twenty students—but that was a selling point of the academy. Yes, they'd scheduled an unusual amount of field trips—particularly in Spanish—but again, a good thing. Who doesn't like field trips? And yes, most of the teachers were passionate about their jobs, but I'd had zealous teachers before. All reasonable characteristics of a private school.

The smell of paint hit me the moment I stepped into the spacious Creative Core art studio, even with the windows cracked open. The front was similar to a typical classroom with twenty desks in tidy rows. However, the back was twice as big and cluttered with tables of various heights, easels piled to one side, and cabinets lining an entire wall.

Ben motioned for me to take the empty seat in front of him near Ryan and Aditi. I slipped into the spot and gave a little wave to my new friends—our second class in a row all together.

Our teacher was writing on the whiteboard in big green, block letters: *Mr. Gary Robbins*. I bet he was the person those sophomores had referred to. Judging from his balding head, graying brown beard, and wire-frame glasses, he had to be in his fifties or so. Unlike all my other teachers, who dressed in business-casual attire, Mr. Robbins wore a loose flannel shirt and blue jeans smudged with a dozen colors of paint.

"Good afternoon. You've *almost* made it through your first day. I'm sure by now you're dying to get back to the dorms. That's the tough part about teaching the final period."

A few students chuckled.

"Lucky for me I teach the fun course." He grinned. "So I hope you won't spend your afternoons pining for the bell."

I smiled. This guy seemed pretty cool and laid back.

Before long, Mr. Robbins began to go off about how we were special and would do great things with our creativity. Then all of a sudden, he stopped, glanced at the doorway warily, and started taking roll.

Someone tapped my back, so I twisted around.

Ben whispered, "Did you see that?"

A chill went through me. He'd noticed our teacher's odd behavior too. I nodded then returned my attention to the front. There had to be a logical explanation. As Dad would say, there's one for everything.

"A good portion of the freshman Creative Core curriculum focuses on visual arts, so I'll teach you the fundamentals of a variety of art forms this year. We'll begin with drawing." While Mr. Robbins continued to speak, he strolled up and down the rows. I peered down the aisle, trying to see what he was passing out. He placed a piece of paper, a ruler, and a sharp pencil on my desk.

We spent the rest of the period learning about one-point perspective and vanishing points. For Aditi and those who had taken multiple art classes, it might have been basic, but I was fascinated these techniques would help us make our drawings appear three-dimensional. The time flew by as I worked on our first assignment: a street scene with the buildings getting smaller and smaller as they converged toward a single point on the paper, giving them the illusion of vanishing into the distance.

****

Sunday night, I finally got ahold of Julia. Her phone had gone straight to voicemail all week. "Hey, what's up?"

"Oh my gosh! This has been the best week of my life! I can't even begin to tell you everything." Then Julia launched into a detailed account of each and every person we knew and all the students she'd met, focusing on the boys of course. "I wish you were here, Autumn. You'd love it. And everyone would know who you were, being Josh's younger sister and all." She barely paused to catch a breath.

Meanwhile, each time she spewed a new story, I swear my body shrank smaller and smaller. Not once did she ask me how I was doing at Dickensen. I'd been dying to tell her about Ben and our frequent walks and hushed conversations. He was suspicious something was up with Creative Core based on Mr. Robbins' comments and a few things he'd managed to pull out of Gabe. I wanted Julia's take on it and also to see if she thought Ben might possibly be interested in me. But she never gave me a chance, and by the end of the call, I had lost my desire to share.

When I hung up, an empty feeling entered my chest. Seattle may as well have been a million miles away. I picked up the phone to call Mom. At least she'd care what was happening with me.

During our conversation, I mentioned I was trying out for cross country the following day. Technically, it wasn't a try-out—there were no cuts—but I wasn't positive I'd enjoy it enough to complete the season. I'd planned to do cross country with Julia at Haller Lake, so at least we'd still have that in common. Mom agreed it'd be a great way to make friends.

Dad picked up after Mom and I said our goodbyes. "So I overheard you're thinking about cross country?"

"Yeah. I thought it'd be nice to get involved."

He paused. "Well, I'm not so sure that's a good idea."

"Why? You knew I was going to join the team at Haller Lake."

"It's different now. I'm not sure you can handle so many changes. You need to focus on your studies. *If* you get a handle on them, you may consider a sport later this year."

"But Josh always does sports."

"You're not Josh."

I swallowed hard. He'd meant I didn't get Josh's grades. "But—"

Mom spoke in the background. "You're being too hard on her, David. Let her try." The words grew muffled. Talk about ironic—as a heart doctor, you'd think he'd be thrilled I wanted to do some form of cardiovascular activity.

"All right." Dad sighed. "But you need to keep up your grades. I want us to talk every Sunday night and go over the materials from the past week. Got it?"

"But…I was only thinking about it."

"Doesn't matter. A weekly review session will be valuable regardless until I can trust you're succeeding on your own."

"Fine." I silently slammed my seat in the phone room. I should never have brought it up. It's not like I needed his permission.

"I'm only looking out for your best interests, Autumn." That was his excuse for everything. "So tell me more about math. Your mother mentioned you might be eligible for tutoring?"

I took a deep breath, then explained what Mr. Yoon had told us.

"Tomorrow, let your teacher know you're interested, and I'll call the school to make arrangements."

"Okay." *Please let this be over.* But he was just getting started. I should've hung up on him, but I was a wimp. Why did I care so much about what he thought?

"Now tell me, what are you learning in science?"

By the end of the call, I was wiped. It was as if I had relived my entire first week of school.

Chapter: 5

After the final dismissal on Monday, I went straight to my room to change into running clothes. I could handle the addition of a sports practice whether Dad believed so or not. If anything, our discussion had spurred me to commit to cross country *and* earn the best grades of my life.

As I pulled my hair through an elastic band, I made one final plea. "Aditi, are you sure you don't want to join cross country?"

She swiveled around from her desk. Her face looked as appalled as if I'd asked her to swim with crocodiles. "I don't even own running shoes."

I laughed. Aditi lived in high heels when she wasn't forced to wear something more practical. She even dressed up for school. Not me. I'd choose jeans, hoodies, and athletic shoes over fancy clothes any day.

"Besides, I'm joining band. Some practices might conflict."

****

About fifteen other girls were waiting on the grass field inside the track. Most were older and chatted in little groups, but two were in my classes and stood off to one side, so I gravitated toward them. Tessa Williams was the towering, lanky one, and Hannah McIntyre was the stunning blonde with a Texas accent.

"Have y'all ran cross country before?" Hannah

asked.

Tessa shook her head.

"It's my first time," I said.

"Me too," Hannah admitted.

My gaze then drifted toward a striking young woman with ebony skin jogging up the hill, her black hair held high in a ponytail. Although slender, the outline of muscles in her arms and legs suggested she was an athlete. She'd been introduced at the *Freshman Welcome*, but I couldn't recall her name.

"Welcome. I'm Ms. Davis, and I teach history. But here, call me Coach Kat." Then she went into a spiel about her background and her goals for the season. She'd attended Lawrence Academy, Dickensen's sister school in Virginia, and this was her third year teaching. After a warm-up lap around the track and some stretches, she broke into an enthusiastic grin, her perfect teeth gleaming against her dark skin. "Let's get running."

We took off down the hill, across the track, and past the pond. The pack began to separate by speed. Although Tessa had never run long distance, she left us in her dust by the time we entered the forest. Hannah and I brought up the rear.

Hannah chatted about Coach Kat and how excited she was to join the team. In school, the girl intimidated me. She'd just sit in class, in all her beauty, and gaze around, rarely talking with anyone. Stuck-up had been my guess. But here, her words tumbled out.

"Who's your roommate?" she asked.

"Aditi."

"Lucky you. She's nice."

I smiled. I was lucky. "Who's yours?"

"Caitlyn."

"Oh." Caitlyn didn't smile, didn't frown. She floated silently from class to class like a ghost. Even her skin and hair were nearly white. The only time she came to life was when she spoke to teachers. "How's that?"

"Um…we get along. I suppose. She does her thing. I do mine."

I'd been curious about Caitlyn but wasn't about to approach her. "Do you happen to know if she's part of the Black family? You know, the one who paid for the library?" My tour leader had used them as an example of the importance of alumni for continued growth and maintenance of the academy.

Hannah laughed. "Don't get me started. I asked her about that when we met. She about bit off my head and made it clear Black was a common last name. That's when I knew I was in trouble."

Soon we both had to stop talking as it became harder to breathe. For most of the two-and-a-half-mile loop, we jogged in the shadows, but every once in a while, a ray of sun pierced through the evergreens, casting swaying geometric patterns of light. The dirt path was wide enough for a few students to run side by side, and the pine needle coverage made our steps soft and quiet. Coach Kat had warned us that when we ran on the narrower paths, we'd need to avoid branches and tree roots.

"Hey, what's over there?" Hannah asked.

I checked where she pointed. Bushes and tall trees filled my vision. Nothing else. Then something silver glinted through the green. "Must be the fence."

"A fence? Way out here?"

"They mentioned it on the tour. Something about keeping wild animals out."

"Oh." Hannah looked around nervously. "Think it works?"

"Hope so." It'd keep out the coyotes and wolves but not the animals that could climb. I kept glancing in its direction. What were the chances it was the fence those sophomores had referred to? I'd have to hash it out with Ben. My brain was too low on oxygen to contemplate.

Several minutes later, Hannah huffed, "I'm fixin' to walk soon. Cramping up."

"I'll walk too." Glad it wasn't just me.

Up ahead, Coach Kat had joined the girls ahead of us. We'd worked our hardest to keep them in sight for the last twenty minutes. But then our coach turned and jogged toward us.

"How's it going?" she asked.

"Okay." What I wanted to say was *I think I'm going to die*!

Coach Kat observed us and probably noticed Hannah wheezing. "Let's take it down to a walk to catch your breath. We're almost back to campus."

The three of us slowed. Unexpectedly, Coach Kat stayed with us and took the time to learn our names and hometowns. "This first week, why don't you try running for ten minutes, walking for two, running for ten, and so on. Make sense?"

We nodded.

"Tomorrow, run slower. If you can't hold a conversation, you're going too fast."

"'Kay," Hannah said.

"Don't worry about everyone else. Go at the pace

that works for you."

I bit my lip. Maybe I could do this.

Soon the campus clearing appeared ahead.

"I'm going to catch up with your teammates. Run back to the track, where I'll guide you through your stretches. After that, practice is finished. Fantastic job, girls!"

Coach Kat ran ahead, her skin glistening as she emerged from the trees into the bright light.

Hannah smirked. "I was right. She's going to be awesome."

****

The second day of practice, Hannah and I were in the back of the pack again. But we took our coach's advice and ran slower as we alternated between jogging and walking, allowing us to talk more easily.

Hannah told me she lived on a ranch outside of Houston and had been homeschooled until now. That explained everything. The poor girl had been thrown in with a bunch of hormonal peers for the first time. I couldn't even imagine starting school in ninth grade. No wonder she'd come across as unapproachable. Turned out she was really sweet, and we had a ton in common. She even loved to write and dreamed of becoming an author.

"You know," Hannah began, "I almost didn't come to Dickensen."

"Me neither. I was enrolled at my brother's high school."

"I meant when they invited me to apply, my parents said no."

I watched her from the corner of my eye. "What happened?"

"I thought a small academy might be good. You know, for my first school." She paused for a moment. "Can we stop a sec?"

"Sure." My heart could use the break too.

Hannah bent at the waist, filled her lungs, and let out the air. Once she could breathe better, we began to walk. "My parents were dead set against this place. Didn't want to send me so far."

"How'd you feel about that?"

She shrugged. "My parents were fixin' to enroll me in public school. Finally. So I had that to look forward to. But a couple weeks later, my parents had this dream about this place, and they changed their tune."

The hairs rose on my arms. "What kind of dream?"

Hannah shrugged. "Don't know. They admitted they were being selfish. Next thing I knew, they'd arranged for my testing and interview."

I glanced behind us to confirm we were alone. "I also had a dream about Dickensen. A couple nights after being accepted. Made me want to come here."

Her mouth dropped open. "You did?"

"Didn't think much of it at the time. In my dream, there were some photos of me on campus…and some with Ben Coleman."

"The Ben in our Creative Core?"

"Yeah. But not that big of a deal. Ben's also from Seattle. We did our testing together. I must've connected him with this academy in my dream." My face was likely reddening. I hoped Hannah attributed it to exercise.

"That's what I figured happened with my parents. They had this boarding school on their brains, so it'd make sense to dream about it."

"Maybe."

"Yeah. Maybe."

I checked the time. "We better start running. That was way longer than two minutes."

As we jogged in silence, millions of ideas circulated in my head. Ben had also dreamed about Dickensen this summer. Maybe there was something unusual about it after all. I remembered the nagging feeling I'd had that Aditi looked familiar. Could she have been in my dream too? Or did she merely resemble someone else?

Hannah and I were the last to leave the track. Now that everyone knew the stretches, runners could complete them on their own after they finished with the trails.

"Looks like Taylor forgot her sweatshirt." I bent down to retrieve it from the grass. Its neon pink had been impossible to miss on her earlier. "Want to help me find her?"

"Sure," Hannah said. "She's got to live in Rogers. Isn't she a junior?"

"Maybe even a senior."

We walked toward the dorm, keeping an eye out for Taylor. I hadn't been in Rogers Hall since the school tour. I wouldn't mind checking it out.

When we got into the entryway, we wandered around, disoriented. From the outside, the dorm looked identical to O'Reilly, but the inside layout was different.

A girl approached us, smiling. "Looking for the campus store? You came in through the wrong door." She motioned toward our left. "You need to enter it from the quad."

"Actually, we're looking for Taylor." I lifted the sweatshirt. "She left this at practice. Do you know where her room is?"

"Sorry. Freshmen aren't really allowed here." She reached for the sweatshirt. "I'll take care of it for you."

"No, but thanks." I clutched the sweatshirt. "We've got it." I moved to go around her, but she stepped to the side, blocking me.

Her smile disappeared and her tone sharpened. "I told you, freshmen are *not* allowed in this part of the dorm." She snatched the sweatshirt from me.

"Okay," I stammered. "Um, thanks."

The girl watched us leave.

"Wow, she was rude," I muttered as soon as the glass door shut behind us.

"Yep," Hannah agreed. "I get the impression the older students don't want to associate with us freshmen."

"What do you mean? Everyone's been nice at practice."

She turned to me. "That's not what I meant. Seems to be more of a group mentality."

I raised my eyebrows.

"You know, like the closed door to the sophomore wing."

I didn't know.

"Haven't you noticed they close the door each night around ten o'clock?"

I shook my head.

"Thought it might be some sort of fire code. But the other night, I tried to open it, and it was locked."

"Doesn't sound too safe."

"Nope. Of course, it might open from their side.

But I was thinking it kept the freshmen out of their hallway at night."

My heart pounded in my chest as if we were still running. The locked door reminded me how Gabe had said the upperclassmen weren't supposed to hang out with freshmen. I started to open my mouth about Ben's suspicions but stopped. That would be the end to my private discussions with him, and Hannah was the last person I wanted to share Ben with. Any guy in his right mind would choose her over me.

Chapter: 6

My hand shook as I held the paintbrush with nowhere to rest my elbow. I'd never worked at an easel. I glanced at Aditi on my left. From a distance her landscape could've been a photograph. Her drawings, like her half of our room, were always precise. Ryan on my right painted with gusto. He used every warm color available to make his sunrise explosive. In his rush, his bright colors mingled into the darker trees.

Mr. Robbins stopped behind us. After a moment, he broke his silence. "Ryan, I love your use of color. Your sunrise makes me feel energetic and eager to start my day. Great art always evokes an emotional response."

"That's what I was shooting for," Ryan replied.

Was he sucking up to our teacher or telling the truth? I studied his canvas. I had a lot to learn about art.

After Mr. Robbins left us to observe some other students, Hannah approached Aditi and me. "Hey, what are y'all up to this weekend?"

Fortunately our teacher didn't care if we wandered around and talked. He encouraged it as a way to generate new ideas for our own projects. It's a good thing because this studio was always loud with chatter.

"I don't know," I said. "I haven't looked at the *Calendar of Events* yet."

"They're having some sort of sports competition

tomorrow," Hannah said.

I was hoping to do something less socially demanding, like play a board game or watch a movie. But that excuse sounded lame. "I have a ton of homework, but I could definitely make time for a run or something."

Aditi put down her paintbrush. "Come on, Autumn. Everybody's going to be there. I'll do it if you do. You've got to be better at all those sports than me."

"Don't worry, guys," Hannah said. "It's supposed to be low key. They even have wheelbarrow races and balloon tosses."

Even those events required skill, but Hannah was likely only trying to get involved. She'd never had a chance to participate in school spirit activities.

Ben spoke up from his position behind us. "You girls should come. Ryan and I will be there."

Everyone wanted to go. I remembered my promise to myself to be more outgoing. "Sure. I'll sign up."

After the bell, Ben caught my arm as Aditi and I stepped into the hall. He whispered, "Hey, I think now's our opportunity to check out the cabinets."

I turned. Mr. Robbins was strolling toward the bathroom. If we were lucky, he might even chat with the teacher next door before returning.

"I just want to take a quick look for anything unusual." He'd told me he'd been dying to dig through the cabinets all week for any clues about the secret Gabe was protecting.

I doubted he'd find anything, but I'd use any excuse to spend time with Ben. Especially alone. "Okay. I'll stand guard."

Ben rushed back into the now empty classroom.

Aditi turned back to me. "Aren't you coming?"

"In a minute. I'm waiting for Ben." I couldn't say anything because Ben and I had agreed not to mention the little confrontation down by the pond. We didn't want to get on Gabe's bad side. Besides, I enjoyed having our own secret. "I'll see you back in our room later."

She grinned at me as she backed away.

I stood in the doorway, keeping an eye on the hallway. Fortunately the art studio was huge, so the opening and shutting of each cabinet door only made slight clicking noises near the entrance. I turned my head back over my shoulder. "How's it going?"

"Nothing so far. Just a bunch of art supplies."

Suddenly Caitlyn breezed past me into the room before I could stop her. After she spotted Ben, she turned to me, her face a blank slate. "You won't find what you're looking for in here."

Then she strutted back out.

What the heck was she talking about?

That fifteen-second distraction was all I needed to screw up my job.

"Hey, Autumn," Mr. Robbins said.

My chest constricted.

"Did you need something?"

I followed him to his desk. "Mr. Robbins," I bellowed, trying to warn Ben and keep our teacher's attention on me. Ben, with his head buried in the cabinets, likely didn't hear him return. "I needed to—"

"Ben?" He furrowed his brow. "What are you doing over there?"

He looked like a puppy caught with a chewed-up shoe. "Um, I misplaced my Creative Core notebook

51

yesterday. Thought maybe someone put it in one of these cabinets."

Mr. Robbins motioned to the other side of the classroom. "Don't you think they would've put it over on the shelves, with the books?"

"Uh, yeah…I already checked there, so I was taking a peek in the cabinets." Ben's voice was flustered.

I expected our teacher to demand to know what we were up to. Or worse, send us straight to the dean. But instead, he smiled. "Let me help."

Together the two of them rummaged through all of the cabinets. Ben never found his notebook. After a while, I suggested he might've left it in the library. Then we thanked Mr. Robbins and scooted out of there to avoid arousing more suspicion.

Only when we arrived at our lockers, two floors above, did we slow down.

Overcome with laughter, I spit out, "You should've seen your face when he caught you. Priceless!"

"What a stupid idea," he muttered. He wasn't laughing. "I didn't even find anything unusual except a dumb, plastic model of the brain. Some science teacher is probably missing it. Ryan's right. I need to let it go."

"I'm just glad he didn't give us the third degree. He actually seemed amused." I started laughing again, unsure if it was because Ben was acting so serious, or if I was simply relieved we hadn't gotten into trouble. "Obviously he's not hiding anything."

He sighed. "I had this hunch there'd be something there."

"Well, I talked with Josh the other day and told him how the freshmen were excluded from a few things around here."

"Uh-huh?"

"He brought up how college fraternities often haze their freshmen in the fall. So I got to thinking, maybe they're doing something like that to us."

Ben rubbed the back of his neck. "Then that'd mean they have something awful planned."

I shrugged. "Not necessarily. Supposedly it's kind of a bonding thing."

He blew out a long breath. "Maybe I just want to believe there's some big school secret."

"Did you notice Caitlyn walk in?"

He shook his head.

"Just for a sec. Said something about how we wouldn't find what we were looking for in the studio. It was strange. She's never said two words to me before."

"Caitlyn's a little know-it-all. Thinks she knows everything because of her brother." Ben bit his lip and nodded. "He's older. Or maybe it's a sister. I never paid much attention." He looked back at me, his eyes bright with curiosity again. "Either way, they graduated from here."

I grinned. "Maybe she does know something."

****

The sporting competition on Saturday afternoon included traditional sports such as volleyball, soccer, and softball and some team-building events. Aditi and I spent most of our time as spectators. While I watched Hannah play soccer with Ryan and Ben, it dawned on me she was integrating into our group, so what was the point of keeping secrets? Maybe together we could make sense of all the unusual things that'd been bothering me.

Ben, Ryan, and Hannah met up with us after their game.

"Do you guys want to ditch this competition?" I asked. "I have an idea."

They stared at me in confusion, although Ben looked intrigued.

"Hannah and I found something in the woods. I think we should check it out now while everyone here is busy."

"Now?" Ryan's jaw dropped. "But the competition is getting good. Looks like we might actually beat the sophomores."

Ben shook his head. "Doubt it. I'm sure it's rigged. I vote for the woods."

"Me too," Aditi said.

Ryan surveyed the field and let out a long sigh before turning to us. "Okay, then."

I smiled as unfamiliar confidence seeped into my body. I'd never been a ringleader, always the follower. But a mere two weeks on campus, and I was leading my new friends on an adventure.

As we made our way to the trail, Hannah and I explained about the fence we'd discovered, the way we were forced out of Rogers, and the locked door between the wings. The guys admitted the third-floor door was also locked at night. Ben flashed me a warning when I began to relay the conversation by the pond. I winked at him before mentioning I heard some students talking about a fence so wanted to check it out. I glossed over the minor detail that Ben was with me.

Once on the forest trail, it didn't take long for the guys to pull ahead about twenty-five feet—Ben's strides were much longer, and Ryan was the type of guy who always sped around.

"It was fun watching the soccer game," Aditi said. "Never seen one before."

"Right," I teased. "You were watching Ryan."

"Okay. True. But you've got to admit he's good. Now I see why he's always raving about the sport. He's got the perfect body for it."

"I thought you liked that guy in science?" Hannah asked.

"A girl can keep her options open." Aditi focused her gaze on Ryan up ahead. "Just look at those legs."

Hannah laughed. "Definitely hot."

"I can see it." I bit my lower lip. "But I think Ben's more my type."

Aditi turned to me, her eyes wide. "I knew it!"

"Did you hear about her dream?" Hannah asked.

"*Shhh*!" I hissed.

Hannah whispered, "I'll distract the guys so you can tell her." Then she ran ahead while Aditi and I slowed our pace to put even more distance between us.

After I told Aditi what I remembered about my dream and Ben's, she asked, "Why didn't you tell me?"

I shrugged. "Ryan made such a big deal about my appearance in Ben's dream that I was too embarrassed. I haven't even told Ben he was in mine."

Aditi's eyes shone. "You should ask him out. It's obvious you like him. And I mean, wow, he dreamed about you too."

My cheeks warmed. "And ask him out where? The dining hall?"

She giggled. "I don't know."

"Seriously, I'd never ask him out. I don't think he likes me that way. What if he said no?"

She smirked. "That could kind of mess up the friendship thing we've got going."

"Yeah." Part of me had hoped Aditi would be more encouraging and tell me I stood a chance. But she was right. It could be awkward. "Besides, now that Hannah hangs out with us, I'm sure Ben doesn't even notice me."

"I don't know. Ben seems different than other guys. More mature. And remember, he dreamed about you. That's got to say something."

"Maybe. But maybe not." I kicked a pinecone out of my way. "Remember how I thought you looked familiar when we first met?"

"Uh-huh."

"I'm thinking you might've been in my dream too."

"You're kidding! That's impossible. I'm sure you just saw some girl with black hair and dark skin."

I shrugged. "I've had this funny feeling ever since I got here that something is off. That's why I want to show you guys the fence. Maybe it'll make sense to you." I went on to explain everything I'd discussed with Ben.

"Wow," Aditi said. "We'll have to convince Hannah to do a little detective work with Caitlyn."

"For sure."

"We're getting close!" Hannah yelled back to us.

They stopped and waited for us to catch up.

Hannah gestured toward the right. "It was somewhere around here."

We lingered for a few minutes while peering through the tree trunks. All the shadows made it difficult to see much.

I pointed to a distant section of fence. "There!"

Ben grimaced. "It's going to be tough to get there." The fence was in a heavily wooded area. Dense bushes covered the ground. "Let's keep walking. See if the trail gets us closer."

When we got within forty feet from the fence, Ryan said, "I think this is as good as we're going to get." Then he left the trail and forged his way toward it. The rest of us followed. Too bad I wore shorts; my legs were becoming a scratched mess.

"Man, this is big!" Ryan cried. "It's got to be ten feet tall."

"High enough to keep out the dangerous animals, right?" Hannah asked.

"Assume so," Ryan said.

When I looked up from the attacking plants, I blinked several times. There were two fences. The closest was chain-link with barbed wire at the top. Based on the rust and the growth of vines covering sections, it had been there for years. But behind it, a silver electrical one gleamed.

Ben studied the fences for a moment. "Guessing they're meant more for people."

"Wouldn't electricity keep out the animals?" Aditi asked.

"Of course," Ben said. "But why go to the expense?"

"On our ranch," Hannah said, "we use electric fences to keep the livestock from pressing up against them."

Ryan pulled a few branches back and peered at the bottom of the fence. "Makes sense."

"And it would keep animals from climbing," Aditi

added.

"True." Ben shrugged. "But some animals can still get over through the trees. Or even by digging."

"Are you saying it's trapping us inside?" I asked, suddenly chilled.

"Well, yes…" Ben said, "or it's keeping people out."

My eyes took in the dark forest surrounding us. "I can't imagine anyone would try to get in this way."

"Maybe there are," Aditi suggested. "This campus is closed to visitors except a few days of the year."

"There are some real crazies out there," Ryan added.

"Y'all, check this out," Hannah said as we returned to the trail. "There isn't any of this salal on the other side of the path. Only near the fence."

I bent over. "You mean this thick groundcover?"

Hannah nodded.

"That's random. You think someone was trying to hide it?" Ryan asked.

"Not necessarily." Hannah squatted down and inspected the greenery. "Planting along the fence would prevent animals from running into it."

By now the slight chill had spread to my entire body. I was freezing and wanted to get out of here.

As we hiked back to school, we debated all types of scenarios for the academy to take such precautions, from keeping out hunters and animals to preventing the students from getting lost. Ben suggested maybe gates were placed along the fence and that's what the sophomores had referred to. Ryan gave the most compelling argument: a secure fence would keep the overprotective parents happy whether it protected us from dangerous animals or random weirdos.

My gut told me two fences were overkill for everyone's theories. Mom had always said I was perceptive. Or were all the changes over the past two weeks simply getting to me?

One thing we agreed on was Hannah should talk to Caitlyn. But by the way Hannah's face paled and she started chewing her lower lip, it was as if we were feeding her to a wild animal.

Chapter: 7

I squeezed through the crowd into Bennett Hall. The room buzzed with excitement. Principal Locke had called a mandatory meeting for all freshmen. I'd never been in this lecture hall. It was smaller than the auditorium but ample for our class of fifty. Aditi and Hannah had saved me a spot, so I worked my way toward my friends and plopped down between them.

"What do y'all think this is about?" Hannah asked.

"Don't know," I said. "But I bumped into Taylor from cross country, and she was grinning like crazy. So guessing it's something good." I didn't say it, but my gut told me this might be what Gabe and his friends had been discussing. Ever since the examination of the fence last weekend, my suspicions had intensified. However, the pieces appeared to belong to different puzzles. Only Ben had remained questioning like me. He sat with a group of guys a couple of rows above me. I caught his eye, and he gave me a conspiratorial grin. Seemed like he too thought this meeting might be something out of the ordinary.

Principal Locke took the microphone. "Good afternoon." He waited for the room to quiet. It didn't take long. He went on about all our accomplishments as we acclimated to Dickensen the last couple of weeks, such as making new friends and establishing routines. His voice grew more and more animated.

"Today, I'm going to shake up your world again."

My ears perked up.

"Let me get right to the point. We're going to discuss dreams."

My throat went dry. It couldn't be. He must be talking about the aspiration type; he was a principal after all. I glanced over my shoulder to check on Ben. He stared at Principal Locke with his mouth ajar. His mind must've jumped to the sleeping kind too.

"Sometimes you may have fleeting images of your dreams upon waking, yet they usually disappear. But sometimes, you remember them. Do you ever wonder why?"

My heart beat faster. Some students were nodding in agreement. Could he be referring to dreams like the one where I took photos on campus?

"Scientists would say whether you recall a dream depends on which stage of sleep you wake and the length of your REM sleep. I don't disagree. That is for most dreams. But what if I told you there are some dreams you are meant to remember? Dreams that can be recalled with clarity months later. Now, not everyone is capable of having these dreams. This is a gift. And I believe you all have it."

What?

"How do I know this? Because someone affiliated with this school gave you a dream."

His words hung in the air while he remained planted with his hands on his hips and watched us react. Murmurs rippled throughout the room. A boy in front of me twirled his index finger near his head and leaned to his neighbor. "The man is crazy."

"You may think I'm loony." Principal Locke

laughed as he twirled his own index finger near his head and nodded toward the student in front of me. "But stick with me for a few moments." The back of the boy's neck turned red.

"During the interview process this past summer, you were each asked to describe a recent dream. All of you recalled it in its entirety."

He's right. How could I have forgotten the steeplechase dream? Not only had the recruiters asked about it, but they'd asked me to draw the images I recollected.

"You may have thought this was a question of your creativity, but it was a test. A test you all passed. Your answers confirmed you have the ability to be *dream receptors.*"

The murmurs grew louder, but I tuned them out and kept my gaze glued to our principal.

"I can tell many of you don't believe me or comprehend what I'm saying. This is not surprising since what I've described doesn't fit with your current belief systems. So today, I'd like to perform another test. Please raise your hand if you recall a dream from last night."

About half of the hands shot up. I kept mine down. It'd been a crazy-busy day. I couldn't even remember what I'd had for lunch.

"Who's willing to share their dream?"

Principal Locke called on a student in the back.

I craned my neck to see the guy.

"I dreamed I was hiking through the woods with a group of people. We walked for miles, circling a mountain lake."

As he spoke, it all came back, and the hairs rose on

my neck. I'd dreamed the same thing. Chatter erupted around me.

After a couple of minutes, Principal Locke raised his hands. "Quiet everyone. Thank you. You, up front. Tell me about your dream."

A redheaded girl stood. "Mine was similar. Our entire grade was hiking together. We stopped along a pebbled beach to skip rocks. Oh and I remember, the day was really warm."

More whispers.

"Thank you. Now, one more. Over here in the front."

The girl who lived across the hall from me spoke. "I had the same dream but wanted to add that you were hiking with us."

Everyone began talking at once. I admitted to Hannah and Aditi I'd had the same dream. When they confirmed they'd had it too, I released the breath I'd been holding. It wasn't just me. We were somehow in this together.

After the chatter died, my attention returned to our principal. He stood tall and smiling. "It appears the majority of you had identical dreams. If not, don't be concerned. I expect if we held this session in the morning, you'd all recall it. It's a talent that has to be nurtured." He shifted his body in my general direction. "You, there in the back."

"So to be clear." My heart quivered hearing Ben's voice from behind me. "What you're saying is someone created this hiking dream and somehow managed to get us to dream about it?"

"Precisely. In fact, *I* created the dream and sent it to you."

My heart stopped as if it'd been hit with a bolt of lightning.

Ryan jumped up next to Ben. "Couldn't you have hypnotized students so some of us think we dreamed the same thing?"

Leave it to Ryan to challenge our principal. But he'd asked a legitimate question.

"Perhaps a hypnotist could produce a similar result. However, I can honestly say I'm no hypnotist."

My ears couldn't be hearing this right. Yet everything he said made sense of my dreams. It was all falling into place. But perhaps I was dreaming now.

Principal Locke strode up and down the aisles. "Now, if you're having a tough time grasping what I've already told you, you'll have an even tougher time with what I'm about to say. We haven't brought you here because you can receive dreams. We've brought you because we believe you have what it takes to create a dream and telepathically send it to someone else."

Telepathy? What is this place? Some academy to train people with supernatural powers?

Someone behind me shouted, "BS! Telepathy doesn't exist!" I whipped my head around. A stocky guy named Quinn was scowling at the stage.

Principal Locke ceased moving and bore an expression my dad wore countless times—a look I'd spent a lifetime learning to avoid. *Uh-oh!*

All side conversations halted.

"I don't expect you to believe me yet. But I *do* expect you to be respectful. Please raise your hand if you have a question or a comment."

After several moments of silence, a girl raised her hand partway. "Principal Locke, could you please explain what you mean by telepathy?"

"Telepathy is the transmission of information from one person's mind to another's without using our known senses. Scientists have been trying to prove its existence for years. However, what we teach is not simply focusing on an object and having another person guess it. What we do takes the notion of telepathy to a whole new level where fantasies can come to life and dreams can be interactive. Therefore we do not refer to it as telepathy, but rather, *Dream Management*."

I leaned forward, my elbows on my thighs. The audience was so quiet one could hear a cat purr.

"Years ago, Lawrence Dickensen discovered pockets of people had this ability, like him. He learned how to identify who had this aptitude and how to cultivate it. His life's work led to the establishment of Lawrence Academy in 1912 and later this school.

"That brings me to you. You've been meticulously selected. Additionally, you straddle the line between child and adult. Mr. Dickensen learned if he found the right people at this critical juncture and taught them through a rigorous instruction process, they could unleash dormant abilities and keep this extraordinary talent alive."

I rubbed the tops of my jeans over and over. Did I really want to be involved with this? It was like I was being asked to produce a class play when I'd prefer to be part of the ensemble cast. But still, those were cool dreams.

"If we chose effectively, and I'm confident we have, then all you must do is climb onboard, and we'll begin a magical journey together. You'll learn more in the coming days, weeks, and months. Through a blend of your Creative Core and language arts classes, you'll create your own dreams, and we'll teach you how to *convey* them to others.

"This is sensitive information, and you are bound to keep it secret. Failure to do so will result in serious consequences."

I wiped my sweaty palms on my pants.

"Expulsion is one of many possibilities. This school is special, and we wish to keep it that way." Then Principal Locke slowed his voice so each word rang clear. "You are our next class of *dream-makers*."

Chapter: 8

I shuffled between Hannah and Aditi toward the exit, leaning on the wooden chairs along the aisle for support. I'd never fainted before, but I was so light-headed I thought I might. Snippets from the crowd broke through my fog. *Can you believe it? I was suspicious all along. Telepathy, he's got to be kidding! Did you have that dream last night?*

Once we emerged into the sunlight, I took a deep breath of the fresh air. Soon I was steady on my feet, and the guys caught up with us.

Hannah's eyes shone. "Do y'all want to find someplace to talk?"

Ben nodded. "You bet."

"There's rarely anyone behind O'Reilly," I suggested.

As we walked around the dorm, Aditi began, "What did you guys make of all that?"

"I think it's real," Hannah said. "I had his hiking dream…and well…" She shot me a questioning look.

"Tell them," I urged.

"Last week, I told Autumn there was something odd about how I wound up here." Hannah went on to explain how her parents' dreams had convinced them to let her apply to Dickensen. While she spoke, we reached the backside of the dormitory and sprawled in a haphazard circle on the cool grass in the shade of a big leaf maple.

I piped in. "I've had a few dreams like Principal Locke described. The hiking dream last night and—"

"Come on!" Ryan interrupted. "You can't really believe him?"

"Let her talk!"

Thanks, Ben. "I also dreamed I was taking pictures of people on campus before I accepted the offer, so when I got here, everything was strangely familiar. Oh, and the night before the interview, I dreamed I was a jockey in a steeplechase. Did any of you have that one?"

"Nope." Ryan scowled. "At the interview, I described a dream about playing soccer at the national championship. Doubt they sent it. I dream of soccer all the time. And I didn't have any dumb hiking dream last night."

"Maybe they'll put you into the remedial dream-making class," Hannah teased.

Ryan scrunched up his face at her. "Ha, ha."

"I had a sports dream before the interview too— about basketball." Ben twirled a large, golden leaf in his hand. "It's a bit fuzzy now. I remember the one about Dickensen better."

"Oh yeah." Ryan chuckled. "The one with Autumn."

I stared at the ground so no one would see my burning face.

"Until now, I didn't see how that dream or Autumn's could fit in," Ben said, ignoring Ryan's comment. "But Locke's crazy Dream Management makes sense of why the freshmen have been isolated. Like Gabe saying we couldn't hang out for a while. Not being allowed into Rogers Hall. And even the locked doors to the sophomore wing."

"Thought you said they were planning some sort of hazing ritual?" Ryan asked.

"It was my best guess. Still, I felt there was something more, but no one besides Autumn wanted to hear it." Ben continued to fiddle with the leaf. "I knew something was special about that dream. But you kept hounding me about it, so I tried to forget it." He punched Ryan in the arm. "See, it didn't mean what you thought at all."

I sucked in a quick breath as if Ben had punched me too. But in the stomach. And harder. He truly didn't want anything more than friendship. My hope his dream had meant something about me disappeared like helium in a popped balloon.

Ryan narrowed his eyes at Ben. "Sure, if you want to believe Locke forced you to dream about a girl, fine."

Aditi elbowed Ryan. "Leave it alone."

"I'm just saying, most kids came here for the art and education. To get into a good college," Ryan said. "You guys can't seriously think there's more to this school than that."

"Do you believe Locke would lie?" Ben's tone was sharp.

"Telepathy isn't real!" Ryan's gaze darted between each of us. "It's got to be hypnotism or something. Locke is nuts. We're going to find out tomorrow we were the butt of some annual, school-wide joke."

I turned away from Ryan. "I believe our principal." It was the only explanation that made sense. "Hannah, have you talked to Caitlyn yet?"

She shrugged. "Kind of. She admitted her brother Tom graduated from here a couple of years ago. But she didn't say anything about dream-making."

"Can you ask her again?" Aditi asked.

"No way! I actually have to live with the girl. You ask."

Poor Hannah. Was her relationship with Caitlyn even worse than she'd let on?

"Doesn't matter anyway," Hannah said. "We'll find out more in class."

"The only thing is," Ben began, "how have they kept this from the rest of the world? You'd think it would've leaked somehow. Gone viral."

"Like I told you, if telepathy was real, people would know," Ryan shot back.

"It could explain the fence," Hannah said. "Maybe it keeps animals *and* curious people out."

"Perhaps no one's talking." Aditi looked slowly around our group. "Principal Locke warned us there'd be consequences if we told anyone."

"They must be bad," Ben said. "That'd explain why Gabe and his friends were freaked when we overheard them."

"Well…" Ryan blew out a long breath. "If these guys can communicate telepathically, I bet there are thousands of ways to keep students in line. Think about it, you could manipulate people's minds."

We sat silent for a moment. A sick feeling grew in the pit of my stomach. I hadn't considered anything like that. Did my dream somehow force me to come to Dickensen? And Ben's? And Hannah's parents? Did we have a choice?

"Come on." Ryan laughed. "I was joking. There's

no way!"

"Well either Ryan is right and there's nothing to worry about—" Ben's mouth turned into a full-on grin, and his gorgeous, blue eyes lit up. "—or telepathy is real. And I'll bet it's pretty darn cool. Let's face it. The upperclassmen were excited to be back after summer break."

Ben's comments broke the tension, and we started to hypothesize about possible dreams. Soon we were talking over one another as our ideas grew more outrageous—time travel, flying like Peter Pan, speaking with animals, and our favorite, creating a clone to attend classes and complete our homework. Even Ryan joined in the fun, although he obviously wasn't convinced.

****

After dinner I tried to call home, but the phone lines were down. The internet too. Seemed a little coincidental. A sophomore informed me it was a frequent occurrence. Dickensen's official position stated powerful gusts of wind coming through the mountain range caused unreliable service. But rumor had it the school shut off all means of outside communication whenever they sensed their secret might be at risk. Tingles in my body affirmed the rumor was true.

I tossed and turned in bed for over an hour. Even though every part of my body needed sleep, my mind wouldn't shut off. I worried someone was peering into my brain right now with the power to control my dreams. But mostly, I wondered how it all worked and if other fantastical abilities could exist. When I was young, Dad had squashed so many of my fantasies and beliefs, using science to prove or disprove everything. Yet now this. No way would he believe in dream telepathy.

Chapter: 9

A new world had unfolded. Throughout the day, I observed the faculty, searching for some unique trait revealing the secret power they possessed. But they taught college requirements, same as before. In the hallways, I studied the older students, but they went about their business, gabbing with friends and rushing from class to class. I had to admit, I was relieved to see normal behavior. The notion of telepathy was thrilling but a little frightening too.

The day dragged on. I found myself reading the same paragraph from my science textbook five times. And then in Spanish, a student had to tap my back to break my trance and let me know Señor Ortiz had called on me. Not my brightest moment. The only thing out of the ordinary was gossip about Quinn spending the day in the school office, presumably for disrupting yesterday's assembly.

At last it was time for seventh period—Creative Core. I slipped into my seat and gazed around the art studio. Mr. Robbins wasn't at his desk. *What if he's sick?* I feared I'd burst with curiosity if I didn't learn more today, and I was already imagining the worst. Aditi and Ryan chatted together, Hannah doodled in her notebook, and Ben chewed on the end of his pencil as he paged through his planner. I doubt he even saw me with his hair covering half his face. I tried to remain calm, like my friends.

Mr. Robbins hurried in as the bell rang and dumped a pile of books on his desk. I strummed my fingers on my binder, waiting for him to get organized.

"Okay, class. Beginning today, this course will take a new direction. I'm now going to devote a portion of our time to Dream Management."

Goosebumps appeared on my arms. I caught Ben's eye and he grinned back. My classmates whispered excitedly.

"To begin, there are three distinct skills within the study of Dream Management." Mr. Robbins began to write on the whiteboard, twisting his body back toward us every so often. "The first is *dream reception*, the second is *dream creation*, and the third is *dream conveyance*." He paused while he finished writing.

"These skills build on one another. You must learn dream reception before dream creation, and you must learn dream creation before dream conveyance."

I scribbled frantically in my notebook to write it all down. When I looked up, a couple of students were raising their hands. Our teacher called on Ben.

"Does everyone have to master dream reception before we start dream creation?"

"Nope. Once I'm satisfied this class has reached an acceptable level of competence, we'll move on. After I've introduced all three skills, individuals can move between them while working toward mastery."

Mr. Robbins walked up and down the aisles, giving us more details about dream reception. He had our undivided attention as he explained how people who are imaginative, artistic, and/or spiritual tend to have the ability as well as young children. A handful of classmates, including Ryan, were clearly not one hundred percent committed. However, Mr. Robbins suggested everyone hang with him for a couple of weeks. Then if they still weren't convinced or didn't believe Dream Management was right for them to consult with him individually.

"Now some of you may be asking yourselves, why would someone even wish to send someone else a dream?"

That's what I'd been wondering. My theory: the school used these unforgettable dreams to convince us to accept. But that idea wasn't comforting.

"There are a variety of uses for these robust dreams, particularly in the fields of education and psychology. But that's years off for you. For now, our focus will be on education and entertainment." He eased himself onto the top of his desk. "So much of life can be busy, mundane, and repetitive, especially when you get to my age." He chuckled. "But we all have approximately eight hours a day when our bodies must rest. A dream can take that time and make it extraordinary."

"How?" Grace asked.

"Perhaps it's a memorable trip, a visit with a relative, or an encounter with a fairy tale figure. There's no limit to what you can create, only your imagination and skill."

I thought back to my dream about racing in a steeplechase. I could still recall the wind whipping through my hair, the sound of pounding hooves, the smell of sweat, the jolts as my horse jumped each obstacle. And of course, the silly grin I wore through it all.

"But what if I told you those hours of sleep could be used productively? This is where you as Dickensen students have a tremendous advantage over your peers in traditional high schools. Your teachers are all dream-makers, and they will use dreams to produce unforgettable lessons. What if your science teacher could send you back in time to view dinosaurs while you were studying fossils? Or what if you could watch a volcano erupt?" Mr. Robbins' voice grew louder, and the prance in his step reminded me of Principal Locke. "Or you could go into space and view the planets up close rather than memorizing them from a textbook. Or perhaps in history, you could watch a Civil War battle unfold or participate in the first Thanksgiving. Even in language arts, you could immerse yourself into the life of a literary character.

"Tim, what would you think of living a day in the life of Huckleberry Finn or Holden Caulfield?"

"I guess it could be kind of fun." Tim shrugged. "I don't know much about them."

"Or maybe Ms. Jenson will up the excitement level and teach something that has made its way to the big screen. Hannah, what would you think of experiencing the 1920s by attending one of Jay Gatsby's extravagant parties as Daisy Buchanan?"

Hannah grinned. "I'm all in."

"The possibilities are endless. Being engaged in an accurate dream created by one of your teachers is simply another method they have at their disposals to make the content of their courses more authentic and to bolster your memory recall." He smiled. "And it's infinitely more fun than traditional learning. By receiving these dreams throughout the next four years, you'll also retain your dream reception ability."

As Mr. Robbins continued on, my fears lessened. I wasn't sure how it all worked. But using dreams to teach seemed safe. Maybe even beneficial if I could actually learn from them.

A flurry of hands began waving the moment our teacher opened it up for questions.

"How often will we receive these dreams?" Ben asked.

Mr. Robbins considered his question. "It'll depend on your instructors. Some may only give you a few dreams throughout the year. Others may give them more frequently."

"How does a teacher give us a dream?" Jacob asked.

"Your question deals with dream conveyance. I'll introduce the topic in detail in another month or two. But to answer your question in simplistic terms, your teachers will create dreams based on content from their curriculums and then focus on their students to convey the dreams. Learning how to convey to a group of students is a high-level skill, which takes years to learn."

"Do all these dreams have the students travel outside the fence?" I asked. "Like the one Principal Locke sent us."

Mr. Robbins chuckled. "Many do. But not all. Guessing you've heard the term *outside the fence*. The phrase has become code around campus for experiencing a Dickensen dream."

I glanced over at Ben. He mouthed, "Good question."

With less than fifteen minutes left of class, Mr.

Robbins said, "I'll take one last question." He pointed at a student in the back. "Caitlyn?"

"Will we learn to create nightmares too?"

The room went silent. *What*? We'd been discussing academic dreams. Talk about a change in direction.

Mr. Robbins didn't answer at first. Instead he stared at a watermark on the ceiling as if he needed time to prepare an answer. "It's not something I teach. In fact, any of you caught attempting to create a nightmare will be expelled or severely punished. At Dickensen Academy, our mandate is to make the world a better place. That's why we were so careful in the recruitment process to select students who not only have the aptitude, but also the wisdom and moral fiber to use good judgment."

As Mr. Robbins explained, Caitlyn stared at him with a strange smile, as if she enjoyed watching him squirm. I glanced to my left at Hannah, who looked mortified. Why did one of the nicest girls in our grade get stuck with Caitlyn as a roommate?

"Okay, class, enough for now. Let's get out your oil pastels and continue where we left off yesterday. We don't have much time left."

A few students moaned, but I was content to switch to art. It would help me relax. Perhaps Mr. Robbins knew that after being bombarded with so much information, yet again, we would need some normalcy. Ending on a discussion about concocting nightmares had taken away some of the peace I'd begun to feel.

"Remember," he said, "we've got to keep up with the art lessons if you're ever going to create settings for your dreams."

I pulled out my crayon-like oil pastels and removed

my drawing from my portfolio. I'd sketched a flowered meadow earlier in the week and was now coloring it in. I loved the smooth, velvety feel of the pastels as I drew on the paper. But using my fingertips to blend and shade was still a strange sensation—I'd never been a kid who liked to get dirty. I looked at my drawing from a new perspective, realizing for the first time it wasn't simply a picture to hang on the wall. It could form a backdrop for a dream I'd create. I shook my head slightly as I worked, still having a tough time believing this was truly happening.

****

As I approached my room after cross country practice, faint, yet familiar, high-pitched buzzing sounds of the sitar filtered from under the door. Aditi often played instrumental Indian music through her speaker dock while she studied—said it helped her focus. But I'm pretty sure she listened to it because it reminded her of home. Maybe she was feeling a little apprehensive too. When I stepped in, she turned down the volume and rolled her chair toward me. "Did you hear the news?"

"What news?" There'd been so much of it in the past twenty-four hours, I had no idea what she might be referring to.

"About Quinn."

I arched an eyebrow. "I only heard he was called to the office."

"Well…" The way she drew out the word told me this was going to be some juicy gossip, so I got comfortable on the bed. "Ryan talked with Quinn this afternoon. He told me Quinn spent *hours* with Dean Rothchild and Principal Locke. They had a discussion about whether he should remain at Dickensen or not."

She stopped mid-story, her eyes wide and her lips smashed together as if she were struggling to keep the words from pouring out.

I threw a wadded piece of paper at her. "Aditi, I'm dying here!"

She leaped onto my bed beside me. "So last night Quinn told some other students he didn't believe anything Principal Locke said and planned to tell his friends at home once the phone lines were fixed. Someone must've overheard and told the faculty because last night he had an awful nightmare as punishment—something straight out of *The Hunger Games,* where people were chasing him through the forest, trying to kill him. His roommate couldn't even wake him while he thrashed about."

My mouth hung open. "Did he get kicked out?"

She shook her head. "He gets to stay on some type of probation. Supposedly he didn't think the school was serious about all this dream stuff. But after his nightmare, he knows it's for real."

I swallowed hard. "Are you even supposed to be telling me this?"

"Get this. Ryan said Dean Rothchild told Quinn to spread the message as a warning." Aditi blew out a long breath. "It's gotten to Ryan. He's totally shaken up. Oh, one more thing. Quinn said don't even think of posting anything related to Dream Management online. Your account will somehow be shut down before you know it."

Chapter: 10

I shifted positions at the wood desk in my dorm room, trying to focus. I'd spent most of the afternoon in the art studio so hadn't gotten much else accomplished today.

I reread page seventy-three of my science text.

The corkboard, covered in notes and photos, hanging two feet from my face, seemed too close tonight. I attempted a calming breath, but the air was too thick to enter my throat.

"Aditi, doesn't the air in here seem a little stale?"

She glanced around our tiny space and shrugged. "It's fine to me. Maybe crack the window."

I shoved it open and returned to my desk. A minute later, I still couldn't breathe right. The slight breeze hadn't made an ounce of difference. Our room simply didn't hold enough oxygen, and I was slowly suffocating.

"I'll be back."

Minutes later, I pushed open O'Reilly's heavy exterior doors. I inhaled deeply for several minutes before my lungs had their fill. Lightheaded, I staggered to a nearby bench. A few tears fell. Using the sleeve of my sweatshirt, I dried my face. I still had fifteen pages of science to read and an algebra worksheet to complete, but I needed a break even though I'd stopped for dinner not long ago.

I couldn't go back to my room. I felt so trapped up there. Taking another deep breath, I leaned back on the bench. The setting sun cast long shadows from the tall evergreen trees. Here I was in a beautiful prison, trapped outside too. The surrounding forest hid an enormous, secure fence. We couldn't leave campus for months. Our phones and internet were monitored. Visitors weren't allowed. But now I knew why. No wonder a general sense of unease tugged at me from the corners of my mind. The overwhelming homework certainly didn't help.

My initial enthusiasm for Dream Management had waned over the last week and a half because we'd only learned some basic theory and history of the discipline. Mr. Robbins explained that cynicism would interfere with our capacity to receive dreams, so we couldn't move forward until the entire freshman class accepted the idea of dream telepathy. Or what remained of us.

Since Quinn'd had his nightmare, nobody else experienced one. However, a pair of roommates mysteriously disappeared within three days of each other. Mr. Robbins only said the boys had chosen to return home. But the less that was said, the more I worried. I was beginning to think these weeks were actually a test. Did the school trust us to keep their knowledge confidential?

The campus had dimmed with dusk. Where could I go now? The game room? Wasn't in the mood. I checked my watch. Maybe I could catch the Saturday night movie later. But those weren't the kind of breaks I needed.

I wanted to go to the mall with Julia. I wanted to meet Josh's new girlfriend. I wanted to take Zoey to the park with Drew and his dog. And I wanted to chitchat with Mom while helping her make dinner rather than have another unnatural conversation on the phone. I even missed Dad when he was in his relaxed-weekend mode—not to be confused with his high-pressure-you-can-do-better mode.

I dragged myself up to the phone room. I needed to hear a familiar voice from my old life. First, I called Julia. Her mother answered, but Julia's voice sounded in the background. She was with a friend, and they were getting ready to go to the high school football game. She'd call me tomorrow.

Then I tried Drew. Same story.

At last, I called home and faked some enthusiasm. Didn't want Mom's homesickness detector to go off. Getting her all sad and worried wasn't going to help. "Hey, Mom. Guess what I did today?"

"What?"

"I took this really cool drawing workshop. I'm finally getting 3D shapes down, so they don't look like an elementary kid's doodles."

"That's great, honey."

"Only problem, it lasted four hours. So now I have all this studying to do."

"Well, I'm sure it was worth it. I'd love to hear all about it, but we were about to leave for the football game. Josh is starting, so we want to get there before kickoff. Your father's already in the car."

"Oh…"

"You okay? I can call back on my cell."

"I'm fine." I made an effort to sound normal. "Just tired." No way was I going to have a heart-to-heart while Dad listened in. "I'll call you tomorrow. Cheer on

Josh for me."

I hung up the phone more miserable than before. The whole world was going to the game except me. It hit me how hard it was to see everyone in Seattle go on with their lives.

As I trudged back to my room, I passed Mrs. Humphrey's doorway. Although she was my RA, we'd never had a real conversation. Maybe she could help somehow. I knocked tentatively on her door. What was I going to say? I started to back away, but then footsteps approached. Too late.

A moment later, we were face to face. I must've been a terrible sight with my splotchy skin and puffy face because she ushered me inside. She led me into a cozy room filled with antique furniture. At one end of the space was a kitchen nook. An open doorway revealed a bedroom with its own bathroom. I'd love my own bathroom! Cluttered with pictures and knick-knacks, the apartment reminded me of my grandparents' home. Not a surprise since Mrs. Humphrey was about the same age.

She gestured toward the old-fashioned sofa. "Have a seat." It turned out to be more comfortable than it looked as it enveloped me in its cushiony softness. "Would you like a cup of tea?"

I wasn't a tea drinker but didn't want to be rude. "Sure. Thank you."

"I hope chamomile is all right. It's my favorite in the evenings, and my girls seem to like it. Not too strong and no caffeine." As she clattered about the kitchenette, she added, "They say it has a calming effect, and I have to agree."

Beside me was an end table covered in framed

photos. One caught my eye. About fifty students posed in front of the school building. Everything appeared the same as now except the ornamental trees in the picture were much shorter and covered in pink blossoms.

Mrs. Humphrey set two steaming, fragrant cups of tea on the coffee table. "Give it a few minutes to steep. Be careful, it's hot." Then she took a seat kitty-corner from me. The tea was in a floral, china teacup—so different from the solid mugs Mom used for coffee. It was like being in another time period. I took a sip. Not too bad, almost like drinking flowers.

She nudged her chin at the photo. "I was part of the class of 1962, the inaugural class."

My jaw dropped. "You were here when it opened?"

"I was," she replied wistfully.

"What was it like back then?"

"Some of the buildings were still under construction. They hadn't even broken ground on Rogers Hall. But we were like you, adapting to being on our own and all the hard work...and the secrets."

My body began to sweat and I unzipped my hoodie. "Did you have a hard time when you came here?"

"Are you asking if I ever got homesick?"

I bowed my head. That was part of it. "Yeah. Kind of."

"Of course, dear. Everybody does. I've been in this position for over fifteen years, and I assure you most of my girls have experienced homesickness at some point. All those restrictions they put on you in the beginning don't help. You'll adjust and make friends. Things will get better soon." She squeezed my hand and gazed into my eyes. "I promise."

A smile spread across my face. "I've actually already made some good friends." Then I went on to explain how in some ways, I felt like I belonged at Dickensen more than at home. There I was often uptight, particularly around Dad. But here, I didn't have the same pressure and was learning to be myself.

"So tell me more about your family."

As I leaned back into the couch, my words flowed and the tension in my chest loosened. Mrs. Humphrey had a knack for opening me up. Or maybe the herbs in her tea were more potent than I had expected. The more at ease I grew, the more I realized I wanted to talk about everything bothering me. I scooted more upright. "I'm not just homesick." I wasn't sure how much to say. But she'd attended school here. She knew what it was like. "It's the whole Dream Management thing. It sounds cool. It does, but…"

Mrs. Humphrey set down her teacup with a faint clink and moved to the couch, settling next to me. "Go on, dear."

"Well, two of my classmates disappeared. And this guy Quinn got this terrible nightmare because he planned to tell some of his friends about Dream Management."

"Oh yes, Quinn. I heard about him. The poor lad. I assume Principal Locke warned you not to mention anything about Dream Management?"

"Uh-huh."

She gave me a sad smile. "It's always tough after the initial reveal. Teenagers like to talk. But I'd guess one nightmare was enough to convince him and the others to remain quiet."

I swallowed hard. "Have you had a Dickensen

nightmare?"

"Heavens no! I had the good sense to know what was expected of me. They're reserved for people who violate the rules. And I imagine the administration has some other tricks up their sleeves if nightmares don't work for a particular person."

A sudden bout of dizziness forced my head into my hands.

"Oh, Autumn. Don't be alarmed. Most people will only experience amazing dreams. As long as you follow the rules, no harm will come. It's like at any other school; there have to be consequences. We happen to have a unique one at our disposal. Punishments like nightmares and expulsion are rare."

After a few deep breaths, I felt a little better. We were warned, and Quinn had flaunted his plan to talk. *Harm. Other tricks up their sleeves.* No way was I going to utter a word.

"But what about the students who disappeared?" I asked at last.

She smiled. "I doubt they truly disappeared."

"Okay, well, moved out without any goodbyes."

"Dream-making is not for everyone. Each year a few students decide it's not right for them, so they choose to leave. They were probably too embarrassed to face their peers is all."

"So I could leave too, if I wanted?"

She patted my thigh. "Of course, dear. Anytime."

Hearing those words was comforting. It made me feel less trapped. Despite the way I'd felt the past few days, I knew deep down I didn't want to return home. Besides, it would prove to Dad I couldn't hack it on my own.

She lifted my chin to meet her gaze. Her gray-blue eyes had lost their warmth. "But if you go home, know there is no coming back."

****

It didn't take long to fall asleep since the flood of emotions had left me exhausted. But then I found myself at Memorial Stadium in downtown Seattle. The night was chilly and clear. My cup of hot chocolate warmed my hands, and I took occasional sips of the sweet, frothy liquid.

The sun had set, and overhead lights blazed down on the football field. I was squished between Hannah and Julia, with Aditi and a girl I didn't recognize on their other sides. Drew, Ben, and Ryan goofed around on the bleachers in front of us as if they were longtime buddies.

The Haller Lake football team had the ball. Josh lined up on the field in his green and gold uniform, number eighty-three. The scoreboard displayed 21 to 24 with the opposing team in the lead. It was second down, and the quarterback completed a long pass to Josh near the sideline. As he sprinted down the field, several opponents in navy and white uniforms chased him. One dove at Josh but missed the tackle, allowing him to run into the end zone. I jumped up and down and hugged my friends. Somehow I didn't spill my drink.

Soon the crowd noise faded away, and I was vaguely aware of the blankets in my bed. Before long, I drifted back to sleep.

Chapter: 11

As soon as I booted my computer Sunday morning, an email from Drew popped up. I smiled. He preferred to text, but without wireless or cell coverage here at Dickensen, he didn't have many options to reach me.

Sept 30 at 10:14 a.m.
Subject: Hi!
Drew Miller
To: Autumn Mattison

~*~

Hey Autumn,
My mom said you called last night. Sorry I missed you. Was at the football game. Great game! We won thanks to Josh. He caught a freaking long pass and made the game-winning touchdown. You should have seen it. Call me.

Miss you :-)
Drew

My mouth dropped open. What the...? I read then reread the email. My brother really did make a touchdown to win the game. *That's what I dreamed!*

I checked the time. Drew's family would be at church, so I called home instead. Funny, but as I dialed, I realized I was no longer homesick, simply curious about the game. The evening with Mrs. Humphrey combined with a good night's sleep had made me feel so much better.

Dad picked up. "Hello?"

"Hey, Dad."

"Morning. We thought you might call today. Your mother said you phoned as we were leaving for the game."

"Yeah. Bad timing."

"You should've seen Josh last night." Dad's rare excitement came through in his voice. "In the fourth quarter when Haller Lake was down, he caught a forty-yard pass and ran it into the end zone. We won twenty-eight to twenty-four!"

Dad continued to rattle off facts about the game, but my mind raced in circles.

"Autumn?"

It was like my mouth was sealed shut with peanut butter.

"Autumn? Are you there?"

I found my voice. "Yeah, Dad. Sorry. A little tired is all."

"How's your algebra tutoring going?"

I faked a yawn. "Pretty good. My tutor is super helpful. I totally get it now." That was close enough to the truth.

"I'm glad math is going better this year. Sorry to cut this short, but your mother is anxious to get on. We'll talk tonight when we do your review."

I gritted my teeth but managed to utter an obedient "okay." A month into school and still the stupid weekly reviews.

"Oh, and make sure you have all your notebooks when you call. It might be a good idea to review science too."

I sighed. It was as if he wanted to relive high

school but at my expense.

A moment later, Mom got on. "Hey, honey. You okay? You didn't sound like yourself yesterday. Then when your RA left a message, I started to worry."

My eyes popped open. "Mrs. Humphrey called you?"

"She said to call when we got home."

Ugh! I hadn't wanted Mom to know I was homesick. And I sure didn't want every bit of our conversation to get passed along. "What'd you talk about?"

"She likes to get to know the families of her girls. We didn't get much chance to talk the day we dropped you off."

I bit my thumbnail. "What did you tell her?"

"A little about us and the reasons we allowed you to attend Dickensen." She lowered her voice. "I mentioned your father puts a lot of pressure on you and is already pushing you into medicine."

My mouth curled into a tentative smile. "Yeah. And?"

"I said I just want you to be happy. And the future is your decision. But I do agree a solid education will open doors for you."

I was full-on grinning now. "Really?"

"Yes, really." I pictured her smiling on her end, holding the phone between her ear and shoulder as she folded laundry or busied herself around the house with some other task.

"Thanks, Mom." Knowing her and Dad's united front wasn't so united was a huge deal. "Anything else?"

"That's about it. We talked about how we'd missed

your call because we were at Josh's game."

I breathed a sigh of relief. I should've known my RA could keep secrets.

After I hung up, a warm feeling of contentment came over me, grateful Mom and I still had a relationship where we could be open and honest…well, about most things.

****

I had a ton of homework to do since I bailed on the library yesterday to attend the Drawing Intensive Workshop, and the night had been a total bust. Ben was my favorite study partner. Of course, I'd use any excuse to hang out with him, especially alone. As a bonus, if I ever got stuck on an algebra problem, Ben would explain it to me in terms even I could understand.

He'd lean over, his blond hair flopping inches from my face. "Here, let me show you." I'd attempt to focus on his explanation but always had a hard time ignoring my body's response to his beautiful olive skin and the lean muscles of his arms, smelling of soap and a hint of some citrusy deodorant. For the first time in my life, I was actually enjoying math homework. Nothing beats having a hot guy sitting next to me going through an algebraic equation. Okay, I could imagine more exciting scenarios, but we hadn't yet made it past friendship—except in my own mind that was.

But math wasn't the problem today. After a long period of staring into space, I asked, "Can we take a break?"

He brushed his hair aside and lifted his gaze. "Now? Don't you want to wait until three?" Every Sunday afternoon the cooks made up a delicious batch of cookies, brownies, and other sweet treats—our standard study break.

I shook my head. I needed his opinion now before everyone in the dining hall offered theirs.

He pushed back his chair from the table. "Let's go." Ben never minded a break. He didn't have to study as hard as me. He had the focus and intellect of an adult crammed into his teenage brain. We left our books in the library. I still had to finish my essay about *The Great Gatsby*, but if I didn't spill what was on my mind, I'd waste the entire afternoon debating the possible reasons I was so much happier today.

As we headed away from the students clustered between the dorms and the library, I poured out the details of my football dream, the email from Drew, and the phone conversation with Dad. "The way it stayed with me reminded me of the photography and hiking dreams. And you know how I've been a bit homesick lately?"

He nodded.

"When I woke up today, it had vanished. Poof! Homesickness gone. It's like I actually visited my friends in Seattle."

Ben motioned for me to sit on a bench along the campus path.

"Do you think Mrs. Humphrey gave it to me? I was with her right before bed. And she knew I was homesick."

He slumped down next to me and rubbed his fingers on his forehead as he stared at the grass. He bit his lower lip and nodded methodically. I was dying to read his mind.

"But how did she know about the score and the catch?" he mumbled. He sat back up after a minute.

"What'd Aditi say?"

I snorted. "She joked that maybe I have ESP."

"Maybe you do." He exhaled while he took in the cloud-covered sky. "Wouldn't that be cool?" Then he looked back at me, eyes wide. "Maybe Mrs. Humphrey can see the future."

"Or into other people's minds is what I was thinking." A notion I found more than a little disturbing. I had kind of hoped Ben would tell me that was impossible.

"Ask her," Ben urged. "You have time. Go now." He practically pushed me off the bench.

I raced back to O'Reilly, praying Mrs. Humphrey was available.

At her door, I smoothed down my clothes and knocked, hoping she didn't think I was bothering her too much. I had chewed up her entire Saturday night.

When she opened the door, her face lit up. "Good afternoon, Autumn. Stopped by for another chat?"

My uneasiness about interrupting left like heat from an oven. Mrs. Humphrey seemed delighted to see me again, and her voice was warm and welcoming—perhaps why she was so popular.

I nodded. "If you have time."

"I always have time for my girls."

I followed her into her apartment and sat on the couch.

"Tea?"

"Sure."

This time she served a chai tea. It was stronger than the chamomile. Probably a good thing. I didn't need to grow sleepy.

After some chitchat, I worked up the courage to

say, "I don't know how all of this dream stuff works…so I have to ask, by any chance did you send me a dream last night? One about a football game?" I hoped she wouldn't think I was stupid or crazy.

She gave a guilty grin, like a young girl. "You got me. I hope you enjoyed it."

My muscles sagged in relief. I was right. "Oh, I did! I feel so much better. As if I'm meant to be here, and my home and school lives can somehow intertwine."

"Wonderful. That's what I was aiming for."

I bit my lip. "But this morning, I received an email from my friend Drew, and he mentioned the football play where my brother scored the winning touchdown. And then later, my dad repeated the same story. Even the score was identical."

Mrs. Humphrey didn't look surprised.

"How'd you do that? Are you a mind reader, or do you tell the future? I don't like to say it, but even though all this dream stuff is amazing, it's also a little creepy. Like someone is watching us."

She gave me a reassuring smile. "It's not like that at all. Dream Management is a respectable talent. I was simply trying to help you overcome your homesickness. Nothing more."

"But what about Josh's touchdown?"

She sipped her tea. "What about it?"

"How'd you know?"

She dismissed my comment with a swat of her hand. "You probably got all these ideas in your head from books and movies. I can't get into your mind or hear your thoughts. I knew about the game because I spoke with your mother."

That's right. Mom mentioned they'd talked.

"Getting to know the families of my girls is the best way for me to create realistic dreams. Besides, last night you needed to experience the power of our dreams. In my opinion, the teachers take too long to dive into their Dream Management curriculums."

I nodded. Maybe if one of my teachers had conveyed something like that I wouldn't have been so tense this past week.

"By speaking with both you and your mother, I gathered enough information to create the dream. In reality, the football play didn't go exactly as portrayed. I only knew your brother caught a long pass and ran twenty yards for the winning touchdown. I believe I had him on the right side of the field." Mrs. Humphrey chuckled to herself. "For all I know, he could've been running backward and on the opposite side. As for the rest of it, I concentrated on the names of your friends, which allowed your mind to insert their images into the dream. A similar method was used to pull an image of the stadium into the background."

"So no two-way communication?"

"None at all. For me this was an easy dream since most of the images already resided in your brain and your mother supplied a portion of the storyline. I only filled in the blanks."

My lower jaw practically fell into my lap.

"I know. I'm way ahead of you." She patted my thigh. "Your teachers will show you how to make it happen."

As with the other recent revelations, it was impossible to process all at once. I could only shake my head and smile.

Soon her cuckoo clock chimed three times.

I must've fidgeted because she asked, "Do you need to go?"

"Well...I have a lot of studying to do."

She winked. "Make sure you stop by the dining hall. It's time for Sunday Snacks."

My cheeks warmed.

She laughed. "They began the tradition back when I was a student." Mrs. Humphrey leaned over and embraced me. It felt so good, like hugging an old friend—well, maybe more like an elderly aunt. I promised to visit again soon, then raced to the dining hall to tell everyone what I'd learned.

Chapter: 12

Aditi shook me awake. "We have to hurry. Mr. Katz said to meet in the quad for the field trip."

My clock displayed 1:12 a.m. She had to be kidding. But my body had a mind of its own and crawled out of bed. We threw on some clothes and jackets and entered the hall where we bumped into Hannah. No one else was around, so we quickened our pace down the stairs, hoping we weren't late.

We emerged from the dorm into the frigid night air, forcing me wide-awake. Three dark figures stood ahead in the center of the quad. As we approached, I recognized Mr. Katz, Ben, and Ryan. Our science teacher was dressed in a hiking ensemble, complete with heavy boots and khaki pants. I glanced down at my jeans and running shoes and shrugged. My friends wore similar clothes as me.

Mr. Katz handed us each a half-empty backpack.

"Where's the rest of our class?" I asked.

He smiled. "It's just us tonight."

"Huh?"

"For your first field trip, I find it's a better educational experience to have an intimate tour. This way I can cater the learning to your needs. You've selected your best friends." Then he spun around and strode across the quad.

Wait, what? I raced to catch up. How had *I* selected

my best friends? He'd chosen them, not me. And how would he know the five of us were so tight? We weren't even in science together. We continued past the far end of the parking lot and down the entrance road. The moon was nearly full, so I could see well enough once my eyes adjusted even without any path lights.

"I've brought you here to study the ecosystems. We've done a nice job studying the coniferous forest in daylight, but it's a distinctive experience at night." After nearly fifteen years of living in the Pacific Northwest, thanks to my science class I could finally identify the firs, pines, cedar, hemlock, spruce, and larch growing in the Cascades near Dickensen and in most of Washington State.

Suddenly, a massive bird with a wingspan of at least four feet dove to the pavement in front of us. I stopped short and Hannah shrieked. Then as quickly as it arrived, it disappeared back into the forest.

"Man! Was that an owl?" Ryan stared at where it had gone.

"Absolutely," our teacher confirmed. "Any guesses on the type?"

We hadn't studied owls in class, but Grandma Clarke collected owl pictures and figurines, which she displayed throughout her house. My grandparents lived in the suburbs, and sometimes I could hear owls hooting there at night.

"Maybe a great horned owl?" I ventured.

"Good guess," Mr. Katz said. "From its size, it could also have been a barred owl. It was too dark to get a clear view."

"How do you tell the difference?" Ryan asked.

Mr. Katz nodded at me so I answered, "The great

horned owl has large ear tufts. I suggested it because it's the most common owl in the state." I couldn't wait to tell Grandma I was the class expert.

Soon Mr. Katz veered right and entered a path through the woods so narrow we had to proceed single file. The moonlight barely reached us through the trees, but there was just enough to make our way without tripping over roots or running into branches. The trail was soft beneath our feet from layers of needles, and the pine scent was stronger than on campus.

"Watch your faces," he warned. He stopped to unlock a steel gate. "Let's remain silent from this point forward."

I clenched my hands. Although I was now convinced the fence's primary purpose was to keep out unwanted human visitors, there had to be more dangerous animals beyond it.

We walked on for another five minutes or so until our teacher froze.

"What are we doing?" Ben whispered.

"Listen," Mr. Katz said.

At first the world was soundless. But then, without my sense of sight, my ears came alive. The forest wasn't as quiet as I'd suspected.

Hoo-hoohoo, hoo, hoo.

After several moments of silence, an echo returned. *Hoo-hoohoo, hoo, hoo.*

I jutted out my chin and stood a bit taller. Two great horned owls. I had been right. Their call sounds like *who's awake? Me too!*

We continued to listen.

Something rustled nearby. My heart skipped a beat. Could it be a bear or a cougar?

Mr. Katz pulled out a flashlight and methodically shined it around. A few of my friends did the same.

"Over there," Ryan whispered.

I followed his beam of light. A gray opossum scampered up a tree.

"We must've scared it. Typically they prefer the ground," Mr. Katz said.

"Don't they hang upside down?" Hannah asked.

"A myth. Their tails aren't strong enough to hang for more than a moment," he said. "Let's turn off our lights but remain quiet. Follow me. We aren't going to spend much more time here." I felt a twinge of disappointment, like when the power goes out during a movie that's starting to get good. Perhaps our teacher thought we needed sleep.

Soon the surroundings slowly grew brighter. Then a familiar sound pattered the branches above.

"Uh-oh," Aditi said. "Rain."

"It's to be expected," our teacher said.

The pungent smell of moist earth replaced the pine scent, and my feet began to squish through mud. My new shoes were soaked. *Great! Mom is going to kill me.* Instead of the coolness I associated with rain, I started to sweat.

Flickering rays of morning light now outlined the trees. It made no sense. We hadn't been gone for more than thirty minutes…or so I thought. Deciduous trees, rather than conifers, now grew near us, and thick vines and plants hung from above.

My shock mirrored my friends' whose mouths hung open as if they were in dental chairs. They twisted around, gazing in every direction. Mr. Katz slipped off his jacket. I did too. The humidity now clung to my exposed arms.

He turned to me as I stuffed my jacket into my pack. "What do you think?"

"It feels like we're in a rainforest, but that's impossible."

"Nothing is impossible at Dickensen."

What is this place? Rainforests covered parts of the Olympic Mountain range closer to the Pacific Ocean, but they held primarily evergreens. Were we in a secluded section of the Cascades that our teacher knew about?

Hang on. Could this be a dream?

I pinched my arm but didn't wake up. Then I remembered Mr. Robbins had warned us not to dwell too much on the fact we may be dreaming because the awareness could cause us to exit the dream, so I focused on Mr. Katz instead.

He quizzed us about tropical deciduous forests. "Could someone tell me which type of flora is most common here? How about the fauna? Who can list the nonliving factors?"

My science knowledge began to click into place. It was so much easier to understand the dependencies between the rainforest's components when I could see, feel, hear, and smell them. When we got to the decomposition of the forest floor, our teacher overturned a huge leaf. I jumped back—the soil teemed with life. But curiosity overcame me. Soon all of us circled around the leaf, bent at the waist, while Mr. Katz pointed out the unique, oversized insects.

After we had our fill of the larger-than-life bugs, he identified the surrounding trees.

"Does the rubber in toys and other products come

from these trees?" Ben asked.

"Yes," Mr. Katz said. "In fact these trees can be tapped for a milky sap called latex, a component in natural rubber, making these trees a significant source of income."

Hannah scrunched up her face. "Doesn't that kill the trees?"

"No. It's more like tapping for maple sap. Rubber tappers, as they're called, do everything in their power to keep their trees healthy. These trees are native to the Amazon but are now being planted elsewhere." He went on to describe how planting rubber trees in areas where they were not indigenous was taking a toll on the environment.

"That's crazy a tree so helpful for some parts of the world can be so stinkin' awful for others," Ryan said.

"Yeah," I agreed. I wished humans would leave Earth's natural balance alone.

Soon we came to a taller tree—a mahogany—and Mr. Katz began to climb a series of wooden slats nailed into its trunk. "Follow me."

"Wonder what's up here?" Aditi asked as she climbed, echoing my thoughts.

Hannah followed. "Maybe a tree house?" She looked down at me, her blue eyes sparkling and her mouth turning up into a gigantic grin.

After a few minutes, we stepped onto a wooden platform. It was much brighter up here, and Mr. Katz continued his lesson about the vertical stratification of the forest.

"Look!" Aditi pointed up. "You really can see how the canopy differs from the emergent section."

I trained my gaze on the birds above. "Yeah. I

never quite got all this stuff before."

Mr. Katz grabbed several vines and held one out. "Who wants to go first?"

He had to be kidding.

Ryan stepped forward, his eyes lit up. "Me."

"Don't let go until you reach the far end," Mr. Katz instructed.

Without hesitation, Ryan grabbed the vine, ran toward the edge of the platform, and jumped off. His joyous screams traveled back to us.

"Who's next?"

Ben and Hannah each took a vine. They both appeared eager. Ben gave the vine a quick tug, presumably to make sure it'd hold his weight. Then he leaped off, followed by Hannah.

I waited for Aditi. She was the least athletic and needed more encouragement. When she left the platform, she screamed like a heroine in a horror film.

Soon my teacher and I stood alone. My stomach tied in knots. I always liked thrill rides, but amusement park rides were designed and tested by experts. I peered up to see where my vine was attached.

Before I could analyze too much, Mr. Katz said, "Let me show you." Then with the confidence and grace of a trapeze artist, he pulled himself up with both arms, held his feet in front of him, and sailed away. Ten seconds later his vine swung partway back, empty.

I wasn't about to stay here alone, so I closed my eyes and jumped. Warm air rushed by me and rustled the trees. Opening my eyes a crack, I hurtled past branches and giant leaves, praying I wouldn't hit anything solid. After nearing the forest floor, I began to fly up. *When do I let go?* As the rope reached its zenith,

I loosened my grip.

Thump. I landed on my back in a pile of scratchy, yellow grass. When I looked toward the sky, an animal hovered over me, staring down. My stomach leaped to my throat. I scuttled backward on my elbows and heels but couldn't move far in the thick grass.

The animal's warm brown eyes gazed into mine. It didn't appear scared; rather, it seemed curious. Its stocky body and curved horns were familiar, but the name wouldn't come. Since it was a herding animal and unlikely a threat, I stood cautiously. *Wow!* Hundreds of them grazed a stone's throw beyond me.

Off to my right was Mr. Katz. Obviously he'd landed on his feet because he stood tall and appeared straight out of a Banana Republic advertisement. My friends, on the other hand, were disheveled and covered in dust and grass.

I spun around. The forest behind me had vanished, replaced by a grassy plain. All I could do was stare in wonder at its vastness.

Ben pointed to the herd of animals. "Are those wildebeests?"

Mr. Katz nodded. "Yes, they're migrating."

"How did we get here?" Aditi asked.

Instead of answering her question, Mr. Katz explained the characteristics of a savanna ecosystem. As we examined unfamiliar grasses and shrubs and the occasional tree, our conversation delved deeper than it could have in the classroom and became more memorable. When we got to the topic of biomes versus ecosystems, Mr. Katz recited a textbook explanation.

"I still don't get it," I said.

"Here, let me show you…"

The next moment I was sprawled on the bottom of a glass bottom boat staring into the murky depths of a stagnant pond. The change in ecosystems reminded me I was dreaming. But as before, I forgot as I immersed myself in the new environment. It continued that way all night as Mr. Katz toured us around the world. Some of the transitions between locations were subtle such as when we moved from one aquatic ecosystem to the next. But some were more dramatic. My favorite was when the sunlight, dancing on the ocean, twisted like a kaleidoscope before my eyes and became glaring crystals of snow and ice.

Our adventure lasted for what seemed an entire day. We delved into far greater detail of the many processes he'd taught during class, including photosynthesis, decomposition, and the food chain, and we discussed how they varied from one ecosystem to the next. I'd never done well memorizing lists of random facts, but the facts were no longer random.

As the sun set in the desert, the temperature plummeted, and I reached into my backpack for the umpteenth time today—or was it night? The treetops in the distance seemed to approach us, and soon the ground changed beneath my feet. A glimpse down showed the sand was giving way to pine needles and dirt. What a relief to walk on something solid after the effort required to trudge through deep sand. As I slipped into the darkness of the forest, I took one last look over my shoulder at the sun glistening on the sand dunes and the long shadows of the camels that had been our most recent companions.

We followed our teacher through the woods back to our dorm. My adrenaline had faded to nothing. Aditi and I were so tired we paused only long enough to remove our muddy shoes and damp coats before crawling into bed fully clothed.

Chapter: 13

I woke, gradually opening my eyes to the morning light.

Aditi stared at me from her bed. "You…you had it too?"

It all came back. I glanced down at my pajamas, half-expecting to see my dirty clothes. I chuckled. "Yeah. I guess I did."

"It's weird. It feels like I got twelve hours of sleep. I haven't felt this rested in forever."

"Me too. You'd think we'd be exhausted."

The dining hall was louder than usual at breakfast with hyped up freshmen comparing notes. All of us had similar dreams. The primary differences seemed to be the people who traveled with us and the length of time spent in each ecosystem. The skeptics now had to accept the concept of Dream Management. Ryan even asked me to describe my football dream in detail—he'd been cynical, to say the least, when I told him about it last weekend.

The entire experience bonded us. I could remember chitchatting with Hannah, as our camel lumbered across the desert, and dying of laughter when she grabbed me from behind to keep me from tumbling over the camel's head when it eased down to the ground. And I could recall the bear sauntering past our raft, shocking us when it plunged into the river rapids and came up with a flapping salmon in its mouth. I'd never shared such memories with anyone. Between last night's dream and the football dream, it was now easier to understand the benefits of created dreams, and my fears continued to lessen.

****

Mr. Katz's light blue, button-down shirt, brown pants, and loafers struck me as odd. Such a turnaround from last night. My impression of him had changed too in the last twenty-four hours—more approachable, yet at the same time, my respect for him as a science expert had skyrocketed.

"Good morning, class. I hope you had a nice, *relaxing* sleep last night."

The classroom erupted in snickers.

"Based on your attitude, it appears I was successful. But first, does anyone not understand what I'm referring to? It's important for me to find out if anyone missed last night's *field trip*." He scanned the room. "Anyone?" No one raised a hand.

"Great. That's what I expected, but sometimes one or two students have difficulty in the beginning. Usually academic dreams go through as intended since they've been created by experienced dream-makers. As you progress, you'll discover this isn't true for all dreams." He smiled. "So, did you enjoy it?"

I nodded with enthusiasm while my more outgoing classmates shouted out. I was so relieved Dream Management was turning out to be positive.

"I created the dream to assist with our upcoming test. I developed it a few years ago and give it to my classes each year when we wind down our Ecology and Environment Unit."

A hand shot up.

"Yes, Daniel?"

"Was it real?"

"Yeah, right," Ryan muttered.

Mr. Katz ignored Ryan. "No, it didn't really happen. It was the first in a series of academic dreams you will receive over the next four years. Before we move on to review the science you learned, let's pause a moment and discuss these dreams in more general terms, since it was your first.

"The primary purpose of academic dreams is to further your education. There are at least three distinctive styles of learning." He wrote *Auditory* on the board in blue marker while I pulled out my pen and paper. "Some of you are auditory learners. This means you learn best by listening. This is helpful in a traditional school which relies heavily on lectures."

He returned to the board and wrote *Visual* in green. "A second learning style is visual. People with this style prefer to see something to learn it. Reading a book, studying pictures, or watching videos are examples."

Next, he wrote *Kinesthetic*, a word I didn't recognize. He underlined it several times in red. "Kinesthetic involves touching or moving. This style is ideal for people who learn best when they are performing an activity. That's why high school science classes often incorporate a laboratory component to get students involved.

"Here at Dickensen, we can create a kinesthetic learning experience in all of our subjects." Mr. Katz strolled back and forth at the front of the classroom. "For example, last night you experienced the ecosystems in a unique way because you believed you were there. Not only could you see and hear, but you were immersed in them so all five senses could be employed. In reality, you didn't leave your beds. It was more of a simulation. Additionally, REM sleep stimulates regions of the brain involved in learning, so by dreaming about the ecosystems, you were simultaneously learning."

He stopped in front of Daniel's seat. "So back to your question. Last night wasn't real. But I did my best to create an authentic representation of each ecosystem we studied, drawing on my expertise as well as my experiences traveling to many of those locations."

Mr. Katz gazed out at the class and smiled. "Of course, some aspects had to be changed from reality. Any guesses on which parts were altered?"

"The temperatures?" Ben suggested.

"Absolutely. I made the tundra a bit warmer. We didn't have the proper gear to survive in the extreme cold. Other ideas?"

"How we moved from place to place seemed almost magical," Aditi said.

"Yes." His eyes twinkled. "I based my transitions on movies to up the fun factor."

Those tree vines were definitely fun, although a bit scary. It would be awesome to jump again knowing it was safe.

I raised my hand.

"Autumn?"

"Did you have the same dream last night?"

"I didn't. However, I did run through the dream in my mind and on my computer as part of the conveyance process. I should mention, so you are realistic in your expectations, not everyone will be capable of sending such complicated, interactive dreams."

"What will we be able to do?" Ryan asked.

"You'll start small by sending a dream to an individual in the same room as yourself. As you advance in your skills, you'll increase the distance you convey and the number of recipients. Eventually, you'll add complex interactions through the use of computer programming."

Once all our Dream Management questions were answered, Mr. Katz guided the discussion to what we learned about the ecosystem. Complaints were mumbled when we switched to academics, but as our teacher said, education was the ultimate purpose of the dream.

Friday was the feared science unit test. The test was a combination of multiple-choice and essay questions. Although the pages seemed daunting, I flew through the multiple-choice section. During the essay portion, I came to the dreaded question: *please explain the interdependencies between biome, ecosystem, and habitat*. I closed my eyes. My skin went cold with the tundra wind, then warmed with the desert sun. Floral scents hung in the air. Parrots squawked from the trees. I ran my fingertips along the sharp needles of the evergreens. When I reopened my eyes, the answer flowed from my pen complete with examples.

Chapter: 14

My shorts and T-shirt stuck to me under a blazing sun. The nearby ocean filled the air with a salty scent. Older homes made of stucco with tin roofs and arched windows lined the street—nothing like the houses I'd seen before. Palm trees and colorful flowers brimming with hues of violet, mustard, and magenta, like the kind in advertisements for Hawaii, grew everywhere. The foreign, unfamiliar environment murmured *you are far from home*.

Joyful shrieks of children came from behind me, so I turned around. I stood on the edge of a dusty playground with several little kids playing together. They couldn't be much older than five or six.

"*Otoño! Otoño!*" a woman called from a park bench.

I gasped. Was she calling me? She'd used my Spanish name, and no one but the kids were in sight.

"Coming!" I jogged over to her.

The woman had thick, black hair and mocha-colored skin similar to Mrs. Lopez, Julia's mother, although this woman's skin was a shade darker. "*Hola Otoño, tengo que ir a mi casa por un largo rato. ¿Podriás cuidar de mis hijos cuando me vaya, por favor?*"

"What?"

"*¿Podrias cuidar de mis hijos, por favor?*"

113

"I don't understand."

"No hablo inglés."

I understood that. She didn't speak English.

"No hablo español," I said. *"Solo un poco."*

The woman pantomimed, gesturing to the children and then to me. She pointed to her watch and held up one finger. *"Una hora."* She repeated, *"¿Podriás cuidar mis de hijos por favor? Regreso en una hora."*

My mouth went dry. Had she asked me to watch the children for one hour? What mother in her right mind would ask a stranger to watch her children? Then I realized it must be a dream conveyed by Señor Ortiz, so I finally uttered, *"Sí."*

"Gracias."

She left me with three boys and three girls. They couldn't be siblings—they were too close in age—but they all had the same beautiful skin, and they conversed in Spanish as they played.

What was I supposed to do? I couldn't even speak with them, so I sat on the bench and observed. Every once in a while, I caught a word I recognized and managed to figure out two of the kids' names. One was Nicolás and another Isabel. But as I listened and got used to their accents and speech patterns, I comprehended more and more. Lucky for me, they used fewer words than adults, and their speech was nothing like Julia's family when they'd all get talking at once.

Nicolás approached me. *"¿Quieres jugar el topao?"*

I smiled. He asked if I wanted to play *el topao*, which looked like a game of tag.

"Sí." I got up and started running among them.

Soon the tallest boy tagged me. *"¡Te agarre!"* Then

he raced off. Tag was the same regardless of your native language. I was now it.

I pretended to run my fastest but often let the boys narrowly escape me. I touched one child. "Um...*te agarre.*" I must've gotten the words correct because he didn't miss a beat and started chasing another boy.

After a few minutes, I began to shout, "¡*Te agarre!*" and copied a couple of their phrases such as "*no me puedes agarrar,*" which I guessed meant *you can't catch me*, and "*corre mas rápido,*" which meant *run faster*. They yelled some other phrases, but I couldn't quite decipher the meanings.

Fifteen minutes later, the boys stopped running and began to dig in the sandbox. By then I was soaked in sweat. I took it as a chance to check on the girls. I approached the one fiddling with a stick. My confidence higher, I introduced myself. "*Hola. Soy Otoño.*"

She turned and smiled shyly. "*Hola. Soy Ana.*"

Ana drew pictures in the dirt and would turn to me with her eyebrows raised and brown eyes twinkling. Aside from *una casa*—a house—I didn't know the Spanish equivalents. I must've butchered more than a few words because some of my guesses made her burst out in laughter. Then I took the stick and began to sketch. After each picture was complete, Ana spoke the Spanish word. I sketched some of the Spanish nouns I'd studied over the past six weeks, but many of my pictures were of objects I didn't know the translation, so I learned several new words.

After a while, Isabel approached with a jump rope. "*¿Quieres jugar con nosotras?*"

"*Soy Otoño. Sí, quiero jugar con ustedes.*" I took

one end of the rope, and we swung the rope together while the third girl jumped.

The girls recited a gleeful song. "*¿Uva, pera, manzana y arroz a los cuantos años me casaré yo? Uno, dos, tres, cuatro, cinco, seis, siete, ocho, nueve, diez…*"

Most of the song was counting, and they'd count until the jumper tripped over the rope, but I had no idea what the beginning meant. I could've sworn it had something to do with an apple.

The girls alternated turns jumping. I tried once, but they were too short to twirl the rope high enough for me. Every once in a while, the tune and lyrics changed. I gleaned a word here and there but mostly hummed along.

Before long, the woman returned. "*Gracias, Otoño. ¿Cómo estuvieron los niños?*" I was grateful to understand she'd asked how it went.

"*Bien.*"

She rounded up the children and told them it was time to leave. Their bodies slumped, and a couple shouted, "*¡No!*" But then they each filed by me saying, "*Adios.*"

Not a minute later, I was snug in my dorm room bed. When Aditi woke, I asked if she had the same dream. She hadn't. Instead, she'd had a completely different dream…in French.

Chapter: 15

Ms. Jenson walked through the classroom, passing out papers. "I've finished grading your Tom Sawyer essays. I have to say, I'm impressed."

She placed mine facedown on my desk. I flipped it over, and a bright red *A* shone up at me. A satisfied smile spread across my face, and I scooted straighter in my chair.

"Now, I'd like to switch gears. We're going to take a break from studying the classics. Instead, we'll focus on our own creative writing."

Finally! I'd been dying to write stories again, but I'd been too busy with all my homework. Besides, I couldn't access my online writing community through Dickensen's network anyway so hadn't had as much motivation.

"This class will begin to tie in with Creative Core. As you may have guessed, these stories will become your first dream assignments."

The class erupted in cheers, and a spike of adrenaline shot through me.

Once we settled down, Ms. Jenson continued. "I will guide you on the story script while Mr. Robbins will advise you on setting design and the process of breaking it into components as he teaches you the fundamentals of conveyance. This first dream will be a simple interaction with your roommate."

I locked eyes with Aditi and grinned.

"Let's get started."

****

When I entered the Creative Core art studio, all the chairs had been moved from our desks to the back of the room where they were arranged in a circle facing each other, half of them occupied by my classmates chatting eagerly.

I slipped into the seat next to Hannah. "What's going on?"

"No idea."

Mr. Robbins stood outside our circle of sixteen. "I heard you began creative writing in language arts today." He smiled. "It's about time! And time for us to make a shift as well. In a couple of weeks, we'll begin dream conveyance."

We all clapped. Ryan whistled.

"It's going to be fun, but it's going to be a lot of work. Conveying is not as simple as memorizing a list of steps. You'll also need to learn to focus without your mind wandering. Now for some of you, that process will come naturally. However for most people, it's a challenge. I have an exercise to illustrate this point." He told us to concentrate on anything in the world besides a polar bear for one minute. And of course, no matter how hard I tried, I couldn't block polar bears from my mind.

"I have two basic meditative exercises to improve your focus. I'd like to spend our remaining time today walking you through an example of each."

He dimmed the lights. "The first is a breathing exercise. Please close your eyes."

I closed them but shifted around in my seat. I

hadn't done anything like this since elementary school. I peeked. Several others had their eyes half-open and were stifling laughter.

"Okay, now keep your eyes closed and focus on your breathing." Mr. Robbins spoke in a slow, soothing voice. "Breathe in and out, in and out. Concentrate on the natural rhythm of your breath. Feel the air fill your lungs and flow back out. Feel your chest rise. If your mind wanders, bring it back to your breathing."

I inhaled and exhaled, quickly at first, but as my breath slowed, my mind wandered. *I hope I did okay on my math test. This chair is too hard; they should buy more comfortable ones.* I took another peek. The students across from me had their eyes closed, so I reclosed mine. I tried to refocus. My stomach rumbled. *What snacks will they have in the dining hall this afternoon?*

"Okay, that's it. You completed your first five-minute breathing meditation."

Five minutes! More like twenty.

"Was anyone able to focus solely on their breathing the entire time?" He chuckled when nobody raised his or her hand immediately.

Then Caitlyn spoke up. "It was easy. I've been meditating for years."

Mr. Robbins nodded toward her. "Fantastic, Caitlyn." He looked around the class. "I hope with practice all of you will soon meditate as well."

I rolled my eyes then glanced at Hannah. Her eyes narrowed at her roommate.

"Now, let's move on to the second type of exercise called guided imagery. Listen carefully and follow the directions."

Our teacher put on a CD. Ocean waves filled the air. A woman's calm voice talked us through relaxing on a beach. She had us focus on each of our senses, one at a time.

The soft sand squished between my toes.

My skin warmed with the sun.

The smell of salt drifted to my nose.

"Okay." Mr. Robbins said when the CD went quiet. "Now open your eyes."

Wow! Guidance made it so much easier. He flipped the lights back on. So blinding. I blinked several times to revive myself. A few more minutes and I would've fallen asleep.

After we moved our chairs to our desks, Mr. Robbins handed out papers with a list of meditation resources. "As homework for the next couple of weeks, I'd like you to spend at least ten minutes a day meditating. We'll devote class time to review your progress and identify potential solutions for the difficulties you encounter."

Great. Just what I needed: more homework.

But as a dedicated student, I checked out the websites and downloaded a few meditation apps to my smartphone.

****

During my Sunday review session with Dad, I let it slip I was learning basic meditation in Creative Core. I braced myself for his response.

"You're kidding. I think it'd be wiser for them to spend class time teaching the curriculum." He muttered, "I guess that's what you get with a private school."

"Oh, Dad, things are different than when you went to school. And it's not like we're having religious discussions or anything. They're just relaxation and visualization techniques." Mr. Robbins had added visualization exercises to our homework this past week to train us to envision the minute details of our stories.

I gave Dad the sound bite I'd memorized from Mr. Robbins to be used in these situations. "Dickensen teaches meditation to help us increase our focus so we can perform better in school. For example, we could visualize acing a test or giving a speech…oh, and there are health benefits too, including reduced stress and better sleep." In reality, who knew if these exercises would help me with anything besides conveyance? But anything to shut Dad up. "I think I'm already starting to see an improvement in my ability to focus."

"*Hmph*, maybe a unique approach will benefit you. Clearly your mind works differently than mine." He probably meant it as an insult, but I took it as a compliment. "Let me know if the time commitment becomes a burden. I don't know about meditation, but I'll admit, there are benefits to visualization. Although I've never heard of it being taught in high school. I often visualize the steps the night before a complicated surgery…"

My eyes opened wide as I pictured Dad in his home office reviewing his patients' notes. I had no idea he was sometimes visualizing surgery techniques and found myself smiling and shaking my head. My good mood continued even as our conversation shifted to algebra.

Chapter: 16

As the month of October progressed, the concepts of dream reception, creation, and conveyance became a new normal, as if they'd always been a possibility. Life on campus was busy, and us freshmen couldn't afford to dwell exclusively on Dream Management. I had tons of homework, research to complete, tests to prep for, and papers to write. The library was always packed.

Each week, I received multiple dreams from the faculty and staff. The playground dream was consistent, but each time I experienced it, I understood more words and conversed better in Spanish. Some of my classmates had moved on to more complex language immersion dreams, but I was still perfecting my interactions with Mr. Ortiz's nieces and nephews in the Dominican Republic.

I also received dreams from my history and language arts teachers. Too bad math facts didn't materialize in any—I could use an extra mnemonic. Even Coach Kat and Mrs. Humphrey conveyed dreams, both of which had nothing to do with school. Coach Kat sent me on a shopping spree with my girlfriends, and Mrs. Humphrey cast me on a Caribbean cruise with my entire extended family.

Although I enjoyed school more than ever before, I lived for the weekends when even studying didn't seem so bad without the time pressure of Monday through

Friday's tight schedule. Fortunately, ever since Dream Management was introduced, it was rare to catch even an inkling of homesickness in the far reaches of my mind. And keeping busy prevented it from ballooning into anything more.

One Saturday afternoon, Ben found me in the library. "Hey, Autumn. Up to anything?"

I grimaced and gestured to the pile of books and papers in front of me. I had four pages of algebra homework and an upcoming Spanish test. That didn't include finishing up an oil painting or the science research I had planned for tomorrow.

"Can't it wait?" he asked. "I have something to show you."

I bit my lip. Aside from the library, I hadn't been alone with Ben in a long time.

He twisted his neck to study my books. "Spanish. We'll get another dream tonight to help with that."

I sighed. "If I don't get kicked out."

Ben raised an eyebrow.

"Last time, I ignored Nicolás' warning and crossed the street from the park to the beach. Next thing I knew, I woke up in bed." I had crossed a *dream boundary*. Mr. Robbins had encouraged us to learn to identify these subtle signs written into the scripts because this knowledge would allow us to remain in the dreams.

Ben laughed. "You're terrible. Now just don't go badgering little Ana to identify complex nouns. I heard that's another good way to get booted."

"Okay, no boundary exploration tonight. Spanish studying. Check." I smiled. "Give me fifteen minutes to finish up this section of problems before I forget everything my tutor taught me today."

"Meet me in the game room when you're ready." Ben turned to go but then spun back to me. "Oh, and wear something comfortable. And warm."

Thirty minutes later, we were traipsing along the trail away from school. The air was crisp, and bright beams of sunlight filtered through the evergreens. A picture-perfect fall day. The birds filled the woods with song, and an occasional squirrel or chipmunk scurried across our path.

"It's so pretty here," I said. "I run these trails all the time but never have a chance to really look around."

Ben nodded. "How's cross country going?"

"Good. We've started weekly races. It's kind of weird since we only run against our teammates."

"I bet you're doing great."

I shrugged. "I'm doing okay." Hannah and I continued to push each other to improve our personal bests, and we were no longer the slowest but in the middle of the pack. Our progress was a definite confidence booster, and Coach Kat rewarded our efforts with ribbons and certificates I pinned to my bulletin board. Since I'd grown up with Josh's golden trophies gazing down at me from the bookshelves, it was nice to discover a sport *I* was decent at.

I placed my hands in my pockets. "So…what did you want to show me?"

He fished through an orange nylon backpack and pulled out a large silver key, holding it up for inspection.

I reached for it. "What's it for?"

"It's a key to one of the gates."

My mouth gaped. "Where'd you get it?"

"Not a big deal. Any of us can now check them out

from the Rec Center. I just filled out a form stating where we were going and when we'd return. Oh, and this hiking backpack they gave me has some sort of GPS tracking device on it."

I screwed up my face. "What for?"

"They said for safety reasons, in case we get lost or something."

"Uh-huh." Was that the only reason? After keeping us in the dark about Dream Management until mid-September, I questioned much of what the faculty told us. For the most part, my fears had proved unfounded. Even the doors to the sophomore wing were no longer locked at night. Now my fear of students being held on campus against our wishes faded too—they trusted us to leave. But were they tracking us?

Ben led the way, veering off the main path and onto a narrow one, occasionally checking a map that pinpointed multiple gates. The smaller trail was overgrown, and we had to push aside some of the sword ferns and Douglas fir seedlings.

The massive steel gate was the same type as in my ecosystem dream, although it was easier to see in the daylight. It would lead us through both the chain-link and electrical barricades. A more distant memory of passing through this specific gate with Principal Locke and my classmates returned to me.

"Be careful," I said as Ben reached toward the lock embedded in the steel.

He laughed. His natural confidence had returned after weeks of paranoia. He inserted the key and pulled it open. "After you."

I released the breath I'd been holding when Ben didn't get flung back from the electrical current. I'd definitely watched too many movies. Then I had to chuckle, loving how Ben acted like a gentleman even out here in the woods.

The trail continued beyond the gate. Although still overgrown, we followed it easily.

"Shouldn't we be worried about wild animals out here?" I asked in an unsteady voice.

Ben shook his head. "I'm sure the fence is for people. Reporters would have a heyday with this academy. And I suppose it keeps the freshmen locked up until we're deemed trustworthy."

I laughed nervously. "But a side benefit has to be keeping out bears and stuff."

"I've been hiking for years with Jim, my step-dad. We only have black bears in Washington. As long as we make noise and don't surprise them, we'll be fine." He smiled encouragingly. "Besides, there's some pepper spray in the pack. Just in case."

My posture relaxed. Relying on a teenage boy's bravado wasn't as reassuring as a true means of protection.

After about a mile, we came to a patch of deciduous trees mingled in with the evergreens. I stopped to take it all in. Could this be a dream? I doubted I was asleep but had a hard time believing this was real. The setting was the same as in Principal Locke's conveyed hiking dream. But this time, with Ben. Alone.

"The leaves on these trees are beautiful," he said.

I nodded. "Ever been to the east coast?"

"Nope."

"You should see fall in upstate New York, near my grandma's." I began to gush about my family, telling stories and sharing experiences. Outside the gate, my mind was somehow lighter and opening up was easier. While we chatted, we descended toward the mountain lake. It measured about a quarter mile across and reflected the blue sky and surrounding treetops, like a giant mirror. We sat side by side on a moss-covered log and continued to talk.

After about an hour or so, Ben said, "We should probably head back."

I glanced at the trail and then longingly back across the lake. But he was right. The days were getting shorter, and the shadows were already growing long. "We should come back with our friends sometime."

"Maybe...but it was kind of nice, just the two of us."

My heart swelled two sizes bigger and remained that way as we began the ascent back to school. Maybe next time, he'd kiss me.

I was still lost in thought when Ben slowed. "Uh-oh."

I leaned to the side to peer around him. The trail split in two. "Which way did we come?"

He blew out a long breath. "Not sure." Ben pulled out his map, but it didn't show the fork.

I studied both options then pointed left. "I feel like we came from there."

I stopped fantasizing about Ben and focused on the trees and bushes, looking for something familiar. Eventually the trail became too overgrown to proceed. A shiver went through me. I wasn't sure if it was the drop in temperature or fear creeping in. Our mistake had cost us at least thirty minutes, and the sunlight was waning.

"Um, Autumn. I promised we'd be back by five."

"*What*?" My watch showed four fifty. How could Ben have failed to mention that little detail? I'd have insisted we leave the lake much earlier.

"Sorry. I wasn't really paying attention to the time and didn't think about getting lost."

We picked up our pace to a jog. If I got into trouble, Dad would kill me.

When we finally arrived back at the gate, Ben struggled to open it because the keyhole was so difficult to see in the low light, and he wanted to avoid getting shocked. After several attempts, the key slid into place and we got through.

Once we reached the wider main trail, Ben grabbed my hand. "Let's run."

It's a good thing he held on tight because I stumbled a couple of times, and his arm tensed to keep me upright. An owl hooted in the distance, and the nearby bushes rustled. Probably just a squirrel or a bird frightened by our presence.

As we rounded a corner, Ben stopped short. A flashlight shone toward us. I turned my head to avoid its blinding light.

"Ben Coleman?" a man's deep voice called out.

"Uh, yeah." Ben's voice squeaked.

A tall, dark shadow emerged.

I went rigid.

"I'm with Dickensen Security. The Recreation Center notified us you hadn't returned."

"I'm sorry," Ben stammered. "We took a wrong turn."

"I'm glad you're safe." He glanced at me. The man was much shorter and less menacing now that I could see his face. "You okay, miss?"

I swallowed hard. "Yes."

He escorted us back to the Rec Center. I didn't say a word as the man lectured us about how the school wants to give students freedom but freedom is based on trust. And the way he harped on boys and girls not being alone together in the dark made it clear he'd thought Ben had been my biggest danger. When the security officer explained he'd only issue us a warning, my legs turned to jelly in relief.

Back in my room, Aditi asked, "Where have you been?"

I summarized the hike and the run-in with security. "Want to go sometime? Earlier of course."

"Thanks, but no thanks. Sounds like it's about four miles too long. Remember." She tapped her head. "I've already been there. But I am curious, what's going on with you and Ben?"

I shrugged and bit down on a smile. "I have no idea."

Chapter: 17

Mr. Robbins wrote in big red letters on the board *Dream Conveyance* and underneath *Variations 1-4*. When he turned around, he announced, "I've been discussing your progress with Ms. Jenson. You're now ready to learn the final Dream Management skill."

I straightened in my chair, gaze glued to my teacher, who plopped down on the front edge of his desk as seemed to be his custom when he wanted to encourage conversation. "You'll be creating six dreams this year with multiple variations of each one. Each dream will contain progressive skills, so by next year, you'll be ready to catapult your friends into dreams where they'll experience things you can only imagine.

"For the initial conveyance, you'll simplify your stories and remove your designed setting. Instead, you'll use a Dickensen location as your background for the first variation of *Dream One*."

He paused to give us time to catch up on our notes.

"Suppose your story involved playing catch with your roommate." He grabbed an orange ball sitting next to him. "Quick, catch!"

I dropped my pen just in time to catch the squishy football. A slow smile spread on my face when I managed to hold on to it. Football was my brother's sport, not mine.

Mr. Robbins nodded at me. "Nice reflexes." Then

he addressed the class. "You could throw the ball on a field at Dickensen or even in the dining hall." I chuckled along with several others. "It doesn't matter, so long as it's a place you both know well."

My story involved piles of fallen leaves. Countless places on campus would work. Which would be best?

"Once you're able to successfully convey this simple dream, you'll insert a piece of artwork into your story. Any suggestions on what could be used for my example?" His gaze honed in on me.

I held up the football. "A specially designed ball."

"Yes, Autumn. That would be the logical choice." He motioned with his hands for me to toss it back. It wasn't a perfect spiral, but at least I threw it on target.

"Any other ideas?"

"Maybe a colorful outfit. Or a comical animal," Grace suggested and then sprang back in her chair as the ball pelted her in the chest.

He grinned. "Creative. Remember, only your imagination and artistic ability are the limits."

Grace tossed the football back to Mr. Robbins.

We brainstormed potential ideas for each variation of our dreams, passing the football to each speaker. Everyone wanted a turn to play catch, so we ended up with lots of suggestions for artwork creations and settings—both real and imagined.

"When you say it takes a while to learn, how long are you talking?" Ben asked.

"Expect a minimum of two weeks to learn to convey the simplest of dreams. For some, it may take months." Mr. Robbins took a long breath. "I may as well warn you a disparity in skill levels will become apparent within the first few weeks. The initial conveyance is often the hardest."

"Mr. Robbins?" Caitlyn spoke in a sickeningly sweet voice. "If we believe we have the skills, can we move straight to the full conveyance of *Dream One*?"

His smile faded and his eyes narrowed. "Caitlyn, you underestimate the difficulty of conveyance. Regardless of your exceptional ability to meditate, this is a challenging skill to learn, a skill most of the world doesn't know exists. Besides, this exercise isn't simply for your own benefit. Remember, it's a partnership."

Caitlyn cocked her head.

"Your partner will need to learn how to accept a dream from an *amateur* and learn to remain in a dream potentially fraught with boundary errors."

I had to suppress my giggles. Mr. Robbins really shut her up.

He hopped off his desk. "Now we need to discuss scheduling. It's best to ensure there aren't any competing dreams. If more than one dream-maker sends you a dream at the same time, usually the most experienced one's conveyance takes over. And sometimes neither gets through. We wish to avoid this situation." He grabbed a slim stack of light blue papers from his desk and began passing them out. "In case you haven't guessed, the majority of freshman dream conveyance is with your roommate, the fundamental reason why roommates are together in this class."

Someone tapped me from behind. I turned around. Beaming, Aditi whispered, "This is going to be so much fun."

I returned the smile. Then my thoughts drifted to Hannah. Poor Hannah. She'd be paired with Caitlyn in this way as well. I shifted my gaze. Hannah was sprawled forward on her desk, her eyes at half-mast, as if she'd just received an F on a midterm exam.

When I received the handout, I flipped through it while our teacher spoke. Pages of monthly calendars were stapled together. *Wow*! All the dates were filled in except most Sundays. Saturdays were assigned to *Foreign Language Specialists*. Wednesdays read *Faculty/Staff*. The remaining dates had a bunch of *As* and *Bs* written in.

"Beginning next week, the older roommate will take Mondays and Thursdays. This will be *Group A*. The younger roommate will take Tuesdays and Fridays. This will be *Group B*. Any exceptions to this schedule need to be requested through the Dream Calendar Application and approved by me. Drumroll please."

My focus snapped back to my teacher, and I put the handout aside. Mr. Robbins started beating his palms on his desk. Soon the entire class was following suit. A few guys hooted, and Ben slapped Ryan on the back. I giggled as lightness entered my chest.

Mr. Robbins stood at the front. "Now for what you've all been waiting for. Time to teach you the methods and procedures of conveyance." Mr. Robbins picked up a whiteboard marker and wrote the number one.

Butterflies fluttered in my stomach. Not nerves. Excitement. Then he wrote and talked us through each telepathy step. Hands flew and he paused his instruction multiple times to answer questions. The enthusiasm was palpable. It was as if we were planning a European backpacking trip rather than a class project. We were really learning telepathy. Who would've ever guessed?

Chapter: 18

It was my turn to meet with Ms. Jenson. She was my favorite teacher, second only to Mr. Robbins. She was young and inspirational, like Coach Kat. I'd been working on my *Dream One*, revising it over and over, striving for perfection and my teacher's approval. We sat at her desk while the rest of my classmates silently edited their own dreams.

"So I've reviewed your story," my teacher began. "You're off to a good start, Autumn. I like how you plan to involve four of the five senses with the fallen leaves. There will be plenty of opportunity to show various artistic techniques in their designs. And raking, running, and jumping are all suitable actions. But this conversation about your favorite bands and musicians needs to be simplified."

I slumped in the chair. The dream was already boring, and she was asking me to make it even more so. "If I cut back on the number of words, can I at least keep the dialogue two-way?"

She shook her head. "Even simple conversations have variables. Remember this first dream has to be elementary to make it easier to convey." She smiled encouragingly. "Be patient. You'll be writing more creative storylines soon."

I frowned. I didn't simply want to add in a real conversation. I wanted to create the fantasy stories I'd been writing for years, but I'd been told I might not reach that level until my sophomore or even junior year.

"So what are your thoughts for the setting?" she probed.

"The first variation will take place below our dorm window. Under the trees, near one of the benches."

"That should work."

I sat up higher. "For the second variation, I'll move it to my backyard in Seattle."

"Has Aditi seen pictures of it?"

"Nope."

Ms. Jenson nodded her approval.

"Then the last couple variations will have a forest landscape as the background setting. I've started a sketch and plan to paint it with acrylics once everything's approved."

"Sounds like a good plan. I'll have to stop by your Creative Core studio soon and have Mr. Robbins show me everyone's projects. I keep hearing about all this artwork and want to see it for myself."

I fiddled with my pen, suppressing a smile.

****

The week sped by. Now that we had a basic understanding of the conveyance process, I needed to convert my story into the proper dream format. I also had to memorize the conveyance procedure and the structure of the brain—Dad would've been thrilled about that component until he found out why. Surprisingly, I found it fascinating, but that didn't necessarily mean I'd ever want to take a human anatomy course like he expected.

I also had to create feedback checklists for each dream variation I'd go through with Aditi, one upon waking and a second during class to access the *stickiness* of each dream—Mr. Robbins' term for how well a dream could be recalled later. Of course, this work was for only two of my classes. My other five marched along like a typical week.

Monday arrived at last. After dinner, I walked to the library with Ben, as was our custom now several nights a week.

"Are you ready for tonight?" he asked.

"I think so. Trying not to get too nervous. What about you?"

"I'm not conveying. Ryan is. He turned fifteen right before school started."

"Oh, I assumed you were older. You're so much more, um, more…"

"Taller?"

"Well, yeah. But I meant you're so mature."

Ben stopped to open the library door for us. "I don't know about that, but compared to my goofball roommate, you have a point."

"I guess that's what I meant." Ryan was always horsing around and could never concentrate on anything for long, unless it involved a ball. Ben was more serious about everything.

"I suppose Ryan has to be laidback to survive in that big family of his."

Now inside, I lowered my voice. "Well, you're not *too* serious. You know how to let go and not stress like me."

"Because I don't have a father breathing down my neck. Don't you talk to him every night? And he quizzes you and stuff?"

I didn't answer at first but rather chose an empty

table and unpacked my messenger bag. "Only on Sundays. Most nights, I talk with my mom or Josh."

"See, that's what I meant. It's your father who stresses you out."

"Maybe. But it's so ingrained in me, I honestly believe it's part of my personality now."

"Hopefully when grades come out in January, he'll back off. You're acing your classes."

"I'm doing pretty well. But we haven't even taken midterms." I squirmed a little. Talking to Ben about my strained relationship with Dad was awkward. "So are you nervous about conveying your dream *tomorrow* night?"

"Not at all. I don't feel any pressure since it's the first. Know what I am nervous about?"

I shook my head.

"Tonight. I don't like the idea of Ryan focusing on my brain while I'm sleeping. Who knows what kind of crazy dream he'll send me? Or what if he accidentally messes up my mind somehow? I doubt I'll be able to fall asleep."

"I didn't think about that part of this exercise. Gee, thanks! Now I have something else to worry about."

Someone tapped me on my shoulder. The librarian reminded us to keep it down.

When she returned to her desk, Ben leaned over and whispered, "If Aditi was my roommate, I wouldn't worry. She'll probably send you princesses and rainbows and roses."

I smiled. I was lucky. Glad I wasn't Hannah. If anybody were going to send something strange, it'd be Caitlyn. But no, she had to go through an approval process with our teachers too, so nothing bad could happen, right? I kept my negative thoughts to myself, as if I might jinx Hannah if I uttered them aloud.

****

My vibrating alarm woke me at one a.m. I yawned, already longing for the day when I'd be skilled enough to convey while the recipient was awake. Aditi was breathing softly—still asleep. *Step one, complete.* I'd been nervous I might sleep through my alarm or it might wake her.

Now for the hard part.

I climbed out of bed and tiptoed across the room to grab my folder and flashlight. I'd memorized the steps but reread my notes, just in case. Pulling a blanket over my shoulders, I slumped into the chair facing her twin bed.

I began with a short breathing exercise to help me relax and focus. Then I followed my checklist, concentrating on Aditi and multiple areas of her brain. My goal was to telepathically place my storyline into the *pons* at the base of her brain, which would then send signals through the *thalamus* and eventually to her *cerebral cortex*.

I simultaneously tried to pull her short- and long-term memories from multiple lobes of her cerebral cortex. She needed to view me, the main character in her dream, as well as the area underneath our window, including the piles of leaves. Hopefully, she'd also hear the rustle of leaves and the sound of my voice; smell the fresh, earthy scent of soil; and feel the cool breeze on her skin—all memories stored within her.

If I performed the conveyance correctly, she'd soon move into REM sleep where my storyline would merge with her memories in her cerebral cortex to create a dream, and her senses would wake one by one when other portions of her brain became activated as the dream played itself out.

Well, that's it. I think I did it right. I glanced at my clock as I crawled back into bed. Only 1:19 a.m. Yay!

I was so keyed up, it took me close to an hour to fall back to sleep.

****

I could barely open my eyes when our alarm rang at seven.

Aditi was already moving about the room, getting ready. What's with her? Oh yeah, we went to bed early at Mr. Robbins' suggestion.

The conveyance! I bolted upright. "Did it work? Did it work?"

She bit her lower lip. "I think I had a dream, but I can't quite remember. And I don't think it was related to school."

The extra energy drained out of me as quickly as it had arrived. Despite Mr. Robbins' warning not to expect success so soon, I'd hoped to be the exception.

Chapter: 19

I woke to the warmth of a sunlit room and Aditi's eager face hovering near me.

"Did you get it?" she asked.

I shook my head as I raised it off my pillow. Relief washed over me—she hadn't been successful either. Moments later, guilt chased it away. I loved Aditi and should've wanted her to succeed. I blamed Dad that my self-confidence was so low that a friend's success made me feel bad about myself.

I offered an encouraging smile. "You'll do it next time. No one gets it on the first try."

As soon as the seventh bell rang, Mr. Robbins popped up from his desk, even more cheerful than usual and with a new bounce in his step. "I've been told we had our first success."

Everyone looked around in surprise, but no one came forward. *Who could it be*? Perhaps Timothy. He was in several of my classes. He could pass for eleven but was a genius. Probably one of those gifted kids who'd been pushed ahead a couple of grades. Or maybe Samantha? She was always distracted but an amazing artist who'd get so into her work our teacher often couldn't get her attention.

"I want to impress upon you this is extraordinary. In my twelve years at Dickensen, I've only had three students successful with their first conveyance. I also want to give kudos to the recipient. Although conveying is the most difficult Dream Management skill, some people are more receptive to dreams, so part of the credit may need to go to him.

"Without further ado, I'd like to ask Ben and Ryan to come forward."

I couldn't breathe. It was like a vacuum had sucked all the air from my lungs. *I can't believe he kept it a secret.* He could've said something during history or language arts. Or what about lunch? Well, that explained why Ryan was missing—he wouldn't have been able to keep his big mouth shut. Surprisingly hurt rather than jealousy devoured me. Hurt he hadn't shared such big news with me. I wasn't as important to him as I'd hoped.

They walked to the front of the room and took a seat facing each other. Ryan wore a cheek-to-cheek smile whereas Ben's face was bright pink, and he studied the tile floor.

Mr. Robbins stood over them, his eyes dancing like a proud father watching his son take his first steps. He handed a piece of paper to Ben. "I'd now like you to go through your *Dream Review Checklist*. I won't make each pair complete this exercise in front of the class, but I'd like to show everyone how it's done and offer these boys some feedback. They successfully completed the *Initial Dream Review* this morning. This more detailed checklist will review aspects not discussed earlier and determine the dream's stickiness.

"Ben, you may begin."

"Ryan, do you remember the dream?"

Ryan nodded. "Yep."

"Where did it take place?"

"Near the pond, here at school."

I sat there watching, trying to calm down, only half-listening. I still couldn't believe he didn't tell me and was annoyed with myself for letting it bother me so much.

"What did I talk about?"

Ryan shifted in his seat. "You said you wanted to take me to the beach near your house. Said it's windy and a great place to fly kites."

"What did I want to bring there?"

"Your dog."

Ben smiled.

Mr. Robbins cut in. "Let's pause there for a moment. Class, the question about the dog was not on the morning checklist. Let's continue."

Ben read the next question. "What happened while I was talking?"

"The kite got caught in a tree, so we started to climb. It was tricky, and I—"

"Ryan," Mr. Robbins interrupted, "remember not to summarize. You skipped past some key details. Only answer what is asked." He nodded to Ben.

"You said the kite got caught in a tree. What type of tree was it?"

Ryan's features went blank. "I don't know. I don't know trees well."

How could he not identify the type after all we learned in science? Then again, Ryan wasn't the most studious.

"It's okay," Mr. Robbins said. "In some cases your recipient won't be able to answer all your questions as intended, so you'll need to improvise. Ryan, where was this tree located?"

"On the far side of the pond."

"Can you describe it?" Mr. Robbins asked.

"It was about fifty feet tall and didn't have many leaves left, except for a few dead ones clinging to it two or three inches wide and kind of circular."

Mr. Robbins turned to Ben. "Is that your tree?"

"Yes, it's an aspen. Sorry, I assumed he'd know the type."

Ryan turned toward the class and raised his eyebrows and shoulders.

Everyone laughed but me.

"This was a perfect opportunity to show the class what to do when you get stuck. Not knowing the answer had nothing to do with a misconveyed dream. Ben, please continue."

Ben asked a few more questions, and Ryan answered them all correctly. When he was done, he laid his paper on his lap and turned to our teacher.

"Wonderful job, boys! Simply wonderful!" The pride in Mr. Robbins' voice rang clear. "You may return to your seats."

A few students gave the pair high-fives as they passed.

"So that's how the review sessions will go. Now let's everyone move to their pottery wheels while I call up individuals to help you prepare for your second attempts."

As everyone gravitated toward the back of the art studio, Ben pulled me aside. "Autumn?"

"Hey. Congratulations." I forced some enthusiasm into my voice.

"Uh, thanks. I was probably just lucky. Maybe Ryan's the gifted one."

"Doubt it."

"I wanted to tell you but thought we were supposed to keep it a secret until class, and I didn't want you to think I was bragging or anything. Besides, there was a chance Ryan would forget about the whole thing by now."

With his words, the tightness in my chest loosened a tiny bit. Enough to breathe again.

"It's okay. No big deal." I caught his eye. "Now you'll have to help me in both algebra *and* Dream Management."

Chapter: 20

"Aditi. Aditi. Wake up! You did it!"

She sat up and rubbed her eyes. "No, I didn't." She yawned. "But happy birthday, my friend."

Huh? I should've known by now how to detect a regular dream from a created one. And it had been her assigned night. But then a comfortable warmth overtook me. Aditi remembered my birthday.

Fragments of the dream replayed through my mind. I realized it was too complex to have been sent by a freshman. "Well someone sent me a dream. I'm sure of it."

"Me too." She grinned. "Mr. Robbins pulled me aside yesterday and told me someone requested Tuesday's spot to send you a"—her fingers curled into air quotes—"birthday gift. He said I should convey tonight instead."

"I wonder who sent it."

"He didn't say. What do you remember? I bet there were clues."

"Well, I woke up in a beachfront condo in Maui. My family was there too." I couldn't help but smile as I relayed the dream while we got ready. "I had the best day. For my birthday I got to squeeze in all the activities I wanted. Even the expensive ones my parents rarely spring for, like zip-lining and a snorkel trip to Molokini."

"That'd be the best."

"I remember going to a luau, and this Hawaiian guy in a bright floral shirt serenaded me with 'Happy Birthday' on the ukulele while a girl in a grass skirt brought me a bowl of pineapple ice cream with fifteen candles. I can still practically taste the crunchy coconut sprinkled on top. So delish."

I flipped through shirts in my closet and pulled one out. "Oh, and we even took a helicopter ride over the island. The pilot kept asking me, 'Where to next?' Wait. That's it!" I chuckled. "The pilot was Principal Locke. He must've created the dream. I wonder how he knew I liked Hawaii so much."

Aditi shrugged. "The Dickensen staff seems to know everything about us."

****

Back in my room after school, I showed Aditi the big, brown package that had arrived from home. The card read *Happy birthday, Autumn. Looking forward to a belated celebration in two weeks. Love, Mom, Dad, Josh, and Zoey.* I pulled out a couple of warm sweaters, a music store gift card, and a bag stuffed with my favorite cinnamon bears candy. I popped one into my mouth, savoring the hot cinnamon taste, and offered some to my roommate.

"Love the sweaters! Those are going to get some good use up here. It's freezing."

"Wimp!" I teased, hitting her with the arm of a sweater. "Such a Californian. You've been complaining since September."

"Hey, what are you up to today?" Aditi asked.

I'd just crammed a handful of bears into my mouth and had to swallow first. "Um, nothing much. I'll probably call home then head over to the library."

"If you can spare a little study time, I have a surprise for later."

I raised my eyebrows.

"I'm not saying. Go do your stuff. Be back here by five fifteen."

****

When I returned to my room after studying, Hannah and Aditi were sitting on the beds with mischief written all over their faces.

"Y'all grab your coats," Hannah said. "Let's go."

"Where to?"

"You'll see," Aditi said.

When we got down to the main floor, we found Ben and Ryan on a couch chatting with Mrs. Humphrey.

She stood and gave me a warm smile. "Happy birthday, dear."

My gaze darted back to my friends. I could've guessed the guys were involved in their plan, but not my RA. Now I was even more curious.

As we traversed the quad, my gaze strayed toward the parking lot. Perhaps Mrs. Humphrey would drive us to one of the nearest towns. Some of the older students with cars occasionally left campus, but I hadn't left once.

"It's not what you're thinking," Ben said, as if he'd read my mind.

Soon Mrs. Humphrey fell behind. She was by no means frail, but she had to be close to seventy years old. Ben fell in step with her, holding her arm, as if they were having an intimate conversation all huddled together. For a split second I wished I could be the one needing his help. And his warmth.

Hannah, Aditi, and I strolled with our arms linked together while Ryan kicked his soccer ball alongside of us. My body felt weightless as my friends guided me along the footpath that led to the faculty and staff housing known as Forest Circle. Already the day had surpassed my expectations. So many people had gone out of their way to wish me a happy birthday, and Aditi had even led our lunch table in a round of "Happy Birthday."

At last, just when I thought my fingers might fall off from the biting cold—I hadn't thought to bring gloves—we began to see log cabins scattered on both sides of the road. Hannah pointed to one of the smaller cabins. "This is it, number nineteen."

My friends pushed me to the front as we stepped across the flat stones leading to the porch. I waited a few moments for everyone to catch up. Then I knocked.

A few moments later the door opened, and Coach Kat stood there wearing a wide grin. "Happy birthday, Autumn!"

I looked behind to my friends and smiled as I shook my head. "You guys! I had no idea."

"Come in. You can hang your jackets on the coat rack right here. Then make yourselves at home."

The warmth of the house was a relief. We stood on the edge of a room with the living space and kitchen combined. Although it wasn't big, the vaulted ceiling made it more spacious than it appeared from outside. A crackling fire provided heat and a cozy ambiance, and the log walls gave the room a rustic feel, reminding me of the cabins near Mount Rainier, where my family would stay for ski weekends.

As I tugged off my coat, a shadow caught my eye. A black lab sat beyond us, his dark eyes appraising me while his tail thumped the wooden floor.

I couldn't help but smile and squatted down on my heels. He trotted right over. I hadn't been around a dog in months. "Who's this?"

"That's Wilson."

As we all moved toward the couch and chairs, everyone except Aditi took a moment to pet him. He just sat there, enjoying the attention. My dog Zoey would've been jumping up and down, running in circles, and barking like a maniac if six strangers showed up at our doorstep.

Coach Kat flitted between the kitchen and the living room while we got settled. My stomach growled when the smell of garlic and oregano filled the air. Italian maybe? She offered everyone drinks, wine for Mrs. Humphrey and soda or water for the rest of us. She even enlisted Ryan to help her serve, and he used a silly French accent, which drove us to hysterics, as he presented cheese and crackers and a tray of vegetables.

At one point Aditi asked, "So have these homes always been out here?"

"Nope. Not until the 1950s." Coach Kat joined us in the living room. "Back when they were building this academy, the School Board still required the faculty and staff to live on campus full time. You know, to keep an eye on everyone since Dream Management is much more in the open up here. So they created an entire village."

"They were building the last of these homes when I began school," Mrs. Humphrey added. "Most are one-bedroom, I believe, but there are some larger ones for the families who choose to stay here."

"Don't all the employees live here?" Ben asked.

"Most do," Coach Kat said. "We're pretty isolated so it's more convenient. But when they loosened the rules back in the '90s, they added bunkrooms to some of the cabins, so when a storm hits, the commuters can stay."

"Why the change?" I asked.

"Well, it's easier to attract qualified faculty if they're not required to stay here full time." She chuckled. "Don't need the adults feeling trapped too."

"I meant, why did the Board change its policy?"

"Technology advancements. With computers and GPS, it's easier to keep an eye on—"

"Katherine," Mrs. Humphrey interrupted in a soft but firm voice. "Perhaps we shouldn't go into all that right now."

A cold tingle went down my spine. Computers? GPS? Keeping an eye on whom?

Coach Kat stared at Mrs. Humphrey like a rebellious daughter before her face returned to normal. In that moment, I realized my coach wasn't much older than us. "You're right, Mrs. Humphrey. But I'm sure these freshmen figured out within a couple of days on campus someone was monitoring the internet."

Mrs. Humphrey gave a polite smile. "Still. That's not for us to decide."

I didn't know who looked more uncomfortable. Mrs. Humphrey for having to use her authority or Coach Kat for being reprimanded, albeit gently, in front of five students. The ticking clock grew louder in the awkward silence. I felt terrible for my coach and silently pleaded with Hannah for help. I'd already asked one too many questions.

"So, Coach Kat, do you like it up here?" Hannah asked.

She smiled, as if grateful for the change in conversation. "It took some getting used to. Adopting Wilson helped."

The lab lifted his head at the sound of his name and cocked his head but settled back down once Ben began to rub behind the dog's ears.

"I feel safer with him, especially out on the trails. So tell me, Autumn, what else have you done for your birthday?"

I described my day and the conversation flowed from there, making it easy to forget the adults' awkward exchange. As I relaxed on the couch, I felt a connection with these people in a way I hadn't with anyone back in Seattle. I could be my true self, not always on edge or pretending to fit in. They had accepted the real me who was beginning to blossom.

"What's for dinner?" Mrs. Humphrey asked at some point. "It smells delicious."

"It's Autumn's mother's turkey lasagna."

So that's why Hannah had asked me about my favorite foods last week. I blinked a few times to keep the tears from forming, touched they went to the effort to plan such a personalized meal. Coach Kat even served red velvet cake. It was like I had a second family stepping in while separated from my own.

Since it was a weeknight, we walked back to campus right after dessert. Although we were still a festive bunch, out in the dark, I couldn't help but shiver. Not from the cold this time but from Coach Kat's words about monitoring dream-makers. I imagined mysterious guardians watching us from the shadows, ensuring their secrets remained protected.

Chapter: 21

Our room was cold and dark. Aditi lay asleep in her bed, her face lit by the faint glow of my flashlight. I'd already attempted to convey twice tonight. Mr. Robbins had assured me in our one-on-one meetings I'd been following the steps correctly, but it wouldn't hurt to go through them a third time.

Nearly half the class, including Hannah, could convey the simplest version of *Dream One*. Many of these students were now working on more complex variations by adding in unique artwork creations. The more advanced students, such as Ben, were already altering their settings. Aditi and I, however, continued to work on basic conveyance. She kept reminding me the more I obsessed about conveying, the more difficult it would become. I even worried perhaps she hadn't been successful because I was a terrible recipient with only the ability to accept dreams from teachers who had advanced conveyance skills.

After completing another short meditation exercise to stop my mind from drifting, I returned my attention to my roommate. *Come on, Autumn, you can do this. Stay positive.* I glanced at my notes, but the words blurred. So tired. I could barely keep my eyes open. But it didn't matter. I'd memorized them weeks ago.

I closed my eyes and visualized the pile of leaves below our bedroom window. The cool breeze touched my face. No sooner did I start than I heard Dad's voice on the wind. "Telepathy is not real. You can't do this." I took a deep breath and pushed those negative words aside. Aditi ran toward me. She was laughing as she approached. But at the last minute, instead of jumping into the leaves, she turned toward me and said in a deep male voice, "Shouldn't you be studying instead of wasting your time on this garbage?"

I took another breath and tried again.

****

During my morning classes, I kept an eye on the snow falling outside the school's windows, hoping the way it was piling up wouldn't impact my one o'clock departure. We'd be dismissed early today, and the final bell couldn't ring fast enough. Between the recent midterms and my growing frustration with Dream Management, I was so ready for a break. The receptionist in the office had coordinated transportation for the Thanksgiving holiday to make it as efficient as possible. A senior named Allison would drive Ben, me, and a sophomore named Tyler home because we lived in the Seattle area. Dickensen preferred to utilize student and faculty drivers to avoid having parents arrive on campus at non-designated times throughout the year.

Tyler and Allison rode up front while Ben and I sat in the back. My stomach tied in knots. I didn't hang out with older students, especially seniors. Now I was about to spend the next three plus hours with these two strangers. As it turned out, Allison had driven Tyler home a couple of other times, so despite their two-year age difference, they knew each other well, eliminating some of the awkwardness. And when Allison gushed,

"I'm so excited to have another girl in the car for a change," my body began to relax. This wouldn't be so bad.

"How do you like Dickensen so far?" Allison asked us.

"Love it!" Ben said. "I'm learning so much, and it's great to be off on my own."

Her gaze shifted for a split second in the rearview mirror to me. "How about you, Autumn?"

"Ditto. And I've made some good friends."

Ben smiled and turned his gaze out his window.

"How do you feel about Dream Management?" she asked. "It can be a bit overwhelming at first."

Ben answered within seconds. "It's so cool! I'm going to miss sending and receiving dreams while I'm gone."

"Oh, so you're one of the lucky ones who can already do it," Tyler said.

"Yeah. But the dreams are pretty basic. I'm sure yours are much more impressive."

I couldn't help myself and added, "Actually, Ben conveyed successfully the first time."

"No way!" Tyler said. "You're the guy? Hey, Allison, we have someone famous in the backseat."

"Really? I thought it was only a rumor."

"It's true," I said.

"Gee, thanks," Ben muttered under his breath, then raised his voice to address the front. "I'm sure it was beginner's luck."

"So what about you, Autumn?" Allison asked.

"Uh, no...not yet."

"Don't worry. It takes time. Sometimes once you get over the initial obstacles, you'll learn the more challenging skills at a faster pace."

"Doubt it. I'm afraid I'm already falling behind."

"No! Don't think like that. I bet some of those classmates can't yet do it consistently. As long as your art and writing techniques keep pace, you'll be fine. There's just the little hurdle of conveying to overcome."

"I don't know if *little* is the right word, more like *mammoth*," I said.

"Maybe. But my point is, once you begin to convey successfully, you'll be able to move faster through more complex conveyances. Those who convey earlier, such as our friend here, won't be able to move as quickly through the freshman Dream Management series."

"Why not?" Ben asked.

"Because after conveying the final variation of each dream, you'll need to spend time developing the next one whereas Autumn's stories, objects, and settings will be complete and simply waiting for her to have the skills to convey."

That made sense. Meeting a senior who had an experienced perspective was refreshing.

"I have a question for you guys that's been bugging me for a while," Ben said.

Tyler turned toward him. "Shoot."

"I'm curious why news of Dream Management doesn't get out? I mean, I know someone is monitoring the internet, and they threaten us with expulsion and nightmares. But it seems like it'd still leak somehow."

Tyler and Allison exchanged a look. Too bad I could only see their profiles.

"Well, I can't say all the methods they use,"

Allison said. "There are rumors floating around. But I can tell you last summer I ran into this guy at the mall who'd been a couple of years ahead of me. He used to drive me home on breaks until one day he disappeared."

Her gaze shifted between Ben and me in the mirror. "It was strange. He didn't recognize me at first. We weren't close, but still, we spent countless hours on the road together. After I reintroduced myself, we had a little conversation. Eventually I asked why he'd left school. But then he zoned out into the distance—said he couldn't recall. Admitted a lot of his memories from Dickensen were hazy."

A chill surrounded me, even though the heater was blasting.

"So I asked what he was doing with the skills he'd learned in Creative Core, and a blank look came over his eyes. It was freaky, like he'd been brainwashed or something—"

"Allison," Tyler interrupted. "You're scaring the freshmen to death."

Both our mouths were ajar, but Ben recovered. "No, it's fine. I assumed the academy must do something like that."

Really, Ben? You're kidding! He'd never suggested anything like that to me.

Tyler twisted around in his seat to face us. "Don't worry, I'm sure they only inflict that kind of stuff on students who do something truly awful."

After a lengthy silence, Tyler asked, "So what are you guys up to for Thanksgiving?"

Chapter: 22

At last, Allison pulled onto my street. We'd gotten stuck in so much traffic, and we had to drop off Tyler and Ben first. Earlier in the week, I'd thought it would be difficult to leave Ben, but when he got out of the car, he barely mumbled goodbye. He seemed miffed I'd bragged about his Dream Management progress. He was so sensitive. But whatever. I was upset he'd assumed the school was brainwashing former students. He was supposed to tell me that kind of stuff.

By the time I climbed out of the backseat, my family was already waiting in the driveway. I ran into their outstretched arms. Soon Zoey was jumping up against my thighs, so I broke free to squat down and give her some love as my parents thanked Allison and confirmed her plans for the return trip.

Josh carried my bags while Dad put his arm around my shoulder and guided me toward the front door. "Let's get you inside." A warm feeling spread through me. He'd left work early…to greet me.

The smell of chocolate chip cookies made my mouth water the moment I stepped into the house. As we all gathered around the kitchen table, Mom placed a plate of freshly baked deliciousness and a glass of milk in front of me—a special treat; she rarely baked or allowed sugary snacks before meals.

Although I'd called home several times a week for

the past three months, I had so much to say as I munched on the cookies. My stories tumbled out in no particular order: my friends, my teachers, cross country, Coach Kat, weekend activities, tutoring, my birthday, my classes, Mrs. Humphrey, and hiking. I'd taken photos with my phone, so I showed them pictures as we chatted.

"So how is class time spent in Creative Core?" Mom asked innocently.

I was prepared for her question. "Well, it's an art class. We started with drawing in September. Then Mr. Robbins taught us about watercolors and other painting techniques." Luckily, there was plenty to discuss, making it easy to leave out the Dream Management portion of the class. I'd thought when the time came to talk about Creative Core, I'd be dying to tell all—not that I actually would—but after the conversation with Allison and Tyler, any desire I had to even hint it was something more than a visual arts class vanished.

"Let me show you." I dug through my messenger bag and pulled out a few assignments I'd been allowed to take home.

Mom leafed through my folder. "These are beautiful, honey."

"Well done," Dad agreed. "Do you mind if I take one to hang in my office?"

My heart swelled with pride. If only he knew the true purpose of the course, he'd be furious they were teaching *such nonsense*, as he was sure to call it, and pull me out of Dickensen faster than Josh could devour a pizza.

"I'm looking forward to next month when we start on ceramics, which will get fired in the kiln."

"Haller Lake has an art class where they do some of this stuff," Josh said. "It's one of the classes kids consider an easy A."

I sighed. "I'm not sure if that's the case at Dickensen. I guess I'll find out in January."

At that, Dad went off about my recent midterm progress report indicating I was off to a good start. He was eager to see the official letter grades, which would be released at the end of the semester when report cards were issued.

Our conversation went straight through dinner. I'd never been the center of attention for so long and relished it. After running out of stories, I asked what was going on at home. The biggest news: Josh had finished all of his college applications. He'd applied to several out of state, but he'd also applied to some local schools, including the University of Washington, Mom's undergraduate alma mater and where Dad had attended med school.

****

Friday morning, Mrs. Lopez pulled into my driveway. Julia hopped out of the car and ran toward me. "You're back!" She wrapped me in a tight bear hug, and we rocked each other back and forth.

On the way to the mall where we planned to hit the Black Friday sales, Julia talked nonstop. Did she always talk so fast, or had I never noticed before? Somehow, Mrs. Lopez squeezed in a few questions. When I mentioned I took Spanish, she switched to her native tongue.

"*Muy bien*," she said, impressed I was able to carry on a simple conversation. "And with a proper accent no less."

At the mall, Julia insisted we go into every clothing shop carrying the latest brands and styles, even though we were supposed to be buying Christmas gifts. She brought outfits by the armload to the dressing rooms. Then she modeled every single item for me. I forced myself to try on a few things, but the focus was on her.

During lunch in the food court, Julia carried on about how much she loved Haller Lake. She talked about the football games and the homecoming dance. She didn't mention schoolwork once. Julia's questions about Dickensen Academy centered on weekend activities and the availability of cute boys.

I told her about Ben and Ryan. At first I said they were just good friends, like Drew. But after Julia started drilling, I admitted Ben might be something more, which led to a game of twenty questions. It was fun for a while until she painted my relationship with him into something it was not. I mean, he hadn't even kissed me, and I wasn't sure if he ever would, especially with the way we'd left things after the drive home.

We hadn't even finished our teriyaki meals when I sensed a presence. Two girls hovered over us.

Julia bobbed in her seat. "Ashley, Jessica, this is Autumn." Then she turned to me. "I hope you don't mind, but I invited them to meet up with us."

I blinked a few times and made a close-lipped smile. "Nice to meet you."

Ashley and Jessica chattered nonstop too. It was like I was with three Julias, only interested in shopping, boys, and the social life of Haller Lake. Had Julia always been so shallow? We used to have deeper conversations. But now, she seemed more interested in impressing her friends and me. Then again, maybe her babbling wouldn't seem so mindless if I knew who she was talking about. We were living in different worlds.

Maybe I'd changed a bit too. I'd grown more independent and didn't rely on Hannah and Aditi to pull me out of my shell the way I had with Julia. The three of us seemed like equals. Compared to Haller Lake, my school centered more on academics. And of course, Dream Management. I'd love to be shopping with Hannah and Aditi instead. Neither of them was so tiring to hang out with and I could be myself. I was reminded of a conversation with Josh back in August when he had predicted Julia and I would drift apart in high school regardless of my school choice.

After an hour with the three of them, I made up some excuse about Josh having to pick me up early.

On the ride home my brother asked, "How was the mall?"

"Exhausting."

"I thought you liked shopping."

"I do, for about an hour or two. Four hours with Julia and her friends was overkill."

"That's Julia. I can only take her in small doses."

"Yeah. I'm starting to agree with you."

We both laughed.

****

When Mom learned Ben was in town, she insisted I invite him to my belated birthday dinner. I suggested he come over early to get to know my family before he was bombarded by everyone at the restaurant. Besides, if he was still mad at me, I wanted time to work it out.

When Ben arrived on Saturday afternoon, we didn't have a moment alone because Mom and Dad met him at the door and whisked him straight to the kitchen where they'd put out a bunch of snacks. I'd never seen Ben with adults, not counting our teachers, but he was clearly in his comfort zone. He entertained them with stories about his family and school. He even got Dad laughing about some stupid antics with Ryan. Then Ben switched the conversation over to my parents and asked them several intelligent questions about their medical fields, acting genuinely interested in their responses. I'd never quite understood the phrase *worked the room*, but I did now.

After enough time passed, I suggested we take Zoey for a walk. On the way out, Mom pulled me to the side. "You've got a smart one there." Then she winked. "I think he even charmed your father."

I bit my lip and smiled.

Outside, the weather was gray and dreary but not as cold as in the mountains. Fortunately it wasn't raining or I'd have to come up with another plan to get out of there. Zoey refused to walk in anything worse than a drizzle.

"What'd you think?" I asked Ben.

"They seemed nice, especially your mom. But your dad was a bit of a shocker."

"How so?"

"From the way you described him, I expected him to be this hulk of a guy." Ben chuckled. "But I towered over him. And he can't weigh more than one-fifty."

I grinned. How did Ben do that? Here he was so happy and carefree, making me almost forget I was annoyed with him.

After a few moments of silence, I mustered up my courage. "Something you said on the drive home has been bothering me. You mentioned the possibility of brainwashing happening to people who left Dickensen. What was that about?"

"Just me and some of the guys debating that kind of stuff. Erasing people's memories was one idea. I was thinking more along the lines of threatening with recurrent nightmares or using them to influence somehow."

"Why didn't you tell me?"

He raised his eyebrows. "Seriously? Remember how freaked you were after Quinn had his nightmare?"

I gazed at Zoey trotting in front of us. Ben was right. Those conversations would've given me nightmares. He'd tried to protect me, not purposely leave me out.

"Doesn't all that talk scare you?"

"Not really. I find it fascinating and can't wait to learn more."

"Oh."

"Do you remember the dream I created for a young child about the train, my *Dream Two*?"

I nodded. I remembered everything Ben had ever told me. His second dream had a railroad engineer inviting the dream recipient into the engine car to drive the train.

"I sent it to Calvin last night. And he got it! You know how kids are. They tell you everything. This morning while I was still in bed, he came hobbling into my room and told me all about it. He was ecstatic."

"You weren't supposed to convey that until winter break. Mr. Robbins said it would be our first opportunity to work with people outside of school."

"I couldn't help myself. It was so easy."

I froze mid-stride.

Ben's eyebrows fell and his tone became gentle. "I'm sorry. I didn't mean it like that. I meant *convenient*. I went in there before bed to say goodnight, but he was already sound asleep, so I made a spur-of-the-moment decision. It wasn't finished. The setting still needs work. But it took less effort than conveying to Ryan. I can't exactly explain, but I felt Calvin latch on to the dream from my mind more tightly. He must be super receptive because of his age."

Once we started walking again, I asked, "Are you going to tell Mr. Robbins?"

He wrung his hands. "I'm not sure. I don't think he'd be mad. He'd undoubtedly be thrilled. But I'm feeling a bit like the teacher's pet."

Guilt seeped into me with his words. "Sorry about telling Allison and Tyler about your successes."

"It's okay. I just don't like to rub it into everyone's face. The whole school doesn't need to know."

Here I was brooding all weekend about a stupid debate Ben had with his friends while he'd already forgiven me.

Soon we came to our neighborhood park. Most of it was covered in grass, but a swing set and a basketball court stood off to one side. I tied Zoey to a bench and inspected the swings. The seats were dry. We swung, side by side.

"I hope it didn't come across to you like I was bragging," Ben said. "But I was so excited that I wanted to share it with someone. Sometimes it feels like you're the only person I can really talk to."

A lazy smile spread across my face. "I'm glad you told me. That's how it's always been between Josh and me." I pumped my swing higher. "Boys don't always connect with their friends the way girls do. Girls like to have deeper conversations." *Wow, did I just say that? He must think I'm a total loser. Time to change topics.*

"So…yesterday I hung out with Julia at the mall."

"How was that?"

"Weird. She's so into the high school scene. I can't relate."

"Yeah, I get it. Most of my friends are into high school sports. I have to admit it would be fun to go to football and basketball games. What about Drew?"

"Haven't seen him yet. He's been out of town until today. I was thinking, maybe we could go over there now? I'm starting to freeze."

****

After dropping Zoey off at home, we crossed the street. Mrs. Miller answered the door and gave me a welcome-home hug. She looked Ben up and down, then bombarded him with questions, explaining her brother had attended Dickensen, and she'd always enjoyed meeting his classmates. She felt there was something unique about them.

She finally directed us downstairs to where Drew and Luke were playing video games on their big screen TV.

"Autumn!" Drew sprang up from the couch. "You're here!" He turned to Ben. "You must be the Ben she's always talking about."

"And you must be the famous Drew Miller."

"Yeah, whatever," Drew said. "I hope you and your friends are taking care of Autumn. She's like a sister to us."

His brother looked up from the couch. "Hey, I'm Luke. Grab a controller."

The four of us played for about an hour before Josh showed up. After introducing Ben, I turned my controller over to my brother. One hour of video games was more than enough for me. By now, Ben was one of the guys. I sank into the couch, relieved Drew hadn't changed a bit.

Chapter: 23

I woke up on Wednesday having dreamed of splashing as I chased Aditi through the shallow pond behind the sports field. With the crystal-clear images still in my mind, I had no doubt it had come from my roommate. She must have seen something in my eyes because she jumped out of bed and flew across the room to grab the *Initial Dream Review* from her desk. It was a breeze to answer her questions. I recalled the laughter, the icy water, and even the gooey mud between my toes as if it had actually occurred last night.

As we walked down to breakfast, I hugged my arms tight to my chest and stared at the carpeted corridor.

Aditi put her arm over my shoulder. "Don't worry, Autumn. It's going to work for you soon. I'm sure it will."

I nodded. "Thanks." Then I painted a smile on my face. Surely Aditi would have been genuinely happy if I'd been successful first. She was that type of person. She didn't deserve my moodiness today.

All day, I did my best to push aside my jealousy, which had taken hold as an acidic burning sensation in my stomach. I couldn't help but dwell on Aditi now being part of the rapidly growing group of successful freshmen.

When would it be my turn?

That was no way to think. My lack of self-confidence had to be part of the problem. I needed to remain hopeful and focus on the positive: her success confirmed my dream reception skills were intact. That was something.

But what else could I do?

Ben'd had an easier time with his little brother. Perhaps I simply needed to start with an easier dream receptor.

During my private session with my teacher, I sat up straight and waited for his full attention. "Mr. Robbins, I was thinking instead of continuing to convey my dream to Aditi, maybe I could start working on a dream to send to a young child over winter break? I'm going to see my cousins. And I could arrange to babysit too."

He raised his eyebrows. "Are you suggesting you skip *Dream One* and move on to *Dream Two*?"

"Kind of...you see, I've been talking to some of my friends, and it sounds like it might be easier to convey to a little kid rather than to someone my own age."

"Ahh." He gave a half-smile. "You spoke with Ben."

My ears went hot. He must've told Mr. Robbins after all. "So," I stammered, "I thought maybe I could focus on *Dream Two* for now, and then afterward, I'd have better luck sending *Dream One* to Aditi."

He put his index finger to his chin and nodded. "Interesting approach. I have to give you credit for thinking outside the box."

His positive reaction urged me on. "I've already fleshed out the storyline in language arts, so I could finish the development over the next couple of weeks."

Mr. Robbins leaned toward me. "Why don't you tell me what you're thinking for *Dream Two,* and we can go from there?"

I spent several minutes reviewing my idea. During our discussion, he helped me understand why it was too complicated for a first conveyance attempt. My planned *Dream Two* assumed I'd attained the skills, knowledge, and confidence that would come from mastering multiple variations of *Dream One.*

I took a deep breath. "But I really believe sending to a little kid might be the answer. A way to change my mindset and overcome whatever hurdle it is that's preventing me from focusing properly. Maybe I could somehow modify *Dream One* so it's appropriate for someone younger?"

"Statistics indicate eventually you'll be successful with the standard plan of moving in chronological order through to *Dream Six.* Although…" He leaned back in his chair and chewed his pencil.

I sat in silence while he mulled it over.

After a few moments he tilted his chair back upright. "I like your enthusiasm. It may help with your attitude and confidence."

I looked down at my hands and smiled. My persistence had paid off.

"How about we leave your *Dream One* and *Two* alone for now. You can begin anew with another straightforward storyline aimed at a younger audience. Why don't you spend the weekend brainstorming and present me with a suggestion or two on Monday?"

"Thanks, Mr. Robbins."

"You might be onto something. Now if this

approach doesn't work, don't worry. I have some other tactics you can try out in the new year."

When I left the art studio, my steps were lighter as I glided back to my locker.

All weekend, I racked my brain to come up with an idea. It had to be not only simple, but one I could unobtrusively confirm with a child whose communication skills and memories weren't well-developed. After hours of scribbling and crossing out potential scenarios, I created a plan to read a picture book at my neighborhood park. I'd chosen the park setting because it was familiar to both my cousins and the preschoolers I babysat, yet it was an unusual location to read a story. Now, I only needed to locate a unique book the kids wouldn't have read, so I could clarify they'd heard the story from me in their dreams. Luckily, I didn't have to create multiple variations of the dream because it wouldn't count toward my grade. The goal was simply to have a successful experience, which hopefully would translate to the required dreams.

****

Snow fell in earnest throughout December, and the campus became a winter paradise. Big white flakes and a postcard-perfect landscape beckoned to me through the windows of the school and dorm. I swallowed my jealousy as other students found time to go sledding or cross-country skiing on the trails. But my fear of failure won out.

Fortunately, the month was also filled with several academic dreams to help prepare us for all the tests my teachers were squeezing in prior to break. The most memorable one, sent by Ms. Jenson, cast me as a member of a jury in a hot and humid Alabama courthouse, watching Atticus Finch defend his client. It helped me better grasp the concepts in Harper Lee's *To Kill a Mockingbird.*

Despite the benefits of the dreams, I was a person who'd always needed extra time when it came to most subjects. So aside from an impromptu snowball fight in the quad, which drew nearly the entire school including Principal Locke, I remained inside to study and work on my new dream. I even skipped the trip to Leavenworth, telling myself I was too busy. In reality I knew it might make me homesick since I'd visited the touristy Bavarian village countless times with my parents. In many ways, it was easier to ignore the holiday season, since I was going to miss out on many of my family's traditions this year. Perhaps someone would send a dream to help with that too.

Chapter: 24

I waited in the entryway of O'Reilly with my suitcase and school bags. Every couple of minutes, another student bustled by, oftentimes with a parent in tow. I had brushed and re-brushed my hair and even put on a touch of mascara and pink lip-gloss. I'd never met Ben's family. They were driving us home. We could've ridden with Allison, but his family wanted to visit the academy, and this was one of the only times it was open for visitors.

The chitter-chatter of a little kid filled the air before the elevator door fully opened. I bit my lip. It had to be them.

Ben, his parents, and brother stepped out of the elevator. Ben leaned down and pointed me out. Keeping my face neutral was a challenge. He had prepared me for Calvin, but his parents shocked me. They were so young, especially his mom. She couldn't have been much older than thirty. Her long, blond hair had definitely not come from a bottle, unlike my mom's. She was vaguely familiar—I must've seen her on the tour months ago. Regardless, I'd have never suspected she was a mother. Most of my friends' mothers were in their forties and mine had turned fifty last year. His mom was tall and thin like him, and she had his same blue eyes. Definitely related.

Before anyone spoke, someone tugged my leg.

173

I looked down.

Six-year-old Calvin clung to my thigh, gazing up at me with two crutches dangling from his forearms. He had the same hairstyle as Ben, but Calvin's was darker and fell back to reveal big brown eyes.

"Hi!" he said, then grabbed my hand and tugged me away from my pile of belongings. Once I started moving, he let go of me, gripped his crutches, and hobbled away, dragging his left leg slightly. "Which way?"

I twisted back toward his family.

Ben grinned. "Sorry. I promised him a little tour before we left." He dropped his luggage next to mine, and the three of them followed Calvin and me.

His mom and step-dad, Jim, introduced themselves as I traipsed alongside Calvin toward the dining hall. By his speed alone, you'd never guess he had cerebral palsy and wore braces under his pant legs.

While Ben pointed things out to Calvin, his parents listened in. Jim hadn't been to campus before either. As I followed along, I couldn't help but recall the dream Ben had before he accepted. It had included a short tour followed by giving me a ride home. Was it simply a coincidence, or could these Dickensen dreams somehow foretell the future or influence it in some way?

A dormitory tour was a nice way to begin with his parents. It gave me a chance to talk about the academy rather than dive straight into the personal stuff. By the time we finished our fifteen-minute stroll through O'Reilly, I was breathing normally again and ready for the long car ride.

"Let's get you guys out of here," Jim said as he

lifted Calvin up to his shoulders while Ben's mom grabbed the crutches. Jim's voice brimmed with excitement. He seemed as happy to take us home as we were to come home. I could see why Ben liked him so much. You'd never suspect he wasn't his real dad. Supposedly Ben's father was a total jerk.

Calvin sat in a booster seat between us in the second row of their minivan. He talked nonstop for the first hour. Although I loved kids, I couldn't imagine living with a kindergartener. It'd drive me crazy after a few days. But Ben entertained him the entire time, obviously destined for his role as big brother. While Calvin was engaged in a serious game of *I Spy* with Ben, I leaned forward to chat with his parents. They asked questions about Dickensen and my family. They knew a ton about me, way more than my parents had known about Ben when I introduced them back at Thanksgiving.

After a while, Jim turned on the radio to some country station. Then he started singing loud and clear along with the musician's low country drawl. I leaned around Calvin to peer at Ben and gasped. He was quietly singing too. When he saw my raised eyebrows, he shrugged then raised his voice to match Jim's. Soon the whole car was belting out country tunes at the top of their lungs. I couldn't help but laugh. After a couple of songs, I found myself humming along. It was so different from the rides with my family where my parents spoke quietly up front, leaving Josh and I to do our own thing, usually something related to a book or an electronic device. Light sounds of classical music or a talk show on National Public Radio were the only noises ever emitted through our car speakers.

Mom had invited his family to stop in for drinks and appetizers before heading home. I hoped my parents wouldn't embarrass me by acting all old and serious, or worse, take this as an opportunity to learn more about Ben and me. They must've guessed that I liked him a lot, but I hadn't said much about our relationship despite Mom's questions over the past month. It was hard enough to explain it to myself, let alone to my parents. And Mom had always been so protective of me, I'm sure she had some boyfriend-warning conversation prepped and waiting. As for Dad, I didn't even want to think about going there.

If my parents were surprised by his parents' ages, they hid it well. Turns out, I had no need to worry. They managed to find lots to discuss and avoided embarrassing questions. Mom got along with everyone, and Dad had so many obligatory dinner meetings, he was pretty good at socializing too—undoubtedly the alcohol helped. *Oh, and I can't forget Zoey.* She probably had the most fun, finding Calvin to be a compatible, high-energy playmate.

As our parents said their goodbyes, Ben spied my bags by the door and mouthed, "Good luck," as he shuffled out with his family. He knew I had homework assigned and my Dream Management notes were buried at the bottom of my messenger bag.

Chapter: 25

My first full day at home, I had volunteered to babysit my cousins. It presented a perfect opportunity to perform my first conveyance on three-and-a-half-year-old Skylar. Since my aunt and uncle lived over thirty minutes away, I planned to spend the night and stay until my family came over for a holiday dinner. This would give me time to determine whether Skylar received the dream.

I'd decided to read *The Polka Dot Penguin* by Anna Nivlac. It was one of my favorite bedtime stories when I was young. I'd selected it not only because I loved its theme of diversity and friendship, but also because I had it memorized so I could finish planning the dream without a copy on campus. And most of all, few people had even heard of it.

The evening was packed full of board games and crafts. Skylar was usually on my team because eight-year-old Alex could only handle so many rounds of *Candy Land* and *Chutes and Ladders.* Her favorite games were too complicated for her younger sister. By the time both kids fell asleep, I still had at least an hour before my aunt and uncle returned. It'd be the worst if they walked in while I was conveying to Skylar. *Awkward.*

The house was silent. I was ready.

Kneeling on the carpet beside Skylar's princess

toddler bed, I clicked on my flashlight and reread my notes. My senses heightened as I concentrated on my cousin and the memories within her cerebral cortex, primarily her memories of me and those of the park where I'd taken her on Thanksgiving. Then I pulled out my ragged book and began to silently read.

Once down south, far across the sea, penguins huddled, trying not to freeze. They sat so close in the cold sun, their eggs soon hatched, one by one. They each came out in puffs of gray. But one did not look quite that way. This one had red and blue-green spots. They named him Little Polka Dot...

Five minutes later, I finished with *they loved each other through and through. Then went to bed, now time for you.*

The next morning, happy·shrieks woke me before sunrise. Although it was hours before I'd normally get up on a weekend, I forced myself out of bed. It wouldn't be smart for much time to pass before I quizzed my cousin.

I followed the noises to the kitchen. Aunt Kelly was busy unloading the dishwasher, and Skylar was eating a waffle at the table. I helped myself to one and sat down beside her, aching for my aunt to leave.

I had to be careful with how I questioned her. Direct questions might arouse suspicion. Although she was only three, little kids repeated everything they heard.

As if in answer to my prayers, Aunt Kelly closed the dishwasher and turned to me. "Do you mind keeping an eye on Skye while I take a quick shower?"

"No problem."

"Thanks, Autumn."

When she left, I returned my attention to my cousin. "Skylar, how did you sleep last night?"

"Good!"

"Did you have any nice dreams?"

She nodded like a bobblehead doll.

"Can you tell me about your dreams?"

She dropped her half-eaten waffle on her plastic plate. "I be a princess, and Alex be a fairy."

"You mean you *were* a princess, and your sister *was* a fairy?"

She shook her head. "No, I want."

Huh? "So…when you dreamed about being a princess, did you mean you *want* to be a princess? Like pretend?"

She jumped up for a second and clapped her hands. "Yes! You be the fairy! Alex sleeping."

"Uh, maybe later. I meant, did you dream something while you were asleep in bed?"

"I dreamed that kind too."

"Do you remember that dream?"

She scrunched up her face and stared at me.

I clenched my teeth. This wasn't going to be as easy as I'd thought. Maybe she was too young, and Alex would've been the better recipient, but the story appealed more to a preschooler.

I didn't have a choice. I needed to ask leading questions. "Do you ever have animal dreams?"

The confusion evaporated from Skylar's face and pure joy replaced it. "Yes!"

"What kind of animals?"

"Doggies and kitties…and ponies." Then she hopped up and galloped around.

"Anything else?"

"Monkeys. And fishes." She continued to circle the kitchen island.

I was about to give up but took a chance. "Do you ever dream of penguins?"

She stopped abruptly. "Yes. Polka dot penguins!"

I did it! Of course, I'd fed her the term penguin, but she came up with polka dot on her own. She must've heard it in her dream.

Time to change subjects—I needed to save some questions for the afternoon. If it went anything like this morning, I'd have to come up with alternate ones. "Do you want another waffle? I could make you one."

"No! I want to play princesses." Then she stomped her foot with more force than I thought possible for a child her size. "Now!"

"Okay, okay." I didn't particularly enjoy pretend play, but I was elated and willing to play princesses all day if that's what she wanted. Once Alex woke, I could switch activities. Or maybe as soon as Aunt Kelly returned.

The next several hours were a blur. I still had to get through a scaled down version of the *Dream Review Checklist*, so in the back of my mind I worked out a revised plan.

After Skylar's nap, I gathered some paper, markers, and crayons and called the kids over to the dining room table. "Let's draw."

Using her whole fist to grip the crayons, Skylar scribbled what might be a house and flowers.

Aware her attention span was short, and thus, my time limited, I said, "Maybe we should all make some animals."

Skylar soon began drawing stick figure cats around

the house. *Hmm, a penguin might be kind of tough. Better try Plan B.* I drew several penguins and outlined them in black like a coloring book, then I slid my paper her way. "Hey, Skylar. Do you want to color these penguins in for me?"

She grabbed the black and white crayons and colored all but one penguin. Soon she picked up a red crayon and made a few dots. Then she picked up the blue and colored a few more. My heart raced. Next came the green, then the purple, and finally the yellow before she proudly announced she was finished.

"Skylar. Your picture is beautiful. I love the colors." I attempted to keep a straight face. "But why did you draw this one with colored polka dots? Penguins are black and white."

"It's Polka Dot Penguin."

I could've jumped up and down right then and there. I probably would when I replayed the conversation with Ben later.

Alex looked up. "That's nice coloring, Skye. You did a good job staying in the lines. It looks like the one in the book."

Skylar nodded.

I froze. How did Alex know about the book? Did the dream convey to her too? Her bedroom was next door to Skylar's, so it was possible. *Wow!* Two people at once. I should've started with children.

"I liked that book too," Alex added.

I turned to Alex. "Really? When did you read *The Polka Dot Penguin*?"

"I didn't. Josh did."

My heart about stopped. "When?"

"Maybe a month or two ago. You were away at

181

your new school. Josh got it from your bedroom. He must've read it three or four times to her. She loved it. I thought it was pretty cute, even if it was for a baby."

My elation disappeared like candles blown out on a birthday cake.

****

When I arrived to babysit at our neighbors, the Davidsons, a few days later, I barely recognized one-year-old Roxanne. In the past four months, she'd gone from a happy, cooing baby to a toddler who'd finished the crawling stage and was now practically running. But as soon as five-year-old Brady saw me, he bounded into my arms and demanded my full attention.

It turned into an exhausting evening. Not only did Brady want to play, but Roxanne did too. She constantly got into his way, knocking over his Legos, derailing his trains, or grabbing his trucks. Memories of Alex and Skylar when they were younger passed through my mind.

It took forever to get them both to bed because Roxanne refused to take a bottle and kept screaming like an alarm with no snooze button. By then, I was ready to burn my babysitter's certificate. Once they were in their bedrooms, I laid on the couch ready to zone out in front of the TV. But then I jolted back upright. I'd forgotten the conveyance. The primary reason I'd offered to babysit.

As soon as they were quiet, I tiptoed into Brady's room and crouched by his bedside, willing my heart rate to slow. It took a while, even with a relaxation exercise. I concentrated on his sweet face. Then I went through the steps, running through the dream in my mind. When I came to the story within the story, I picked up my book and mouthed the words *once down south, far across the sea, penguins huddled, trying not to freeze…*

When I finished, I leaned over and gave Brady a peck on his cheek, as if a kiss might help seal the dream inside of him.

****

I broke dream review protocols the following day. Since it was impossible to be at the Davidson's house when Brady woke, I didn't have a choice but to merge the two reviews and hope I could somehow get him away from his parents. Mid-morning, I took Zoey for a walk toward their house. *Please be home.* Lucky for me, sounds of screaming kids greeted me before I even reached their front porch.

Mrs. Davidson opened the door. "Autumn, good morning." It didn't look like she was having a good morning. Her hair stuck up on one side, and dark circles had formed under her eyes.

"Hi, Mrs. Davidson. I think I might've left my purple scarf here last night."

"Oh yes, you did. I found it on the couch. Just a sec."

So far, so good.

A moment later, she returned with the scarf.

"Thanks so much. Um…so I'm taking Zoey to the park and thought maybe I could take Brady off your hands for a little while? I know he loves dogs. I bet he'd like to play fetch with her."

She pressed her palm to her heart. "He'd love to. Roxanne has been fussy this morning, and I haven't been able to give him much attention. Give me a moment. I'll bundle him up."

Relief flowed through my body. I wasn't sure what I'd have done if she'd said no. Besides, it felt good to help her out. Mrs. Davidson had always treated me well.

Brady and I strolled along the sidewalk while Zoey tugged us faster, as if she were pulling a sleigh in the Iditarod. Brady giggled at her doggy antics while I held her leash firmly.

"I sure had a blast last night with you and your sister," I said. "Did you have fun too?"

"Yeah."

"What was your favorite part?"

He considered my question for a while. "Playing with my trains."

"Uh-huh. What else did you like?"

"Playing Legos." Then he frowned. "Until Roxy knocked them over. She's always getting in my way."

"That was tough. But someday, she'll be big like you and can help you build towers and spaceships." He brightened at that prospect. "So did you like the story I read?"

His eyes glazed over. "What story?"

"You know, the one about the animals?"

He shook his head.

I had a bad feeling, so I gave him more hints. Maybe he couldn't differentiate yesterday from last week. "Have I ever read you a story about penguins?"

"Maybe…I have a zoo book Daddy reads me."

"I meant another story. Have I ever read one about baby penguins?"

"Maybe."

What the heck does that mean? "Well, do you remember the color of the penguins?"

Brady looked at me like I was crazy. "Of course, silly. Penguins are black and white."

"Yes. And baby penguins can be gray. Were there any different-looking penguins in the book?"

"Penguins are always black and white. I know. I've seen them on *Animal Planet*."

So much for that.

Ben was so lucky he had a brother, who was young enough to receive dreams and old enough to discuss them. *I'm the one who needs a Calvin to practice on, not Ben.* The logistics to arrange babysitting and follow-up visits were too complicated. I tried to console myself with the fact I had made some money, but all I could do was dwell on the entire month of December being a total waste.

For a day I moped about, not even bothering to change out of my flannel pajamas. Mom kept asking what was wrong, but there was no way to explain.

The following day I forced a smile upon my face. We were squeezing several activities into the week before Christmas to help make up for the three weeks of December I'd been away, so I had to get dressed and out of the house. And I'm a girl who loves Christmas. Within a couple of hours, the excitement of the holidays won out and helped push all those negative thoughts to the side…at least for now.

****

My parents always rented a condo in Whistler, British Columbia for the week between Christmas and New Year's—one of my favorite traditions. I had breathed a sigh of relief when we drove away from our house. After being on my own for four months, being back home was stifling. It's not like I had many more rules, but I felt the same tension that hung in the air in the days leading up to finals. Dad would often grill me about school or suggest I pull out my textbooks so I wouldn't forget anything. At Dickensen, I had the freedom to manage my own schedule, and I'd done a darn good job. But I rarely pushed back or argued because excelling in school seemed to be the best way to prove I was worthy of his love.

Dad was different on vacations—more relaxed— and Mom had persuaded him to allow me to leave my books behind. She'd always acted as our buffer and frequently reminded me Dad loved me as much as he loved Josh. I wasn't naïve. Parents often fed their kids that kind of crap. And she was probably telling the truth. But no doubt, Dad would *like* me better if I performed to his high standards.

This year we skied together in the mornings, but in the afternoons I'd take off with Josh. Long ago, we'd passed our parents' abilities. We preferred the challenge of the black and double-black diamond runs, whereas Mom and Dad were more cautious and content to remain on the groomed, blue runs.

It was fun to spend time together on the lifts without our parents hovering nearby. I chatted about Dickensen, while Josh went on about his upcoming high school graduation and college. He'd been accepted into a couple of schools, but he'd have to wait a few months to hear from the rest. He planned to follow in our parents' footsteps and go on to medical school straight from college.

During one of our lift rides, Josh announced, "I'm going to accept at the University of Washington, if I get in."

My eyes bulged. "UW. Why?"

"It's a great school, and my counselor said chances are high I'll get in based on my grades and test scores."

"But what about the schools where you applied *early action*? I thought those were your top choices?"

"They were, but now I'm leaning toward staying closer to home. I can always go farther away for med school."

"I thought you wanted to go away?"

"I did. But now I'm thinking it might be best to stick nearby. Most of my friends plan to stay in state. Besides, I don't know if Mom and Dad are ready to have two kids far away."

That hit me like a well-spiked volleyball. *He must hate me.* I had to turn away and focus on the skiers below for a moment before responding. "So you're saying I'm the reason you want to remain in Seattle?"

"Not exactly. But it opened my eyes to how it'd be. You're not around for so many things. Plus eight years of school will be expensive. Mom and Dad have saved for college, but med school is on me. If I go to UW, they said there'd be money left over from my college fund to apply toward med school."

I let out a long breath, the vapors visible in the frigid air. "Now I feel guilty."

Josh shook his head. "Don't. I'd never go there if it wasn't such a strong school. Besides, Mom and Dad know so many doctors in the area, they'll be able to arrange volunteer opportunities. Hospital experience is nearly as important as your GPA for getting into med school."

"I guess that makes sense." My stomach still felt sick. I was the reason for his change of heart, even if there was logic behind it. "I always assumed you wanted to get away to have more freedom."

"You're confusing me with you. You and Dad are like oil and water. He leaves me alone because I actually want to become a doctor. I'm not faking it, like you. And it's not like I'd live at home. I'd stay on campus."

"What do Mom and Dad think?"

"Mom would love for me to be a Husky like her. I don't think she really wants me to go away. Dad gets my rationale. Besides, he's always looking for a good deal. And remaining in Washington is so much cheaper. It's where you graduate from med school that's most important."

The lift neared the summit, and we pushed up the bar and prepared to dismount. The wind was biting, and it was hard to see much of anything here in the clouds.

"Of course," Josh said, "I haven't gotten in yet. But I've applied to a few others in the Puget Sound area."

Josh seemed set on UW. I agreed it was a well-thought-out plan. But would he have reached the same decision if I still lived at home?

When we arrived at the top of *Seventh Heaven*, Josh yelled, "Can't catch me!"

Thoughts of college disappeared. I was one hundred percent focused on making it down the steep run Josh had picked and didn't want to lose him in the white haze. Maybe I could even beat him. *Yeah, right...only in my dreams.*

Chapter: 26

The bus trudged up the mountain pass, packed with students chatting quietly or napping. Snow fell outside the large windows. The timing was perfect for a ski trip since we'd only been back in school a few days, and I wasn't yet in the studying groove. Moreover, my initial joy at seeing my friends after the winter break had been replaced with jealousy as I learned about so many freshmen's recent conveyance successes.

Ben had made progress with his brother. He conveyed *Dream Three* in which Calvin saw Santa Claus unpack gifts and place them under the Christmas tree. In the morning, Calvin gushed about his dream, and it didn't arouse any suspicion since he had been talking nonstop about staying up to see Santa.

As for Aditi, she had sent *Dream Two* to her younger brother *and* sister. However Aditi could only confirm the dream had made it to Rohan. She skipped the dream review with Shilpa because Aditi was scared her sister, at nearly fourteen, might somehow figure it out.

At least Ben and Aditi were nice enough to downplay their successes in front of me, but I couldn't say the same for some others, including Caitlyn. She somehow managed to brag to the entire class as she asked Mr. Robbins a carefully phrased question.

But luckily today, as I shared in the anticipation of

a fun-packed day, those awful jealous feelings melted away. I needed to think more like Ryan. Although he continued to have difficulties, even with all those younger siblings to practice on, he remained positive.

Ryan leaned forward from where he sat with Ben and popped his head between Aditi's and my shoulders. "The snow's going to be fantastic! They've gotten eleven inches in the past twenty-four hours!"

Ben grinned. "Yeah. And the temp is supposed to peak at twenty-nine, so it should last."

"Twenty-nine degrees?" Aditi wrinkled her nose. "Isn't that a little cold?"

I shook my head and chuckled. "You should be plenty warm in *that* outfit." Aditi wore four thick layers and had a scarf wrapped around her neck, and she hadn't yet put on the ski jacket she'd borrowed from a classmate.

The bus made a slow, wide turn and bumped over a pot-holed, gravel-and-ice-covered road. We passed a sign reading *Stevens Pass Ski Resort*, and the busload erupted in a chorus of cheers.

"I'll meet you guys at the end of your lesson," I said to Hannah and Aditi. Then I joined the rest of the experienced students as we collected our equipment from the side of the bus.

Ryan was mind-blowing on his snowboard—no surprise—as he tore it up in the terrain park. Ben was a skier like me. Having grown up in the Northwest, he'd also skied for years, so we were compatible on the slopes. Point number twenty-seven for Ben as a potential boyfriend...not that I was keeping a list.

Near the end of the day, in a moment of good intuition, I asked Ben to help me take Hannah and Aditi up the beginner chairlift. Ryan admitted he'd be little help on a board—just as well since the chair was two-person. I rode with Aditi, while Ben rode with Hannah.

Right before we arrived at the top, Aditi announced, "I'm really not good at this." Sure enough, she collapsed in a heap the moment her skis hit the snow. The lift operator had to stop the chair while he picked up her scattered equipment, and I helped her scramble away from the exit ramp. She cringed with embarrassment.

A minute later, Ben and Hannah skied toward us. So far, Hannah remained upright.

Ben nodded at me. "Why don't I stick with Hannah, and you head down with Aditi?"

Aditi and I went first. I led the way, checking over my shoulder every so often while she attempted to stay in my tracks. On the second turn, she wiped out again. I covered my mouth with my glove to hide my reaction. I hadn't skied with a beginner in ages and had forgotten how difficult skiing could be at first.

"I'm so sorry, Autumn."

"You're doing fine." I plopped down in the snow near her boots. "Let me hold your skis in place while you stand up."

Meanwhile, Ben and Hannah skied past us. She was able to complete some basic wedge turns behind him.

He shouted over his shoulder, "We're skiing to the chair! Let's meet at the rental shop instead!"

"Okay!" I called as he sailed away.

"I'm so sorry you have to stay with me," Aditi said.

"No worries. I've skied all day. You'll get it."

We continued down the bunny hill. It was slow going, and every few turns she fell. Skiing straight to the rental return instead of the chair seemed like a better option because I doubted there'd be time for a second run. Besides, Aditi looked beat.

As I was helping Aditi out of her skis near the shop, Ben and Hannah skied toward us. Hannah made a controlled wedge stop in front of me. "That was so much fun!"

"Hannah was amazing!" Ben said. "We did the run three times, and each time she improved. She's a natural."

Then he noticed Aditi, soaked through with snow, and grimaced as if he'd bitten into a lemon.

No one else said anything. Poor Aditi. She wasn't a natural. If only we had a better way to teach her.

Chapter: 27

"I don't get what I could be doing wrong," I complained. Ever since I'd returned from winter break, I'd been trying to convey *Dream One* to Aditi, and it was the same each time: failure.

Hannah, Aditi, and I huddled around a table in the corner of the game room playing *Ticket to Ride*. Although the room was crowded as usual on a weekend, the constant noise gave us privacy. My friends' eyes offered sympathy, but I just wanted to scream in frustration. They had no idea what it felt like.

"Maybe I'm the problem," Aditi said. "It might be tougher to get through to me for some reason."

"Doubt it." I couldn't even convey to preschoolers, which was supposed to be the easiest.

Aditi held my gaze. "Mr. Robbins says conveying is like any other skill; everyone learns at a different pace. Take me and Hannah learning to ski."

She had a point. Hannah was picking it up far more easily than Aditi, but that didn't mean Aditi would never ski well. After a moment, I shook my head. "That's a stupid comparison. Who cares if you never learn to ski? But if I don't get this conveyance thing down, I could get kicked out of school." I blew out a breath. "Then they'll erase my memories or something."

"Oh, Autumn!" Aditi leaned over to hug me.

"Don't even go there."

She should be mad at me for what I'd said about her athletic abilities, not empathetic. But the realization only made me feel worse. "I'm sorry. I didn't really mean that. It's just, no one else is having this problem. Even Ryan's figured it out."

Hannah picked up a blue train card then looked up. "You're not the only one."

"Yeah," Aditi agreed. "How about Samantha and um, Jacob. And I'm sure there are more in Mr. Robbins' other periods."

Hannah nodded. "And look at me. I can convey, but I've been having problems with reception lately."

I shot her a questioning glance. "Since when?"

"Y'all need more confidence." Hannah placed a new card in the empty spot, ignoring my question. "All this negative talk is bringing you down."

I shrugged. "Well I blame my dad for that."

"Forget your dad," Aditi said. "You're doing great in your other classes. Latch on to the positive."

"But that's just it. I can't. And it's not only a self-confidence thing. It's the way he raised me."

Aditi laid down several red pieces to claim a train route. "What do you mean?"

"He's so scientific. My whole life he's been teaching Josh and me about physics and biology. He could never take us to the zoo to simply look at the animals. It always turned into a lesson on evolution or something."

Hannah laughed. "That's not all bad."

"No. But I think it's part of my problem. Sometimes I question everything they're teaching. I mean, is this all real? Are we truly doing telepathy?"

Aditi sucked in a breath. "How can you not believe? You get the dreams. Even mine."

"Oh, I do," I gushed. "When I'm immersed in them, I totally believe. But when I sit down to convey in the middle of the night, my mind wanders and I start to question it all. Telepathy doesn't fit in with all the science my dad's drilled into me. Sometimes I wish Dickensen was a normal prep school so I wouldn't have all these worries. And seriously, what are we going to do with dream-making once we graduate from here anyway?"

"I'm sure there's more to it than education and entertainment," Aditi said. "They only parcel out what we need to know."

I stared at my cards, but my mind couldn't return to the game. "So, Hannah, what's this about not being able to receive dreams?"

"Yeah." Aditi placed her cards on the table facedown too. "I thought you and Caitlyn were doing great. Mr. Robbins talks about your skills as a pair almost as much as Ben's."

"Not a big deal," Hannah said. "I'm still receiving them. But a few times, I've woken with this strange sense of fear. I even got a few scary images the other night."

"Like what?" I asked.

"A crazy mask popped out, and I heard some loud shrieks. I'm starting to get nervous at bedtime."

"What does Mr. Robbins say?" Aditi asked.

Hannah narrowed her eyes. "I haven't told him. I answer Caitlyn's questions correctly. Her dreams are coming through fine."

"Do you think Caitlyn might be sending those

images?" I probed. Ever since she first asked about nightmares months ago, I'd been concerned for my friend.

Hannah shook her head. "I don't see how. They're completely unrelated. It'd take a lot of skill to integrate them into her dream. Besides, we've been getting along better lately."

"Yeah. She has seemed nicer. I've even seen her crack a smile couple of times." I chuckled.

"It's probably because I'm helping her ace Creative Core," Hannah admitted. "But I'll take it. It's better than when she despised me."

****

Adrenaline shot through me, and I bolted upright in bed.

What was that? Was someone at our door? Aditi was also awake and climbing out of bed. I crept across the floor in the dark, still half-asleep; it might be part of a dream.

Aditi flipped the light switch and opened the door. As I squinted against the bright light, something knocked me back, and my heart leaped in my ribcage. When my eyes adjusted, a flannel-clad Hannah hung over my shoulders. I definitely wasn't dreaming, but Hannah must have been.

She sobbed uncontrollably and most of her words were incoherent, except for the name *Jake*, which she repeated over and over.

Who the heck is Jake?

With Aditi's help, we eased her trembling body onto my bed.

Aditi began smoothing her hair. "Hannah, wake up. You're dreaming."

After a couple of minutes, Hannah's tears stopped and she blinked. Her eyes were wide and her pupils darted side to side.

"You were having a nightmare," I said, voice wavering. "But it's over. You're okay now."

A classmate tapped on our open door and leaned in. "Everything okay?"

"Yeah," Aditi said, getting up to close the door. "We've got this."

"Horrible," Hannah began. "At the beach. Buying ice cream. Jake ran off." Her words came out in whispered spurts, punctuated by heaving breaths. "Chasing something. Pulled leash away. Called him. He wouldn't stop." She sniffed. "A car flew around the corner. He kept running. The brakes screeched. All in slow motion."

"It's okay," Aditi soothed. "It wasn't real."

Hannah dabbed her watery eyes with her pajama sleeve.

"You should stay here," I said.

Hannah curled up on my bed and fell back to sleep soon after we covered her up.

I pulled down some extra blankets and pillows from the top of our closet and made a bed for myself on the floor. I gritted my teeth. "I bet Caitlyn did this. Remember how she asked about creating nightmares that one time? And she's always had it in for Hannah."

"I don't know," Aditi said. "All this dream-making stuff could be messing with Hannah's head."

****

I woke to Hannah's whispers. "You guys. What am I doing here?"

"You don't remember?" Aditi asked.

197

She shook her head.

We went through the events of the previous night, but Hannah couldn't recall much. She only remembered standing in line to buy ice cream at a beach.

At breakfast, I could almost feel Caitlyn's icy blue gaze boring into my backside. Each time I glanced over my shoulder, she was sending evil glares to our table from where she sat with Tessa, across the dining hall. Hannah told Aditi and me she'd confronted Caitlyn when she returned to her room. She denied sending her a nightmare and was so furious Hannah had jumped to that conclusion she stormed out. Obviously, she was angry with Aditi and me too.

****

One afternoon Hannah, Aditi, and I stayed after school in the back of the art studio, painting scenes for our assigned dreams. Mr. Robbins worked at his desk up front, head down, well out of earshot.

"I still keep waking with this weird sense of fear," Hannah explained. "But it's every morning now, not just the times Caitlyn conveys. I don't get it."

I set my paintbrush down and rested back on my stool. "Have you talked to her again?"

"No way!" Hannah painted hastily as if she were taking her frustration out on her canvas. "She's avoiding me more than usual. Guessing she's still upset."

Aditi pointed her thumb at our teacher. "You've got to tell Mr. Robbins."

"Or what about Dean Rothchild? Or even Principal Locke?" I said.

"I don't have proof it's her," Hannah explained as she continued to paint the yellow-green grass of a huge ranch. "And if it's my own fault, I don't want our teacher to know. He might stop my conveyances. I want a good grade."

"You could keep notes," Aditi suggested. "Perhaps you'll find a pattern and figure out why you're having those dreams."

"Yeah. A sleep journal might help your case," I said. "If you can convince Mr. Robbins she's sending nightmares on purpose, she'll get in trouble."

"That's a long shot." Hannah lowered her brush and glanced toward our teacher, still busy at his desk. "He loves Caitlyn, all the teachers do. She's so two-faced. Always raising her hand and participating in class discussions. Then the moment she's alone, she acts like none of us exists. What I really want is a new roommate." She sighed. "If only I could stay with you every night."

"I wish," I said. But school rules didn't permit three freshmen to a room because everyone needed a dream partner.

"Come on." Aditi nodded toward the front of the room. "This is the perfect time."

Hannah glanced up at our teacher, then back to us. She closed her eyes tightly and nodded. "'Kay."

"Mr. Robbins," Hannah said after I nudged her left arm. "I had a terrible nightmare last week and was hoping we could talk."

He gave a sympathetic smile. "Sure. Sit down, girls."

"Well…" Hannah began once we got seated around his desk. Then she launched into a recap of what she could remember and what we'd told her. Aditi and I clarified as needed, so he got the complete story.

"Sounds like a night terror."

"A what?" Aditi asked.

"It's a technical term for a type of nightmare that can't be recalled but usually involves sleepwalking and the appearance of being awake." He shook his head. "I can't imagine something like that could've come from another freshman. Instilling a sense of fear in a benign dream is a high-level skill."

He pulled out a file and studied the papers within it. "Caitlyn's Dream Management notes only describe how Hannah was supposed to be buying ice cream at the beach. And you said those parts went through?"

Hannah nodded.

"Caitlyn has no motive. She knows the rules. Sending a nightmare is cause for serious discipline."

"But Caitlyn has had it in for Hannah from day one," I argued.

His eyebrows shot up.

Hannah caught my eye and shook her head slowly, so I lightened my tone. "They've never been good friends."

"Not everyone is best friends with his or her roommate." He sighed. "I've never heard of any problems with her. She's been a model student."

While I listened to Mr. Robbins, I noticed out of the corner of my eye Hannah had tuned out and was chewing her fingernails.

Suddenly her voice made him stop mid-sentence. Hannah spoke softly, almost to herself. "Reminds me of when my dog got run over by a car."

Mr. Robbins rested his chin on his fingers. "When was this?"

Hannah looked up. "My ninth birthday."

"I'm sorry to hear. And what was your dog's name?"

"Jake."

Aditi's mouth fell open. Why hadn't Hannah mentioned the coincidence before?

He nodded. "Seems likely something in Caitlyn's dream triggered a memory in your cerebral cortex."

"But it hasn't happened to anyone else," I insisted.

"Don't be so sure, Autumn."

Hannah fidgeted. "I think we should go. That had to be it."

"Come back if this happens again. I don't want my students affected by nightmares. I may need to give you a break from conveyances if this continues."

Dream-making could accidentally trigger nightmares? I shuddered. I preferred to think it had to be a malicious act—mean girls I understood. The idea we could be tampering with each other's brains scared me much more.

****

All my classes were gearing up for semester finals as January came to a close. Like before other tests, most teachers sent dreams to reinforce the course materials. My teachers even used Sundays, typically a night off. Not everything was covered during the academic dreams; therefore, we still had to study hard. But it was always a pleasant surprise to receive one delving deeper into a particular subject.

My weekly Spanish dreams had moved well beyond the simple playground dream. I now received one where I was eating dinner with a large Dominican family. Ana and Nicolás still starred in the dream as two children at the table, but I was learning more complicated interactions as well as many nouns and verbs related to food.

But the best dream by far this month was a language arts dream where I attended an outdoor Shakespearean festival on a warm summer evening, complete with a magnificent sunset and later, fireflies. I watched *Julius Caesar*, the play we'd studied in class, performed live. But the dream also allowed me to select a second one to watch, just for fun. I chose *Romeo and Juliet.* Best thing—Ben sat right next to me the entire time.

I had to do well on my final exams because a significant percentage of my grades depended on them, and my parents were impatiently awaiting my first report card. Every time I had spoken with Dad these past few weeks, he'd remind me how my grades would become a permanent part of my record. Good thing I didn't have Grandpa Clarke's blood pressure, or I'd probably die from a stress-induced heart attack.

All the extra work was taking a toll on Hannah too. One weekend afternoon during a much-needed break in my room, Hannah opened up to Aditi and me.

"I'm starting to worry about Creative Core," Hannah muttered.

"What? You've been doing great," I said.

"Until lately. I keep messing up my conveyances. They aren't going through. Caitlyn's having a tough time answering my questions."

"What do you think you're doing wrong?" Aditi asked.

Hannah shrugged. "Probably too stressed out. It's nonstop studying lately."

"Uh-huh," I agreed.

"And Caitlyn's making it worse."

I caught Hannah's eye and gave her a sympathetic smile. "I thought the nightmares stopped."

"Mostly. But she's still so mad I accused her of creating that dog nightmare. She's always mumbling these snide comments." Hannah gave a half-grin. "Good thing she doesn't know we spoke to Mr. Robbins. The only time she treats me like a human being is during our dream reviews. She's not about to let her anger affect her grade."

"What does Mr. Robbins say in your one-on-ones?" Aditi asked.

"Says it's normal. As the dreams grow more complex, it can be a struggle to learn more advanced skills, so often the dreams don't go through in their entirety. And he agrees the stress of finals could be my problem."

After several more minutes of discussion, Hannah sprang from the bed and started pacing. "Ugh! I'm so frustrated. It's been so easy until now." When she caught my eye, she sucked in her breath. "I'm sorry to say it that way, Autumn, but really, I don't understand what's changed."

"It's okay. I'm sure I'd feel the same if I'd been conveying as well as you."

"I can't trust myself anymore," Hannah explained. "It feels like Caitlyn's mind is latching on, but my dreams have lost their stickiness."

"Do you think Caitlyn might be up to something?" I asked.

"Like what? I'm obviously not getting through to her. Maybe I'm not cut out for this dream-making stuff…"

Aditi and I let Hannah continue to vent, but my mind clung onto her last comment. Maybe *I* was the one not cut out for dream-making.

Chapter: 28

I raced up the stairs to the second floor of my dorm, careful to avoid falling into the stampede of freshmen and sophomores. My heart pounded, thanks to both anticipation and the unexpected exercise. Two minutes ago, I had been enjoying my Friday night watching TV when a student announced report cards had been sent. Within fifteen seconds, the room had cleared.

Breathing hard, I plopped in front of my computer. The unread message taunted me from the top of my inbox. When I was ready, I held my breath and clicked.

****

February 1 at 5:58 p.m.
Subject: Semester 1 Grades—Dickensen Academy
Joan Rothchild, Dean of Students
To: Autumn Mattison

~*~

Autumn K. Mattison
Year 1—Semester 1
History: A-
Science: A-
Physical Education: A
Spanish 1: A-
Algebra 1: B
Language Arts: A
Creative Core: B-

****

I released the breath I had been holding, thrilled to earn so many As and grateful for the B in algebra. I'd received several Cs during middle school. Too bad I got a B minus in Creative Core. But considering I hadn't yet conveyed successfully, it was somewhat expected, not to mention I had a couple not-so-stellar marks on my earliest art projects.

An hour later, a classmate knocked on our door. "Autumn, there's a call for you on line three. Said it's urgent."

People seldom called the dormitory phones to reach students. They were typically used for outgoing calls. I jogged to the phone room at the end of the hall. Who could it be? My parents usually waited for my calls. Perhaps it was Drew? When I picked up the phone, my heart skipped a beat when Dad's critical voice came through the line.

"I received your report card. We need to talk."

Dread filled my body like wet cement.

"What's this B minus in Creative Core? I thought it was an art class. An *easy A*. How the heck did you manage to get a B—make that a B *minus*?" His voice was on edge like he was about to lose it, which was out of character.

"I...I don't know, Dad."

His voice sharpened. "What do you mean, you don't know?"

I truly didn't know. At the beginning of the year, Dream Management hadn't been introduced, so we weren't told how it would factor into our grade. But how to explain? "Um...we haven't gotten some of our assignments back."

"I didn't send you all the way to Timbuktu to have art mess up your grades. Do you realize this class lowered your GPA more than algebra?"

"Yes, Dad." *Do you think I'm that stupid?*

"I'm not going to allow you to stay at some fancy school if you're required to take so many art classes to graduate and you can't earn As in them. I permitted you to go to Dickensen because they promised their creative curriculum would supplement college prerequisites. Never in my wildest dreams did I consider an elective might hurt you."

Creative Core was far from an elective, but I wasn't about to correct him.

"I want you to speak with your teacher and find out what you need to do between now and the end of the semester to bring your grade up to an A. If you can't do that, we'll have to reconsider where to send you next year."

Both his words and his tone burned my heart. My legs gave out and I slid down the wall. Cowering on the floor, I forced my voice to remain strong. If I cried, it might come across as having given up. Then he might make me transfer to Haller Lake mid-year.

I took a deep breath and spoke deliberately. "I was going to talk with Mr. Robbins on Monday. I promise to work harder. I swear. And I'll do extra credit if I need to."

The receiver went quiet for several agonizing seconds. "Okay...okay." His tone softened as his anger subsided. "You can do this, Autumn. But I'm serious when I say I want to see an A next time."

I remained silent.

"Call me after you meet with your teacher."

My voice almost broke as I said goodbye.

I held the phone to my ear long after the click. Still in shock, I sat there incapable of even replacing the handset on the receiver. Eventually, blood surged back through my body, and I tore head down through the dorm to my room, where I dropped on my bed and wadded my pillow.

Aditi was still there. "Are you okay? Who called?"

"My dad. I hate him!"

She sat beside me and placed her hand on my back. "What happened?"

"He was furious about my Creative Core grade. Stupid B minus. It was my worst grade."

"That's not so terrible."

I sat up, leaned against the wall, and let out a deep breath. I hadn't cried, but I'd come close. "I think he'd have been fine with a B minus in algebra. It's what he expected. But he views Creative Core as a useless elective. Something you could drop at any other high school."

"Is that what you want? To drop it?" Like it was even a choice.

"Of course not. I love it. Well, at least the art. But I'm so frustrated I still can't convey. And the worst thing, he warned if I don't earn an A in June, he might make me switch schools."

"He wouldn't do that."

I shot her a look. "You don't know my dad."

She mulled it over. "Well, you'll just have to get an A, then."

I swallowed. "Can I ask what you got?"

Aditi looked down. "An A minus." She raised her eyes to meet mine. "But I got a B minus in French.

Even with all those immersion dreams, I still struggle to get it right. I have this Hindi-American-French accent going on. Maybe because I never learned Hindi properly. But I doubt my parents will care or even notice. I'm the least of their problems." She tucked a strand of hair behind her ear. "I promise, I'll do whatever I can to help."

****

Later in bed, I tossed and turned. I seethed with the anger that had been brewing all night. Dad hadn't even said anything positive about the rest of my grades. He knew it was by far the best report card of my entire life. But he was so focused on that one low grade I could scream. Mom would be proud, but I wanted Dad to be proud too.

I tried to calm down by meditating, but my mind fixated on my future instead.

What would happen if I left Dickensen? Haller Lake for the next three years was a given. But what about my mind? Would I be plagued with nightmares for the rest of my life? Or would my memories of this place be destroyed like Allison's friend? I could promise Principal Locke never to reveal the secrets…but maybe it'd be best to forget everything.

As I debated the merits of persistent nightmares versus brain tampering, my thoughts drifted to Hannah and her recent nightmares. It seemed possible dream-making was messing with her mind. Maybe Dream Management wasn't as harmless as the faculty made it out to be. All those fun field trips might be masking dangerous consequences that could afflict us for the rest of our lives. But no. Many students before me had gone through this curriculum. If awful side effects were occurring, the school would've shut down Dream Management. But if that assumption held true, then Caitlyn was sending nightmares on purpose. But how?

Dickensen-created nightmares were supposedly much more difficult than freshman dreams. However, Caitlyn was a solid dream-maker—one of the best in our freshman class—and she had a brother. Could he have helped her? Was that even allowed?

I was overtired and still furious with Dad. In the safety of my bed, my anger gradually transferred to Caitlyn. My suspicion she was behind Hannah's problems grew to enormous proportions. No one else was having a setback like Hannah. I had to know more about Caitlyn's brother.

I hopped out of bed and opened my laptop.

When I typed *Tom Black* into the search engine, it came up with a million results, reminding me how Caitlyn had lectured Hannah about her commonplace last name.

I narrowed the parameters. He was undoubtedly a Thomas anyway, so I typed *Thomas Black and Dickensen Academy*. Two pages of results. That was more like it.

I clicked on the most promising item and read.

Expecting to learn about a guy in his teens or early twenties, I read about Thomas Black, a man appearing to be in his forties from Texas. Toward the end of the article, I spotted the names of his children, Tom and Caitlyn. I wiped my sweaty palms on my pajamas, then pulled up another webpage dated six years ago: *Thomas and Michele Black Donate $1,000,000 to Alma Mater, Dickensen Academy in Washington State*. The piece said the money was slated for a library renovation.

I pressed back against the chair and tried to breathe regularly. I had to do something or I'd go crazy. Should I wake Aditi? No. She was fighting a cold and needed sleep. Besides, this didn't necessarily mean Caitlyn was doing anything wrong. But she was hiding the significance of her family and had flat out lied about the library.

Finally I grabbed a piece of paper and a pen. Using the glow from my computer screen, I wrote frantically, making sure to disguise my handwriting.

To Caitlyn,

Word around school is you sent that terrible nightmare to Hannah. I've heard you're behind the conveyance problems she's having now, but Hannah is too sweet to suspect anything. It's just a matter of time before you get caught. You're being watched. If you try anything, I'll tell Mr. Robbins even if Hannah won't.

Sincerely,

A Friend

P.S. I know about your family.

When I finished, I sealed the envelope and peeked out our door. The hallway was empty. I tiptoed toward Caitlyn and Hannah's room.

Silence.

I kept going. Suddenly footsteps approached from my left and a growing shadow appeared on the wall. Could it be one of the RAs? Rumor had it they patrolled the halls at night, and I had no reason to be in this area. I dashed toward my right, trying to be both fast and quiet. Only when I locked myself into a bathroom stall did I dare take a breath. I crouched near the toilet, my feet freezing against the icy linoleum—I hadn't bothered with slippers. After about five minutes, I reentered the carpeted hall and walked toward my room. It was now silent, so I continued past my room. No one saw me as I slipped the paper under their door.

Once I was safely back in my warm bed, my mind returned to the contents of the note. Even though it was a stupid and immature thing to do, I was proud of myself for standing up for one of my best friends.

If only I could do the same for myself.

Chapter: 29

The bell rang and students rushed from their seats. Mr. Robbins stood at his usual post near the door, saying goodbye as everyone left. It'd be so easy to follow them out, but I had to get this conversation over with. It had hung over my head all weekend.

I waited up front, swaying side to side, hugging my notebooks tight to my chest. Once the room cleared, I asked, "Can we talk about my grade?"

He nodded toward his desk. "Sure."

Once we were both seated, I said, "I'd like more information about how my grade was calculated so I can earn an A next time."

"Good question." He leaned back in his chair. "And a good reminder for me to review my grading system with my classes. I always forget how much some students care about their grades. Personally, I believe what you learn is more important. If it were up to me, I'd do away with letter grades."

His answer didn't shock me. Mr. Robbins acted contrary to my other teachers from day one: less organized, less strict, and a lot more fun.

"Well, of course I want to learn, but you see…it's my dad. Grades are extremely important to him, and he expects me to get an A. He sees Creative Core as a regular art class, which would be optional at other high schools. And of course, I can't explain what actually goes on here. He threatened to pull me out of Dickensen if I don't bring it up."

"Oh my." He scooted his chair toward his desk. "Well then, we have our work cut out for us. Let me start by reviewing this past semester."

"Okay, but was it my art projects? I know my skills aren't so great, at least compared to Aditi and some others."

He reached for his grade book, found the proper page, and ran his finger down to the middle. "Let's see, I gave you a B for Visual Arts. As you can see here, your project grades have improved since September. If you keep that trend up, you'll be on track for an A there."

I studied the book. A neat row of Bs and a few As followed my name. The only Cs were from months ago. I'd worked my butt off to improve my art skills.

"My apologies for not sharing your recent grades. But the last two projects were so impressive, I got ahead of myself and tacked them straight up in the hallway. I should've let you look at their grades first."

I forced a close-lipped smile.

"But you should know Dream Management had a slight impact on your grade. For this class, the score is based predominantly on your ability to convey a dream. The script writing goes toward your language arts grade. For the first semester, I gave you a C minus."

Mr. Robbins continued to rattle on about grading, but I tuned out as the realization sank in: my final grade could've been a whole lot worse. The C minus barely affected it.

Then he said something, breaking me from my trance.

"Could you please repeat that? Sorry, I missed the last part."

"I said, for this current semester, Dream Management is going to weigh more heavily. It only accounted for a small percentage of your grade last semester, which is why I neglected to bring it up. Also, my expectations are higher going forward. Everyone should be able to convey dreams by summer break. I pride myself on having over a ninety-seven percent success rate."

My hands went clammy. "What if I can't?"

"Don't worry. This semester I'll have more time for individual consultation since most freshman procedures have been taught. Our recruiters do a terrific job selecting candidates, and everything should click into place for you soon."

"But if I can't? I need to know."

"Technically, it's possible to flunk Dream Management and walk out of here with a passing grade of perhaps a C minus or D plus. That sometimes happens to a student or two, but they'll be asked to leave the academy."

I trembled. My dad would kill me for getting that kind of grade. After a moment I recognized there might be something even worse than Dad's wrath. "What would the school do to me if I left?"

Mr. Robbins tugged his ear a couple of times. "I can't say. It's not up to me."

"Please..." My voice shook. "What would happen?"

He sighed, then looked around the room as if to confirm we were still alone. "All I know is disciplinary actions are determined on a case-by-case basis, and the committee does the best they can to minimize detrimental impacts to departing students. *If* memories need to be adjusted, they usually don't erase much more than Dream Management knowledge."

Usually?

"Honestly, Autumn, you don't need to worry. I see how hard you work and your enthusiasm as you complete your scenery. And I've read your stories. You've got talent, but you need to start believing in yourself."

I gave him a half-smile. That was so much easier said than done. And although he said I had no reason to worry, simply the idea a disciplinary committee even existed caused my anxiety to rise.

"I'm more concerned you're falling behind. Most students are working on their second or third dreams, so even if you're successful soon, you'll have some catching up to do. Many freshmen don't complete all six dreams in all of their permutations by June. These skills can be mastered in the sophomore year. However, if your father requires an A, not only must you learn to convey, you must finish all six dreams. Make sense?"

I nodded.

"Good. Now as I mentioned before winter break, there are some nontraditional routes we can take to push you harder. I'd like to propose you switch partners."

"You mean roommates?" He couldn't be serious.

"Yes and no. What I suggest is Aditi remains your roommate, but for the next couple of weeks, I'd like to alter your sleeping arrangements on conveyance nights."

My mouth dropped open as he explained.

"There are a couple of reasons for this suggestion. First, Aditi may be a tougher dream recipient, requiring a more advanced dream-maker. Second, a new partner will wipe out some memories of failed attempts, which may course through your mind during the conveyance. It can reset your mind to how you felt back in November, but you'd have the advantage of knowing the steps inside and out."

"Makes sense. But who do I switch with?"

"It needs to be somebody in this class. I prefer to switch you with another pair where both partners have found success. So in here, that would be..." He scanned his grade book. "Either Caitlyn Black and Hannah McIntire...or Grace Nguyen and Tessa Williams. Would you be comfortable with one of these girls?"

"Hannah," flew out of my mouth without thinking. A split-second later, I backpedaled. Partnering with Hannah would mean Aditi would get stuck with Caitlyn. "But...I don't know if Caitlyn would want to help me. We're not really friends. Maybe Tessa or Grace would be a better choice."

"Leave that to me. There'll be benefits to everyone involved to make up for the inconveniences."

"There will?"

"We'll go through it all together when I inform them about the switch."

Guilt weighed me down. *Why did I suggest Hannah?* "Please consider Grace or Tessa. I think I'd prefer to switch with them."

"I'll look at all the options. Now don't mention this little conversation to anyone until after I make a decision."

I nodded and stood to leave.

He rose along with me and smiled. "Stay positive, Autumn. This should work."

As I dragged myself through the empty halls back to my locker, I envisioned Dad's face seeing my next report card. It'd be summer and I'd be at home. I couldn't face him if I brought home a near-failing grade. And I might have to face a disciplinary committee too. Would I sit before them and plead my case while they determined my trustworthiness and doled out an appropriate punishment? I shuddered.

I cautiously climbed down the frozen stairs of the school building. I breathed in the crisp air while my eyes adjusted to the sunlight reflecting off the snow-covered world. My thoughts shifted to working with another partner, and my pace sped up. Perhaps I could do it. Most students ultimately learned. It'd be a fresh start. I was only behind by two dreams with four months to catch up. I just had to get over this stupid stumbling block, the first conveyance—the simplest and yet the hardest, at least for me. If I could actually convey, catching up was simply a matter of spending more time on schoolwork and less on everything else.

When I walked back into our room, Aditi stopped reading. "What'd he say?"

I relayed most of the conversation, leaving out the part about switching partners. I was dying to tell her about Caitlyn's family too but had been waiting for a time when I could tell both my friends at once. Since I stayed late after school, Hannah was already at her indoor soccer practice.

At the library later with Ben, an awful idea hit me. What if Caitlyn thought my note was from Aditi? Then she might send Aditi some terrible nightmare while she partnered with her as a favor to me. It'd be all my fault. I was so stupid to have written it. What was I thinking?

But maybe it'd be okay. Although Aditi and I had to be high on her list of suspects, lots of students liked Hannah, and Caitlyn had rubbed many people the wrong way. I'd phrased the note so it didn't necessarily point to either of us. All I could do was pray Mr. Robbins switched me with someone else. At least I hadn't mentioned anything about Caitlyn's family yet to my friends. No doubt Caitlyn would catch wind of it, and it looked like I might need her help with Dream Management.

****

My fingers carefully sorted through the colored glass fragments, searching for the perfect purples to form the petals on a flower in my mosaic piece, when Mr. Robbins called, "Autumn, Aditi, Caitlyn, Hannah. Would you please join me at the front?"

My stomach went sour. So much for my prayers.

Soon we were all seated around his desk. Everyone's gaze darted around the circle while I avoided my friends' questioning glances. Clearly, Mr. Robbins was springing this on them now. Perhaps a good strategy to ensure cooperation.

"I have a surprise in store for the four of you. Starting next week, I'd like you to participate in a little experiment. You're going to switch dream partners."

His words hung in the air. Hannah had her mouth pressed shut, but her eyes showed delight. Aditi's and Caitlyn's faces were unreadable.

"As you probably know, Autumn is having difficulty conveying. Switching partners will be a fresh start for her. But there will be benefits for you as well."

"Will it help my grade?" Caitlyn asked.

Mr. Robbins nodded. "I plan to give the three of you extra credit. But more importantly, a new partner will improve your conveyance skills."

"How so?" Aditi asked, her lilting voice both sweet and curious.

"Every recipient is unique, and the dream-maker can feel the difference during the conveyance, requiring subtle changes. As your skills increase, the modifications become second-nature, but for you as new dream-makers, even a slight change may be a challenge." He smiled. "And of course, you'll be exposed to broader styles of dreams. Always helpful for generating ideas."

Our teacher leaned toward us. "Beginning next week, Autumn and Caitlyn will switch rooms right before bed, four nights a week. Then in the morning, you'll switch back."

Caitlyn's face puckered as if she'd bitten into a sour candy. "Me?"

He clamped his mouth shut for a moment before answering. "Well, I thought that would be simplest. Since this experiment is primarily for Autumn's benefit, I thought she should be one of the students to move. And for various reasons, I believe Hannah would be an ideal partner for her."

"Uh-huh." Caitlyn coughed. "Um…well. I'm not so sure I'll be able to fall asleep in another student's bed—"

"I'll do it," Aditi jumped in. "That'd work too, right? I mean if Hannah is also willing to move."

Hannah nodded enthusiastically.

"Would that work for you, Caitlyn?" Mr. Robbins

asked. "To convey to Aditi in your own room instead."

Caitlyn gave her angelic, only-for-teachers smile. "Yes, Mr. Robbins. Of course."

"Great. Then it's settled." He sighed. "I know there won't be any problems, but as per school policy, I need to remind Hannah and Aditi not to touch any belongings while sleeping in the other's room."

"How long will we continue?" I asked.

"It depends. I'll keep close tabs on the status of all your dreams and will call off the experiment if it causes any undue hardship. I anticipate you'll continue for two, possibly three weeks. That'll give each of you at least four opportunities to convey with a new partner.

"Now, I'd like you to come to a consensus on the timing of each switch. I don't know your nightly routines, so you four can come up with the best solution. But I recommend consistency. I'll leave you to it." Then he pushed his chair away from his desk and left to monitor the rest of the class.

As the four of us worked out the logistics, I began to freak out. I hadn't even told Hannah or Aditi about the note. If they didn't know, they'd act innocently if Caitlyn ever confronted them. The butterflies in my stomach morphed into vampire bats biting my insides. At one point, I almost had to race to the bathroom when bile crept its way into my throat. But I managed to swallow it back down.

After class, I tapped Caitlyn on her back as she closed her locker. "Caitlyn, hey, can I talk to you a sec?"

She looked surprised. "Sure, what's up?" Her pleasant tone caught me off guard. No wonder the teachers loved her; she could turn her moods on and off like a light switch.

"Well…I wanted to say thanks for helping me out."

"Oh, that." She bent down and heaved her backpack onto her shoulder. "Well, it's not like I had a choice." Then she strolled away.

Did I have the nerve? My thoughts went to Aditi, always the cheerful roommate. I didn't wish to be the one to spoil that. I took a deep breath then chased Caitlyn down the hall.

When I caught up, I said, "One more thing."

She turned around. "What?"

"I sent the note."

"You?" Her face contorted as the news sank in.

"Yeah, it was stupid and mean. I'm so sorry. You see, I was—"

"I didn't think you had it in you." She strode right up to me so we were face to face. "I figured your roommate did it. She seems a lot stronger than you. *Hmph*, got to give you credit for doing a little research and sticking up for your friend. But you're wrong. I haven't done a thing to Hannah. It's all in her head. Just because we aren't besties doesn't mean I'd try to screw her up."

I didn't know what to say. It was so much easier to be brave on paper than in person.

"Well, you're not as smart as you think." Caitlyn's tone sharpened. "It was *really stupid* of you to get on my bad side. And I wouldn't go around blabbing about my family. Mind your own business." Then she strode away again but turned around one last time. "Best of luck next week, Autumn."

Then she was gone.

****

As Aditi and I lay in bed, we chatted about the upcoming week. I was relieved I'd talked to Caitlyn, especially since she'd suspected Aditi had sent the note. It'd taken me a while to calm down, but I'd rather have her do something rotten to me than to Aditi. Plus, what could she do? I didn't have to convey with her.

"So are you nervous to work with Caitlyn?" I asked.

"A little. But it could be interesting."

"I'm so sorry," I gushed. "I know I'm the problem. I'm sure Mr. Robbins is only saying how beneficial it'll be so I don't feel so guilty."

"Don't worry. You'd do the same for me. I just hope it works. You're stressing me out with your constant worry. Switching partners seems like a great idea. You know, change it up." How lucky was I to have such a supportive friend? "Besides, it'll be a nice break for Hannah. I'm sure the stress of rooming with Caitlyn is causing all her Dream Management problems. This'll be like a vacation."

"Maybe. But it might make it worse later."

"At least it'll be that much closer to June. I heard as a sophomore, you create a list of people you'd like to room with. So next year, she'll get a roommate she likes. We all will."

I prayed I'd return next year. I could easily envision Hannah and Aditi becoming roommates if I remained in Seattle. "While you're with Caitlyn, see if you can find those creepy images Hannah used to talk about."

"I hope not. I'm not a fan of nightmares."

"Me neither."

"But I'll tell you one thing," she said seriously. Her

silhouette turned toward me in the dark. "If I receive anything suspicious from her, I'm not about to let her walk all over me."

Chapter: 30

The tension hanging over me had dissolved. Finals were over, and I had a new strategy in place for Dream Management. Except for the weekly foreign language dreams, the academic ones had halted after January's onslaught. Although they were interesting and provided us with ample sleep, they were taxing because they crammed our brains with so much data. Wednesdays and Sundays were now either dreamless or filled with light-hearted experiences.

Coach Kat sent me one in which I ran along the beach with Zoey and Wilson, who occasionally veered into the breaking surf to play. Clearly she was spurring me to run again once the snow melted. Then the boys' PE teacher sent his class a skydiving dream. It was all the guys could talk about the following day. I'm not sure if I would have enjoyed it so much—more of a nightmare in my opinion.

Saturday, I went up to Stevens Pass again. After weeks of begging, Hannah had convinced me to sign up for the trip. She'd skied most weekends, regardless of schoolwork, and was anxious to show me her progress. We'd tried to convince Aditi to join us, but she refused, saying, "Skiing isn't fun for me." I could relate—it's no fun to do something when everyone else can do it better.

After a quick run with Hannah, Ben and I took off

on our own. During a chairlift up, I said, "I've been thinking of this idea for a dream."

"Yeah?"

"I was wondering if a ski dream might somehow help Aditi learn to ski."

He lifted his goggles to look at me.

"Maybe a dream with lots of nice, easy turns might help her overcome her fear. If she could feel herself skiing down the slope, perhaps it could become part of her muscle memory."

Ben's eyes lit up. "That's a great idea. Seriously, if she could go down the hill without falling twenty times, she'd love it."

I laughed. "That's what I was thinking. I hated leaving her in the dorm this morning...like I was leaving her out. And at the rate Hannah is improving, she'll be skiing all day with us soon." I sighed. "Do you think it would work?"

"Well, you're not really using your muscles in your dreams," Ben pointed out.

"No, but maybe if you believe you are, you could rewire your brain somehow."

"It's worth a try."

I frowned. "Only problem, I can't even convey a stupid dream about leaves. I'll never be able to send something so complicated."

Ben smiled. "I have a good feeling about your dream partner switch. You just need to focus those green eyes of yours, like you do when you're writing, and it'll happen."

Despite the freezing temperature, my body core warmed. He had faith in me. If only it was that easy, but my mind always strayed and filled with self-doubt.

I stared down at my skis and tapped them together, unleashing a flurry of snow. "Would you create it for her?"

Ben shook his head. "I don't want to take your idea, Autumn."

"Hey, I have dozens of ideas I can't do a thing about. You'd be doing me a favor if you could get Aditi back on the slopes. I just want to ski with my friend."

He blew out slowly, the vapors visible in the frigid air. "Well, I was looking for an idea for *Dream Five*. I have no doubt I could send something like that to Ryan. But your room is on the floor below. Sending it through walls is a sophomore skill."

This was my time to be encouraging, so I smiled. "If anyone can do it, it's you. Besides, you could always send it to her next year if it doesn't work out."

"Or maybe you could?"

I chuckled. I had about a hundred other conveyance skills to learn first.

Ben pointed to a skier flying off a huge ski ramp. "What do you think if I added in some jumps and rails?"

I laughed. "Ryan would love it, but you might freak out Aditi. I want her to learn to like skiing, not be more terrified."

"I'd only put those elements in the advanced version. I'd keep the basic dream simple."

I had definitely asked the right person. Ben was already tying dream skill progression with ski skill progression. "Maybe while you're at it you could create an intermediate run for Hannah. Something to help with her form. You know, keep her skis more parallel and her pole planting in sync."

He grinned. "You got it. Any other advice?"

I batted him with my mitten. "You don't need my help. Sounds like you've already designed half the dream."

****

Monday night, Hannah knocked on our door at ten p.m. as planned. She came with a small bag of clothes so she could go straight to breakfast before returning to her own room. That would provide a large window of time to ensure Aditi and Caitlyn finished the *Initial Dream Review* if Caitlyn was successful.

Aditi ran her hands through her thick, black hair a few times before she grabbed her own overnight bag. "Well. I guess I should get going."

"Good luck," Hannah said.

I bit my lip. "Thanks so much."

Aditi straightened to her whole five feet then turned to leave.

Three hours later I woke to my vibrating alarm and climbed out of bed. As I sat in the shadows with only a soft, blue glow from our digital clock, I prepared to convey. I was calm. The dark cloud had lifted and confidence had taken its place.

I'm going to do it this time.

No sooner had I thought those reaffirming words than negative ones began to compete for my attention. I pushed them aside and refocused. The pressure mounted and my heart quickened, pulling me from my relaxed state. I could no longer keep the nagging thoughts at bay. This time it wasn't Dad speaking inside my brain. Instead it was Mr. Robbins explaining how I needed to convey soon or I'd never earn an A. I refocused. I had to do it this time. Then worse, I heard

Mr. Robbins say I might fall into the three percent that would never convey successfully and be subject to the disciplinary committee.

The next morning, Hannah gave me a weak sympathetic smile before I even opened my mouth.

I turned away.

At breakfast, I scanned the dining hall for Aditi and Caitlyn. My legs jiggled nervously until Aditi arrived at our table. I looked up from my cereal to see her beaming. Caitlyn's dream had obviously come through, and there'd been nothing to fear. Part of her smile had to be relief, knowing her dream reception skills were intact. I was the problem, not her. But Aditi, of course, was too polite to mention that revelation.

Later in Creative Core, Aditi successfully completed Caitlyn's *Dream Review Checklist*. The benefits of this experiment for my friends were now apparent, which made me feel even more incompetent.

****

The following night, our roles reversed. It was Hannah's turn.

My alarm clock rang in the morning. I slapped it off with one hand, still half asleep.

My heart continued to pulse rapidly, as though Ben were near. I closed my eyes to savor the sensation before fully waking to reality. I could still see him on the back of my eyelids. But it wasn't Ben. Based on his Texas accent and the blond hair sticking out from under his cowboy hat, it had to be Hannah's older brother.

As I blinked myself awake, guilt crept in for being attracted to another person. Crazy. It wasn't like Ben was an official boyfriend. And it was only a stupid dream. It's not like I would ever even meet the guy. But it was much more complicated and emotional than the dreams I'd been getting from Aditi. Must've been because Hannah was a full dream ahead of her.

I sat up and shook my head while the dream moved from my present state of mind to my recent memory. Hannah lay across from me in Aditi's bed, still sound asleep. Her dream had come through in high definition. She would be so relieved.

I shook her gently. "Hannah, time to get up."

She rubbed her eyes and yawned. "Well?"

I took a deep breath and nodded. All my friends soaring ahead in Creative Core was tough enough. Being so intimately involved in their successes was even tougher.

Her eyes lit up. She reached for her notes and put on her glasses—she wore contacts during the day.

"Question number one," she began. "Where did the dream take place?"

"A huge, flat ranch. Was that your home?"

"Yep."

"Cool." Now that I'd experienced it rather than simply viewed the painting, I wanted to know more. But my questions would have to wait.

"Were there any animals in the dream? If so, what kind?"

"There were a couple of dogs—border collies, I think. And lots of cows or maybe they were bulls."

"Anything else?"

I chuckled. "Oh, yeah. Horses."

"How big was the herd of *cattle*?"

I shrugged. "Maybe fifty or so. I didn't count."

My answer must've been close enough because she smiled and continued down the sheet. "What were you doing?"

"I guess I was rounding up the cattle. But honestly, the dogs and the guy were doing most of the work."

She put away her paper.

"That's it? What about the guy? Was he your broth—?"

"*Shh*! That's for later." Her eyes narrowed and she scanned my face. "No way! *Ew*. Not my brother."

My face warmed. It wasn't my fault he was so darn cute.

Later during class, I finished answering all her questions.

"I can't believe it," Hannah said. "You got them all right."

I made a you've-got-to-be-kidding face. "Uh, yeah. They were easy."

"*Hmph*, it hasn't been like that with Caitlyn. She usually does fine with the morning questions, but by the afternoon, she always misses a few."

"Did you do anything different with me?"

Hannah tapped her fingertips to her lips for a second while she considered my question. "Nope. I'm positive I did it the same way. It even felt the same when you latched on."

"Maybe Caitlyn is just stressing you out, making the dreams less sticky?"

"I used to think that. But now I'm thinking she was lying."

I raised one eyebrow at her. I'd suggested that before, but Hannah had never wanted to hear it. She'd survived the horrors of middle school through homeschooling so didn't quite get some girls could just be plain mean.

Hannah put her head in her hands for a moment. When she looked up, she blew out a long breath. "My reception problems started after I accused her of sending the dog nightmare. She was so mad about that, and I bet she was suspicious I snitched on her. I'm going to pay closer attention next time I convey to her. If I can prove she's lying, I'll tell Mr. Robbins."

"If I were you, I wouldn't mention today's success to Caitlyn. Better chance to catch her in the act later."

Her eyes widened. "Good idea."

****

My horse moved quickly from side to side beneath me. Steadying myself, I touched the smooth, chestnut hair on his neck, hot with the sun. I was more involved in the cattle herding this time. Although I'd never done anything more than a trail ride in real life, my body somehow stayed mounted. After a few minutes of riding, my confidence grew, and I sat higher in the saddle and held on with just the insides of my legs.

Soon I saw a guy in a cowboy hat approach from across the grassy field, and my heart sped up. When he turned toward me, I drew in a sharp breath. It was Ben.

I woke with a gasp, pulled up on my elbows, and looked across to Hannah who was fiddling with the alarm. "How'd you change your brother into Ben?"

Her hand flew to her chest. "It worked?"

"You did it on purpose?"

"Well, I didn't want you to go and fall head over heels for my brother. That's not going to help you with Ben. So I thought I'd surprise you."

My mouth dropped. "You can do that? Change the dream on the fly."

"Yep." Hannah's blue eyes gleamed with pride. "I

232

made a quick revision last night. But don't tell Mr. Robbins I went off script. I wasn't sure if I'd be successful."

I flopped back down on my bed and stared at the ceiling. "You make it sound so easy. Maybe I can be a professional dream receptor instead. Forget conveyance." Really, it wouldn't be so bad.

****

As I stuffed notebooks from my locker into my messenger bag, I peered at Ben, twenty feet away, doing the same. I'd felt on edge, in a good way, all day. Watching for him to pass in the hall. Anxiously awaiting the classes where we'd be together. I couldn't get my mind off him. Or the dream. Nothing happened, but still, I spent a good part of last night alone with him.

I grabbed my heavy bag, moved over to him, and leaned against the wall of cold metal lockers. "How's it going?"

"Hey." He glanced at me for a second, his face radiating glee. "Robbins gave me the go ahead to send the second ski dream. Ryan liked the first the other night. When I told him it was your idea, he admitted it was his favorite. He's going to love it when the skiing becomes extreme."

"I'll bet."

"And get this. Robbins let me reserve several upcoming Sundays in the *Dream Calendar Application* to convey to Aditi."

"Really? That's great." I was relieved Ben had official permission. I hadn't thought through the logistics when I originally suggested the idea.

"Yeah. He thinks it's admirable I want to push myself." He shrugged. "But he admitted chances are slim I can learn to convey to a separate floor without the instruction we'll get next year."

I smiled. "Well, if anyone can do it, it's you."

Ben blushed and looked away. He had to know he was good but still couldn't take a compliment. He shut his locker with a bang, and we walked toward the stairs. Few students lingered in the wide, tiled hallway.

"So how's it going conveying with Hannah?"

I was in such a strangely contented mood his question didn't even phase me. "Not great. I actually hit Hannah yesterday when it didn't work."

Ben's face turned white.

I grinned. "I pegged her with a stuffed animal. Good thing I didn't have anything heavier near my bed."

He laughed. "What does Robbins say?"

I ran my hand along the lockers we passed. "Hang in there. Says it can take a little while to get used to someone new. But he's satisfied with the other three's progress. Good thing because it has to be a hassle for them."

"You'll get it."

I nodded. "So did you have a dream last night?"

"Yeah. Ryan and I raced drones through the woods. It was pretty darn cool."

"Sounds like fun." I didn't care much about drones, but I had to confirm something. "Any other dreams?"

He shrugged. "Not that I remember. Why?" His expression grew worried. "Did you get an academic dream?"

We started down the stairs. "Oh, no. Just a question."

Logically, he couldn't have been in Hannah's

dream, regardless of how realistic it felt. Was I supposed to be disappointed we hadn't truly interacted? Or should I be elated I'd get to spend two more nights with his doppelganger without having to stress about saying or doing the wrong thing? I smiled to myself. Both options had their benefits.

Then, before I had time to think of the myriad of reasons why not, I blurted, "Any chance you'd like to go to the Winter Dance with me?"

If I could have sucked the words back into my throat and swallowed them forever, I would have. I was going to kill Hannah. It had to be her dream making me act this way. I wasn't a spontaneous person. I was quiet and cautious. When the posters went up about the dance last week, I'd never thought for a moment of asking Ben, though I had hoped he might ask me.

Ben didn't respond at first. I had more time to second-guess my question than I'd taken to form it—if I'd even consciously done so. He was probably as shocked by my proposal as I was.

But then he grinned and said, "Yes."

I hugged my books to my chest to keep my body from exploding with happiness. Maybe I'd have to thank Hannah instead.

Chapter: 31

Hannah and I had moved our easels near the windows to capture the natural light. We were experimenting with oil paints to color our dream backgrounds. It took much longer to cover a large canvas with the tubes of thick paint compared with the thinner watercolors and acrylics. Students were scattered today working independently on their projects. I kept glancing at Caitlyn who stood at an easel across the room, near the cabinets.

Mr. Robbins had called off the dream partner switch yesterday, so last night Hannah conveyed to Caitlyn for the first time in over two weeks. She'd told me she found inconsistencies in Caitlyn's answers during this morning's dream review as well as the one she completed at the beginning of class. Hannah was now certain Caitlyn was lying. On top of that, Caitlyn had flat out told her she'd rather convey with Aditi.

"So are you going to talk to Mr. Robbins?" I whispered.

Hannah shrugged. "What can he do? It's probably best to just hang in there. It's only three and a half months 'til school's out. I'm hardly in my room anyway." My friend wore the saddest expression. Like she'd been beaten up, but her bruises were hidden beneath her clothes.

"He's got to do something now that you have

proof." But could he? Mr. Robbins was only a teacher. Since Caitlyn's parents had donated one million dollars, the administration was likely willing to turn a blind eye to their daughter's infractions.

"Maybe it won't be so bad. At least I'm not getting nightmares any longer."

My gaze bounced back and forth between Hannah and Caitlyn. "But she's going to screw up your grade."

"Autumn," Mr. Robbins called from his desk.

I leaned in close to Hannah. "We'll talk later."

She nodded. "Good luck."

I wound my way to the front of the classroom, grabbing my notebook along the way. Time for my one-on-one session. No idea what he'd suggest today.

As I sat down, he gave a half-smile. "I'm sorry, I had to call off the experiment. But after five tries, I think we need to change course."

"No biggie. It's not your fault."

"I honestly believed working with Hannah would be the key for you." He pulled my file from his drawer and picked up a pen. "Let's start by reviewing Monday's conveyance."

After going through my last failed attempt in painstaking detail, he said, "Here's a suggestion you might find interesting. I'd like you to set aside *Dream One* and skip ahead to the simplest version of *Dream Two*."

"But won't that be harder? It has even more complicated components."

"True. However in some cases, it's not the difficulty of the skills involved, but some other obstacle. You need to learn unwavering focus. An alternate dream might be the ticket by giving your mind more steps to focus on so it doesn't wander." He shuffled through my papers. "Let's see if I can find your *Dream Two* assignment. Off the top of my head, I can't recall your plot."

My teacher bowed his head and read from the script I'd submitted earlier. It had already been approved in language arts. "Oh, yes. The one where the child opens gifts under the tree." That's the dream I had planned to send to my cousins at Christmas when I thought I would have moved beyond *Dream One*. He sucked in his breath and glanced at me. "It's against school policy to send a dream with religious undertones to someone of a different faith. I'm guessing Aditi isn't Christian."

"It's okay. I discussed that with Ms. Jenson when it looked like I might have to send it to Aditi instead. Her family exchanges gifts on Christmas."

"Oh, good. Then it should be fun for her."

We spent the next five minutes discussing the dream, with Mr. Robbins offering me additional tips and suggestions.

"I printed out some new meditation exercises too." He handed a sheet of paper to me. "I'd like you to spend at least fifteen minutes a day on them."

He studied my face, which likely revealed my guilt, then frowned. "I know most students have become a bit lax with meditation by this time in the year. But trust me. The exercises should help."

I nodded and uttered a quick "thanks" as I stood to leave. But then I hesitated and plopped back down.

"Something else, Autumn?"

"Um, yes. I mean no." *Do I say something or mind my own business? What would a true friend do?* I glanced about the room. Everyone was still in the back of the art studio. "If I told you something about another student, would it remain confidential?"

"It depends."

"Well, what if I told you about something going on between Hannah and Caitlyn? Would you tell either of them?"

He intertwined his fingers and leaned toward me. "Let's say this. I'd never reveal you as the source. But, Autumn, if someone is being hurt or violating school rules, I need to know."

My gut said to trust him. I took a deep breath. "I think Caitlyn is lying during the dream reviews and somehow messing with Hannah when conveying dreams."

Mr. Robbins closed his eyes for a moment, as if to ready himself for an unpleasant discussion. "Why do you suspect this of Caitlyn?"

"Well, she's never gotten along with Hannah and treats her terribly. She kept bringing up nightmares last semester. And Hannah says her dream review answers have been inconsistent. And then on the internet, I found out her parents donated a bunch of money to Dickensen…and I know her brother went here." Now hearing myself cite the reasons, the evidence didn't sound as compelling as it had in my mind.

"Her brother Tom was in my class five, maybe six years ago. He was an amazing dream-maker." He smiled. "I was wondering when a student would stumble upon the library donation. It is public knowledge. But since I've never heard any mention of her family, I assumed Caitlyn didn't want anyone to know—"

"Because she didn't want kids to know she was getting special privileges."

"Mm-hmm." He caught my eye. "Do you think maybe that's why she didn't want her peers to know? Sometimes students like her have to work harder to prove they aren't getting special privileges."

"Oh." He had a point.

"Furthermore, most students here do not come from wealthy families. Some students struggle to even pay for flights to and from school. Perhaps Caitlyn was simply trying to fit in."

Point two for Mr. Robbins.

"But none of that changes the fact Hannah is miserable with Caitlyn as a roommate. I suspected it. But without a complaint from either girl…you did the right thing, coming to me. Tonight, I'll read carefully through their dream reviews for anything illogical."

A boulder lifted from my chest.

"What'll you do if you find something?"

"That's not something I can discuss with you. You've let me know there's a potential problem. I'll take it from here."

****

Hannah burst into our room one afternoon as Aditi and I prepared to go to the library. "Y'all, guess what!"

"What?" we both said.

Hannah closed the door and lowered her voice. "I'm switching rooms."

I raised my eyebrows, but a smile was already forming. "You're kidding!"

"Nope."

Aditi moved to the floor, leaned against her bed, and patted the spot next to her—the floor was the best place for the three of us to sit close and talk without worrying a neighbor was listening through the thin dormitory walls.

"When I was leaving Creative Core, Mr. Robbins slipped me a note saying to report to the office."

"And?" I probed.

"Dean Rothchild accompanied me back to the principal's office. He told me they'd had a couple discussions with Mr. Robbins about my partnership with Caitlyn and wished to hear my side."

Aditi urged Hannah on with a quick nod.

"So I went through everything, including the nightmare where I ended up in your room." She looked at me. "I even explained how I couldn't convey with Caitlyn yet had no problem with you."

"Good."

"The dean and principal quizzed me about our relationship. I basically said she hated me from day one, but it got worse after I accused her of sending me a nightmare."

"What'd they say?" Aditi asked.

"They said it wouldn't help my education, or Caitlyn's, to keep us together when we don't get along."

"Now what?" I asked.

"I'm getting there. They said freshmen aren't allowed their own rooms, but they're fixin' to make arrangements for a switch."

I bit my lip. "I wonder who."

Hannah shrugged.

"Why don't they ask Caitlyn what's going on?" Aditi asked. "Seems like she's getting off easy."

"I'm sure she's been talked to," Hannah said. "But

they won't tell me anything."

I began to breathe more easily—the administration could keep secrets.

"Well, I'd love to keep chatting, but I've got to pack. See y'all."

Then she skipped off to her room.

****

Two hours later Hannah joined us at dinner, carrying a tray heaped with spaghetti and garlic bread. Her eyes danced with excitement.

"Did you hear anything?" Aditi asked when she sat down.

"Yep. Switching with Tessa, so Grace'll be my new roommate."

"She's so much nicer," I said.

Hannah sipped her milk then nodded. "She usually hangs with Lucy and Rachel and asked if they all could join us for meals. I can't remember the last time I sat with Caitlyn."

"Is Grace okay with all this?" I asked.

"She's good but has to be relieved she's not the one to move. Her side of the room is decorated all fancy with colored lights and mirrors and stuff. It'd be a pain to move all that." Hannah swirled her noodles with her fork. "Grace gets along fine with Tessa, but it's not like they're super close or anything. But Tessa is Caitlyn's best friend."

"More like only." I snickered.

"It sounds perfect," Aditi said. "When do you move?"

"Tonight. Tessa's packing up. Maybe y'all could help us move?"

I nodded. "Sure thing."

Right after dinner, Aditi and I joined Hannah upstairs. With our help, Hannah and Tessa traded places in under fifteen minutes. Shockingly, Caitlyn helped too. She must've been as grateful as Hannah to get a new roommate because she was actually somewhat friendly for a few minutes. But would it last?

Chapter: 32

The day of the dance finally arrived. Aditi and I had decided to get ready in Hannah and Grace's room. They'd set up a folding mirror on one of their desks with curling and flat irons heated and ready to go. Grace also had nail polish in every color of the rainbow—with a heavy concentration on the reds—and huge, professional-looking makeup trays.

"Where'd you get all of this?" I asked, a bit overwhelmed.

"I've been collecting it for years. I bought most of it, but my sister gives me her things when she buys new stuff."

"So where do we start?" Aditi asked.

Hannah opened the closet. "Let's find Autumn a dress." Lucky for me, Hannah, who wore my size, had several. Seems I was the only one who didn't have any dresses on hand—should've thought of that before I asked a guy on a date. After trying on a few, the consensus was a snug-fitting, jade green one, which brought out the color of my eyes and hit mid-thigh. Then Aditi dashed back to our room to retrieve what she deemed the perfect necklace to complement it from her vast collection. I had hoped Aditi would've also brought a sari from San Jose for our one semi-formal dance, but she claimed she only wore them to weddings.

While we painted our nails, we chatted about the guys in our grade and analyzed who should dance with whom. No one else had a date.

"You've got to dance with Will tonight," I told Hannah. She'd had a huge crush on Ryan's friend all year.

"I want to so bad." Hannah blew on her nails. "I swear I'm going to ask him this time."

"We'll help," Grace said. "What about you, Aditi? Still got your list?"

Aditi tapped her forehead. "Yep, right here. Four guys are on my must-dance-with list."

I chuckled.

"But I'm thinking maybe I should move Quinn over from a maybe to a must."

"What about Ryan?" Grace asked.

Aditi shook her head. "There's no point."

"The guy doesn't know what he's missing," I said. Poor Aditi. She'd flirted with him for months, but she couldn't get his attention away from sports. He needed to mature a bit. Make that a lot.

"There's always next year," Hannah said.

Aditi didn't look too bothered. "Remember to keep an eye out for my hand signal. I don't want to get stuck with anyone for too long."

"So you think this might be the night?" Grace asked me. "You know, when Ben finally kisses you?"

I shrugged, feigning indifference, and continued to focus on my nails, but my cheeks warmed. "I don't know…he's such a good friend, it might be awkward. Besides, it's not like *he* asked me." Ben had said yes, but then everything between us had continued the way it'd been for months. Aditi and Hannah knew I was disappointed our relationship had stalled and were blown away I'd made the first move.

Grace rolled her eyes. "But do you want him to?"

"Maybe, I mean…" I'd never voiced my true feelings about Ben to anyone outside of Aditi and Hannah. I'd always told everyone else he was like a brother, in part to keep my hopes down.

"Come on," Aditi urged. "You've been holding back all year. Tell her what you really think."

I gave a little smile. "I like him. A lot. But I'm sure he only thinks of me as a friend."

Grace raised her eyebrows like she didn't believe me.

"Seriously, there are so many better-looking girls at this school."

"I don't see Ben hanging out with any other girls," Grace said.

"He talks to lots of them," I insisted.

Hannah smiled. "He's just being nice."

Grace looked up from her nails and caught my eye. "Leave it to me. When I'm done with you, he won't be able to keep his hands off."

I giggled. What did Ben truly think? But regardless of what he thought, my heart was full. I had close girlfriends who'd be there for me no matter what happened with him.

When our nails dried, Grace took charge of our hair and makeup. Curls for everyone except Hannah, who chose to flat iron her long, blond hair. By the time Grace finished with Aditi and Hannah, I barely recognized them with their smoky eyes and full lips.

I coughed as Grace doused me in hairspray. "Can I see?" I asked as she began to apply my makeup.

"Not yet," she said while Aditi and Hannah put finishing touches on their faces in the other mirror.

My stomach filled with butterflies. Most days, I tied my hair in a ponytail or let it hang straight—a couple of French braids was as fancy as I'd get—and used only a touch of dark brown mascara. And of course, I typically wore warm, bulky sweaters paired with jeans. But tonight, I was like a princess dressing for a ball.

Finally Grace announced, "You're done."

I stood and twisted my body to each side to get a better view in the small mirror. I couldn't believe it was me.

"I wish I could pull off a tight dress like that," Aditi admitted. "You look fantastic!"

"More like gorgeous," Hannah said.

Grace smiled proudly. "Ben is going to eat you up."

My reflection turned beet red, which made everyone burst out laughing.

Grace led me to their closet and opened the door, revealing a full-length mirror.

I stared at myself. Even I had to admit I looked hot.

****

At 5:45 many of our friends were meeting up with us in O'Reilly's sitting room. Ben hadn't arrived, so we had fun taking pictures. Good thing because my social media needed some serious updating next time I could access the sites. Besides, I'd promised to email some home. Mom was thrilled about my first date. I hadn't exactly told her I had done the asking. I didn't want to get into it with her. She was convinced Ben liked me.

After several poses with at least six different

cameras, I lifted my gaze. Ben had arrived. Alone. He wore a navy sports coat, khaki pants, and a red and blue striped tie. His blond hair was gelled into place, and a faint hint of cologne hung in the air. He always looked good, but tonight he looked amazing.

"Hey, Autumn." His voice was so low I could barely hear, and my stomach fluttered. Then he turned his attention to my friends, as they showered him with compliments.

Soon Hannah was clicking pictures of Ben and me. "These are the best!" She shoved the screen of her phone into my face.

At last, the two of us stepped outside. I shivered as the frigid air hit my bare shoulders.

"You okay?" he asked. "You look freezing."

"I'm fine."

He took hold of my arm. Good thing because my body was tense, and I had to concentrate on each step to keep from falling. Aditi's heels didn't help.

We were going to Rogers Dormitory for dinner. Normally their tables were reserved for juniors and seniors for breakfasts, snacks, and studying, but tonight the Dance Committee had transformed it. The overhead lights were dimmed, and tea lights flickered at each table. Jazz played in the background.

A lady in a white blouse and black pants greeted us with a smile. "Right this way."

I was curious and a bit worried about who we'd be seated with since my best friends had arranged to sit at a table of girls. But when she led Ben and me to a round table, I breathed a sigh of relief to see freshmen I knew fairly well, including Lucy and Jack. Lucy was a close friend of Grace's I'd been getting to know since the roommate switch, and Jack was a friend of Ben's. No sign of Caitlyn, thank goodness.

Everyone was on their best behavior, trying to impress their dates, speaking politely, and using the proper forks and all that. Most of the conversation centered on speculating what the dance would be like.

"I hope the music is better tonight," Lucy said. "There was too much rap last time."

"I loved the music at the last dance," Jack said.

"Fine." Lucy sipped her drink. "But you have to admit it was hard to dance to."

And on and on they went.

I mostly listened and picked at my food.

"Come on, Autumn, eat something," Ben said. "This is the best food we've had all year."

It was silly. It was only Ben. I nodded and forced myself to eat a bit more. By the time dessert came, I felt almost like myself and could speak more than a few words at a time.

After dinner, we went to the gym. Ben held my arm again. This time I was more relaxed and able to enjoy the closeness. Even through his blazer, I felt his biceps flex as they held me steady. Blaring pop music reached halfway across the quad, and the bass vibrated through my body, competing with my beating heart.

"Love this song," I said.

"Me too. It's great for dancing."

I grinned to myself at the thought of us dancing together. We'd danced before in a large group at the informal dance held in the fall, but tonight it felt different.

We entered a crowded gym, the dance floor packed and students strutting their stuff in groups here and there. We stood off to the side taking it all in. The Dance Committee had worked hard here too. A maze of black and white balloons and crepe paper streamers, along with colorful lights, gave the spacious room a magical feel. I was a princess after all.

"Stay close to me," Ben said. "I don't want you spraining an ankle."

I smiled to myself. I'd have to thank Aditi for insisting I wear such high heels. And I'd assumed making my thin calves look shapelier was the primary benefit.

Ben nodded toward the side where long tables covered with snacks and drinks lined the wall. "Um, do you want to eat or something?"

We'd just eaten. Apparently, I wasn't the only one nervous. "No. I'm good."

Hannah and Grace emerged from the shadows and ran up to us.

"We've been waiting for you!" Hannah shouted over the music, as she grabbed my hand and dragged us to the center of the dance floor. "Come on!"

I glanced over my shoulder at Ben. "I guess we're dancing."

He nodded and kept hold of my other hand.

In seconds we found ourselves among many friends while the disco ball covered us with glimmers of light. My body finally relaxed completely as I found the beat of the music and began to sing along with the lyrics. Ben grinned and twirled me around.

After several songs, he nodded to the professional photographer in the corner. "Let's get some pics before I ditch this jacket."

"Okay." I was getting hot, even in Hannah's

spaghetti-strapped dress.

The photographer made us stand in awkward formal positions with our chins facing *just so* as if we were mannequins. So not the romantic experience I'd expected. When the photographer returned to his fancy camera, I could no longer keep a straight face, and the poor man had to come back and readjust my position. Then Ben cracked up too. Oh well. At least we got some decent pictures back at O'Reilly.

After the photos, we weaved our way back to our friends on the dance floor. The group had expanded while we were gone. I took a closer look at my friends. Hannah radiated even more beauty than ever, although her eyes were focused on Will's feet across from her, as they shuffled to the music. I turned to Ryan and nodded toward Hannah.

Ryan leaned over and practically yelled in my ear. "Turns out Will's been wanting to dance with her too!"

Nearby, Aditi danced with yet another guy who had been on her list. Looked like she was going to check everyone off and then some. I turned back to Ben as we continued to bop along to the song.

Toward the end of the night, while I sipped a bubbly fruit punch and chatted with Aditi, the DJ put on a slow song. In five seconds, the dance floor cleared, leaving the couples behind.

"Come here." Ben held out his hand.

I winked at Aditi while I set down my drink. Ben led me to the center of the gym.

I'd never slow danced with a guy. I'd skipped most of the dances in middle school. But Ben knew what he was doing and brought my hands to his shoulders and placed his hands on my waist. A tingle of excitement went through me. We'd never stood so close. Then we swayed to the music. I felt like everyone's eyes were on us, so I kept him between the onlookers and me.

Ben's lips began to move, but I couldn't make out what he'd said even though the music was softer than before. I was concentrating too hard on the unfamiliar sensation of his hands on my waist.

Finally his words formed a coherent sentence in my mind. "Having fun?" he'd asked.

I nodded. "Are you?"

"Definitely," he said, eyes shining.

My mind drifted, filling with thoughts of him as we continued to turn slowly. I forgot about the people around us and enjoyed the moment. I still couldn't believe after all these months I was actually in his arms. I wanted to pull him closer and wished for a kiss. But it was impossible. Chaperones were stationed all around. And who knew if he'd kiss me back?

After the song ended, the volume ratcheted back up. It was a school favorite, and everyone stampeded to the dance floor. Our friends found us, and the spell was broken.

Soon the music faded and people started to leave. Was I supposed to walk back with Ben or with our friends? We were all together, so I followed the crowd with Ben at my side.

When we neared O'Reilly, Ben pulled me away from the swarm. "One more thing." He took my hand and walked me toward the far corner of the building. My heart pounded.

Once we rounded it, he stopped and turned toward me. He leaned closer and gave me the lightest kiss. I could've sworn an electrical shock passed through our lips.

"I've been wanting to do that all night," he said, gazing into my eyes.

Without a word, I put my hands on his shoulders and pulled him down to me. I leaned in, parting my lips slightly, and kissed him as I'd longed to all year.

Chapter: 33

I dragged my feet across the quad on Friday afternoon. The dirty gray snow and freezing drizzle—evidently typical for mid-March in the Cascades—was a perfect reflection of my mood. I had just met with Mr. Robbins. He'd mentioned he had discussed my progress, or lack thereof, with Principal Locke. I supposed if I were to flunk Dream Management, the principal needed time to plan how to keep my mouth shut. Mr. Robbins didn't have any new suggestions today but promised he would come up with something. He even planned to call his counterpart at Lawrence Academy to brainstorm solutions.

In many ways this had been one of the best weeks of my entire life. After longing for Ben all year, I could finally call him my boyfriend. And despite the miserable weather, we'd even snuck out to the forest a couple times to make out. But the closer I grew to Ben, the more anxious I became—afraid I'd lose it all.

Time was running out for me to figure out conveyance, not to mention catch up with all the dream assignments. My improvement was slower than a sloth. Last week and again on Tuesday, Aditi received a fleeting image where she recalled opening a gift, but by mid-afternoon, she'd forgotten. And then in the wee hours of this morning when I conveyed, I couldn't keep my mind on the script. My thoughts kept drifting to

Ben—more like kissing Ben. Needless to say, I didn't get any images across. Right now, a boyfriend wasn't the smartest idea in terms of my focus and my grades. But maybe it didn't matter. Maybe I should simply give up and enjoy the next three months of school as Ben's girlfriend. I was probably going to get pulled out and have my memories erased regardless of how hard I worked. But would my memories of Ben and all my new friends disappear along with Dream Management? I didn't want to even begin to contemplate how it might work.

Without thinking, my body veered toward the phone booths rather than my dorm room. Talking with Mom about our plans for my upcoming spring break might cheer me up. A chance to escape this campus couldn't come soon enough. A mindless trip to the mall or the movies might be exactly what I needed.

Mom picked up. "Autumn! Your timing's perfect! Josh just came home. Hold on. He wants to talk."

Huh. What's up?

"Hey, sis. I got in!"

I took in a sharp breath. "UW?"

"Yeah. Got my letter today. I'm so pumped."

"That's great." Josh got everything he wanted, so I was far from surprised, but I forced my voice to sound cheerful and tried to push my jealousy aside. "I knew you'd get in."

"I thought so. But you never know. Such a relief to actually hold the letter."

"So you'll accept?" Part of me thought he might change his mind now that he'd made it in.

"I'm filling out the forms tonight." The grin on his face came through the phone as clearly as his voice.

"And get this. Luke got in too."

Even better. "Maybe you can be roommates." Drew would be overjoyed to have his brother attend college a mere fifteen minutes south. And at the rate I was going, I'd be staying in Seattle next fall too. One bright spot would be having Josh nearby. I had truly missed him this year.

****

I sat squished in tight on the couch in the TV lounge on Saturday night, wolfing down popcorn and snickering with my friends. A romantic comedy was playing, and I needed a few laughs. Mid-movie, Samantha tapped me on my shoulder. "Autumn, you need to see Mrs. Humphrey."

I leaned toward Hannah beside me. "I'll be back in a few. Let me know what I missed."

Minutes later, I knocked on my RA's door. Instead of inviting me in as usual, she stepped into the hallway. "Let's go to your room, dear." The older woman's mouth was set in a straight line rather than her typical, turned-up smile. She grasped my arm and guided me down the hallway.

"Is everything okay?"

"We'll talk in your room."

The dorm suddenly seemed too hot, and I tore off my hoodie. It had to be about Dream Management. I'd told her my problems, including the threat from Dad. Maybe Principal Locke had spoken with her too. What if she planned to warn me I was about to be kicked out of Dickensen? I took a few deep breaths while she ushered me into my room. She closed the door, sealing us in like a coffin. Mrs. Humphrey pulled out one of the desk chairs and swiveled it toward where I sat rigidly on the edge of my rumpled bed.

My words tumbled out. "Is this about my inability to convey? I've been trying so hard. And I came close not too long ago." I didn't dare mention my new relationship with Ben might be an issue.

"Oh no, dear. I wish it were only that. I received an urgent call from the office. There's been an accident. Your brother is in the hospital."

Shock traveled through my spine. "Josh! What happened?"

"I don't know the details except he was in a car accident and taken by ambulance. He's having surgery tonight."

Tears sprang to my eyes. This couldn't be happening.

"Your parents are with him."

"Were they hurt too?"

"No, they weren't in the car. But it's serious, and they want you to come home immediately."

I trembled.

"The school is arranging transportation. We need to get you packed."

In a daze, I nodded but couldn't move my arms or legs. I'd talked with Josh only yesterday. I should've been happier for him. What if he died and our last conversation had been tainted with jealousy? His reasoning to accept at UW to remain close to home now made total sense. All I wanted was to be there with him and my parents. Mrs. Humphrey moved to my side and pulled me into her soft arms.

Minutes later there was the faint sound of a key twisting in the door, and then Aditi popped in. Her eyes widened. "Is everything okay?"

I broke free from my RA's grasp. "It's Josh! He was in a car crash."

Aditi gasped as her hand shot to her mouth. She raced over to embrace me.

Mrs. Humphrey spoke up after a moment. "Aditi, can you go retrieve Autumn's luggage from the storage room?"

After she left, I moved as fast as I could, stuffing my messenger bag with thick texts and notebooks. Soon Aditi returned and began to haphazardly toss clothes into my suitcase while Mrs. Humphrey supervised.

Someone knocked—Coach Kat. "Autumn, I'm so sorry about your brother." She studied my half-packed bags. "I've moved my car to the school lot. I'll drive you to Seattle when you're ready."

I nodded through my tears.

Soon everything was packed. I put on my coat and blindly followed the adults with Aditi at my side. Out in the hallway, several girls rushed up to me, but Mrs. Humphrey shooed them away. They had to know it was serious for me to leave at nine o'clock on a Saturday night, and I'm sure they could tell by my tear-streaked face I'd been bawling.

Halfway across the quad, someone ran toward me—Ben. "Autumn! I heard you're leaving." He gave me a tight squeeze, holding on for several long seconds while I choked out what had happened. I could barely breathe, but I needed his hug. Then he grasped my hand and led me to Coach Kat's car. After many hurried, teary goodbyes, I left. Only after passing the gatehouse did a small part of my mind begin to question if I could ever return.

Chapter: 34

Why Josh? What happened? Maybe the accident wasn't that serious, but Mom and Dad knew I'd want to be there. Coach Kat encouraged me to sleep, but sleep was the furthest thing from my mind. The questions kept coming as I stared out the car window at black nothingness. *What was the surgery for? Was anyone else hurt? How long will I be home?* When we came to an open area, the stars shone down, and I made a silent wish for my brother's recovery.

After the longest drive of my life, the city lights glowed ahead. When Coach Kat asked her phone to provide directions to Harborview Hospital, I shuddered. As a child of two physicians, I knew it was the place for the critically injured.

We arrived in the Emergency Room a little before midnight. I was vaguely aware of my coach asking for directions and guiding me through a maze of corridors smelling of disinfectant. Soon we came to a waiting room with a bench and few dozen chairs, most of them empty. A TV hanging from the ceiling in one corner provided background noise, but no one was watching. My parents huddled side by side. Mom fiddled with a wad of tissues in her hands, and Dad stared blankly at a nature print on the wall. When they spotted me, they hurried over. Dad's puffy eyes met mine. He pulled me into a tight embrace.

I'd never seen him cry.

When he pulled back, he wiped his eyes and quickly recovered. "He's going to be in surgery a couple more hours."

After brief introductions and a couple thank yous, Dad took off with Coach Kat to retrieve my bags.

I turned to Mom. "What happened?"

"Let's sit, honey." Once we settled on the bench, Mom closed her eyes and began to speak. "Josh was driving with three of his friends. They'd gone to dinner to celebrate their college acceptances and were on their way to a movie."

"Which friends?"

"Luke and—"

I gasped. Luke was like a brother to me.

Mom nodded. "And Kellan and Jeff. The police officer said Josh ran a red light and an oversize SUV slammed into his driver's side." Mom spoke with little emotion, like she was recounting a news story about something occurring far away. "The other driver was unharmed, and her SUV had only minor front-end damage. But Josh's little car was totaled." She took a deep breath. "Luckily, Luke and Jeff were only bruised and shaken."

Thank God.

"Kellan, who sat behind Josh, was admitted with a shoulder injury and a concussion. He's expected to be released soon." Mom closed her eyes again and a lone tear leaked out. She grabbed my wrist. "Josh was seated in the worst position. Right where the other vehicle struck."

Mom stopped talking and broke down. I wrapped my arms around her. After a moment she took a deep breath and continued. "He suffered a brain injury."

I clamped my palm over my mouth.

"He also fractured his left arm in a couple of places, dislocated his shoulder, and broke a few ribs."

My throat went dry. I hadn't thought the news could get any worse.

"He was knocked unconscious." Mom cleared her throat and offered a thin smile. "The doctors hope he'll wake after surgery."

I hugged Mom and let my tears fall until we were both reaching for tissues.

When Dad returned, he looked wiped. He turned to Mom. "Any news?"

"No, David. Nothing."

****

I was jarred awake when Mom moved my head from her soft lap to the hard, vinyl bench.

"Dr. Mattison and Dr. Clarke?"

I pulled myself up to my elbows. My parents stood five feet away, holding hands, talking to a man in light blue scrubs.

"…let you know he's out of surgery. He's stable, and you'll be able to see him soon."

"Thank goodness." Mom's knees buckled and Dad steadied her.

"How did it go?" Dad asked.

"The surgery went as planned. During the craniotomy, I removed the hematoma and drained the excess cerebrospinal fluid to reduce his intracranial pressure…" The doctor threw around so many medical terms, I was completely lost. At least my parents were both doctors. They'd understand without needing to ask a million questions. "…I was able to replace the bone flap, and then…"

I moaned unintentionally.

Mom glanced back at me and her eyes went wide. Her lips were pursed so tight together, the red had disappeared. She whispered to Dad, and they moved farther into the lobby, out of earshot.

Dad eased down next to me when they returned. "That was Dr. Johnston, the neurosurgeon who operated on Josh. He's out of surgery. We'll be able to see him soon."

I scrambled to a sitting position. "Is he awake?"

"Not yet. They've given him some medication to keep him asleep so his body can rest. The surgery went well. The orthopedist positioned his shoulder back into the socket, and she repaired his arm with a few screws."

Hesitantly, I asked, "And his brain?"

He gave me a weak smile, and the lines on his forehead creased deeper. He reached out and held both my hands. "His head injury is pretty severe. They removed a blood clot and put in a drain to remove some fluid. Josh's brain is swelling, and their number one priority is to keep the pressure low. He's being moved to the Neuro-Intensive Care Unit, where they'll monitor him around the clock."

Dad took a deep breath. "There's a chance he might need a second surgery if the drain and the medication don't do the trick. But they're trying to avoid another one." He squeezed my hands. "So let's not worry about that yet."

My head spun and I had to lie back down. But I couldn't fall back to sleep. I couldn't get the image of Josh with a gaping hole in his skull out of my head. More questions floated through my mind, but I kept coming back to: *Was he going to be okay? What would I do without my brother?*

****

Over an hour later, a young nurse escorted us to the Neuro-ICU. She kept her face blank and stood stiffly. Looking at me, she said, "Normally this late at night only parents are permitted in the Neuro-ICU." She smiled thinly. "But I know you've waited a long time, so we'll make an exception tonight."

As we followed her, our shoes squeaking on the polished tile floor echoed down the empty hallway. I glanced left when we passed an open door. A woman was weeping near a patient's bedside. I whipped my face back forward and swallowed hard.

The nurse stopped before we entered Josh's room and addressed me. "I want you to be prepared. Your brother will look different from what you're used to." Then she gave a tight nod.

The room was so full of equipment that it took some finagling to surround his bed. The nurse's words of warning did nothing to prepare me for the scene before my eyes. No words could have. He was my *big* brother, but in the bed he looked smaller and nowhere near age eighteen. His head was shaved, and he was black and blue, particularly on his left side. A large, white bandage covered more than half his head. His left arm was in a cast lying on top of his sheets. Multiple tubes and wires were attached to his head, arm, and chest, and a machine made robotic breathing sounds while computer screens flashed and beeped.

Tears streamed down my face. This was serious. He could die, and I could only watch, helpless. Dad cried openly too. Mom leaned over the edge of the bed, took Josh's hand, and whispered something to him.

The nurse broke the moment before long. "It's best for your son to rest, but if one of you wishes to stay the night, we can arrange it."

My parents looked at each other in silent communication before Dad said, "Liz, I'll take Autumn home. Call if anything changes."

Mom nodded then gave me a tight squeeze. "I love you, honey. Glad you're here."

"Love you too, Mom."

Dad kissed Josh on his head, and I attempted to give him a hug. But so many attachments were in the way, it was more of an awkward body touch.

I could barely stay awake. The clock showed it was after three in the morning when we got home. I didn't even bother to brush my teeth but simply pulled on an old pair of pajamas from my dresser drawer and collapsed on the bed. I closed my eyes, hoping this was all part of some student's sick and tasteless dream.

Chapter: 35

Half asleep, I fought to open my eyes. Where was I? Was this a dream?

The events of last night slammed into me like a wayward soccer ball to the gut: I was home and Josh was at Harborview. The pain in my heart had me snuggling deeper into my warm bed to avoid starting what might be another terrible day. The rain pelted the roof, and the trees outside my bedroom window bent in the wind. *Perfect*. I couldn't bear it if today had been sunny. It would have been cruel with my brother in the hospital fighting for his life.

After several minutes more, I crawled out of bed. Although it was around eleven in the morning, the house was silent and dark as I plodded downstairs. I turned on the kitchen lights and found a note on the counter near the coffeepot.

Autumn,

Returned to the hospital. Your mother or I will be home soon.

Love, Dad

Part of me wished he had brought me along, but I was also grateful he'd let me stay in bed. My stomach rumbled, so I nibbled on cereal while my body revived, feeling guilty I'd slept while my parents sat vigil.

When I returned to my room, my suitcase and bags glared at me from the center of the floor. *What should I do with them*? I shoved my unopened backpack and messenger bag near my desk. As if I were in any state to worry about something as trivial as homework. Opening my suitcase, I removed my toiletries and some clothes for the day but left it propped open, so I could grab what I needed, as if it were a weekend trip. A wave of optimism washed over me. Josh might wake today. His brain injury might turn out to be minor, and I'd return to school in a few days. But then reality crept back, and the memory of Josh's bruised and bandaged body in the Neuro-ICU shattered those thoughts. I grew dizzy and eased myself onto my mattress until my lightheadedness passed. He had to get better. I needed my big brother.

Suddenly, paws pattered across the hardwoods and grew louder each second. Moving my bags must've woken Zoey from wherever she'd chosen to nap. I peered out my doorway, crouched to the ground, and opened my arms to a joyful ball of fur. I tried to enjoy my dog's enthusiastic greeting, but all I could think about was when Zoey was a puppy; my seven-year-old self and ten-year-old brother would toss stuffed toys up and down this very hall with our new *sister* racing between us. What would Zoey think if Josh never came home? He was her brother too.

After a long, hot shower, I found Mom in the kitchen. She sat with a mug of steaming coffee, staring off into the distance. She looked horrible. Her eyes were puffy with hints of purple beneath them, not to mention the raccoon effect from smudged mascara, and wisps of her typically perfect, highlighted hair stuck on end.

"Hi, Mom." I gave her a hug and pulled up a chair.

"Morning. How'd you sleep?"

"Okay, I guess."

"I'm glad someone got some rest. Your father was back at the hospital by seven. He couldn't sleep."

"What about you?"

She shrugged. "Not much. The Neuro-ICU isn't set up for visitors. A nurse insisted I lie down in the waiting room for a couple hours and promised to get me if anything changed."

"How's Josh?"

A shadow far gloomier than the weather outside passed over Mom's features. "About the same. He's still stable, which is a positive sign. It's impossible for him to wake up right now because they've got him sedated."

"Did they say *if* he's going to wake up?"

"Oh, honey, I don't know. The doctors warned us he's in pretty bad shape. But they're encouraged because he's young and otherwise healthy. The next few days are critical."

"So that's good?"

"I think so." Mom sipped her coffee. Only the rhythmic, metallic sounds of raindrops hitting the gutters filled the kitchen. Finally she said, "Just yesterday, we were standing right over there"—she nodded toward the counter—"chatting about baseball before he left for dinner with his friends. They finished tryouts last week. And he was so elated about UW." Mom's voice faltered. "What was he doing? He's always been so attentive on the road."

"Maybe he can tell us when he wakes up."

****

An hour later, we were back in the waiting room,

267

and Dad came out to meet us. He appeared not only exhausted but defeated in a way I'd never seen before with his posture slumped and his eyes glassed over. Mom was always more expressive, so I was used to her emotions. Dad, on the other hand, was stoic. He could handle anything. But not this. And that scared me more than anything. I almost gave him a hug, but then I thought better of it. If he fell apart then what would I do?

Dad collapsed in a chair. "Why don't you two go in? There's really not enough room for three. I'm going to grab a coffee in a sec."

Mom nodded. "Come on, Autumn."

She led me back through the Neuro-ICU. More alert and prepared than the night before, I paid closer attention today.

I took a sharp breath when we entered his room. Josh looked even worse. His bruises were darker and his body more swollen. I teared up but kept it together this time.

Mom went into what Josh and I'd always referred to as physician-mode and explained the purpose of all the equipment in a detached manner. She pointed out one machine monitoring his blood pressure as well as heart and oxygen saturation rates. Another device measured his temperature. He also had continuous EEG monitoring to view his cerebral function and another recording its pressure. She explained why he had a breathing tube and how the machine worked. Then she pointed to the IV and described how he received multiple medications to control pain, seizures, and intracranial pressure as well as one to keep him comatose. Of course, he was given fluids to stay hydrated. The nurses at the station outside his room had monitors to alert them of any changes.

"Josh will be kept here for a while." Mom pulled a chair to the side of his bed, sat down, and picked up his hand. "It could be days or weeks. Eventually, he'll move to a larger, more comfortable room when his brain pressure stabilizes, and he can breathe for himself."

"Does he know we're here?"

"Probably not. But it's possible. Doctors don't know everything. But more importantly, I know we're here. I want to make sure someone is always with him. I couldn't live with myself if he was left alone for long." Mom caught my eye. "When you're a mother, you'll understand. I'd do anything for you two."

I wasn't a mother, but I could understand as a sister. As I sat there, I realized as long as Josh was in the hospital or needed me in any way, I'd remain in Seattle. Nothing was more important to me than my family. My heart told me he'd wake up and be fine, but an idea began to form: maybe I wouldn't return to Dickensen even once he came home. All I wanted was to be near him and to have the old Josh back.

Mom and I stayed with him for what seemed an eternity. We didn't speak much, but I could feel the love in his room. I hoped Josh would wake up so he could feel it too.

At last she announced it was time for a late lunch, so we made our way down to the cafeteria after Josh's nurse assured us she'd call if anything changed.

We didn't expect a call.

After lunch, we returned to the waiting room, and Dad went in to sit with him. The entire day went like that, alternating turns going into his room. One of my parents always accompanied me.

Time passed sluggishly. I found counting holes on the ceiling tiles to be a highlight of my day. *Seriously, it's quite a challenge*. But I felt important in a way I hadn't been before. I prayed he'd wake up and believed my physical presence might somehow encourage him to heal.

****

Monday was more of the same. Tuesday as well. Each day dragged. My parents suggested I take a break. Perhaps visit Julia or Drew. It'd been months since I'd seen them. But I wasn't in the mood. Besides, being at the hospital mattered. Josh never made any outward sign he sensed my presence, but I felt he did, just the same.

On Thursday, Dad planned to drop me off at Harborview on his way to work. He was returning on a limited basis because many of his own patients' appointments and surgeries couldn't be postponed. I suspected losing himself in his job was his way of coping with this nightmare. Before we left, he joined me in the kitchen while I was finishing up breakfast. Although his face was freshly shaved and his hair neatly styled, his pale, dull skin betrayed his exhaustion.

"Autumn, we need to talk about school." His typical assertive tone when discussing anything academic had been replaced with a hesitant one.

"What about it?"

"Your mother and I've been talking. She called Dickensen Academy yesterday and told them your return date is unknown since Josh's condition is touch and go."

I dropped my spoon, which clattered on the ceramic bowl. "What'd they say?"

"They want to work with us. Your teachers will communicate your assignments by email."

"I can't do homework! I can't think about anything but Josh."

"I know. It's just this whole thing with Josh might go on a long time, and we don't want you to fall behind. Regardless of what happens, you need to finish your freshman year."

The traces of milk and corn cereal went sour in my mouth. How much hadn't they told me about his injuries? I took a deep breath. "Is Josh going to die?"

Dad was supposed to immediately say *no*. Instead he sat there, looking stunned. And speechless—another first.

Finally he spoke. "I know it's going to be hard, but homework might be a good distraction and will make it easier when you return to school."

"You mean to Dickensen?"

"Dickensen, Haller Lake..." He put his head in his hands and leaned forward. After a moment, he sat back up and concentrated on a bird outside the window. "We don't know at this point."

Did he mean he didn't know about school or he didn't know about Josh? I wasn't about to ask. Dad looked beaten. I couldn't believe he was returning to work. I hope he didn't have surgeries planned for today. But knowing him, he'd drink another coffee on his drive and magically transform out of his father role as he strode through his own hospital's doors.

I didn't question him further. Instead, I added a few

textbooks to my bag before we left.

As we rode in silence, a new thought flashed through my mind: if Josh died, the pressure on me would skyrocket since he wouldn't be able to fulfill Dad's dream to have another doctor, if not two, in the family—as if the pressure weren't already high enough. Visions of me back at home with Dad hovering over my shoulder, expecting perfection, whooshed the air from my lungs, and I shuddered. But the moment that scenario hit me, I struggled to forget it. What a terrible sister I was to have such a selfish thought.

****

After a full week at home, the daily hospital visits had become my new life, although my homework reminded me I had another one far from here. Had Ben learned to convey to Aditi? Were things still working out with Hannah and Grace as roommates? Was Caitlyn bothering Hannah? Did they miss me? I was curious but wasn't up to talking to, or even emailing, anyone. They wouldn't understand. So far my memories of Dickensen were clear, but I wondered if some awful memory wipe might be in store for me if I didn't return.

Over the weekend, Luke and Drew Miller visited. Drew rushed over and hugged me tight the moment he spotted me beside Josh. "I'm so sorry," he said with tears in his eyes.

Luke's eyes were full of fear, and his hands trembled when he stepped into Josh's room. I'd never seen him scared of anything. Luke's bruises were fading, although his neck was still sore. He informed us he'd also visited Kellan, who was recuperating at home. Fortunately, he was going to be fine. Josh, as the driver, was liable for everyone's injuries. It was hard to believe things could be worse, but they would have been had his driving severely injured or killed one of his friends.

After several minutes of awkwardness, Drew suggested we leave Josh with Luke and take a walk. Although cold and windy, the fresh air was a relief. We found a sheltered bench in a courtyard between buildings and sat huddled together.

I'd forgotten how much I missed him and appreciated the comfort of a lifelong friend.

At last he said, "Hope I didn't upset you back there. I'm such a wuss. But I've been thinking all week it could've been me in your position."

"What do you mean?"

"If that SUV had come from the opposite direction, it would've smashed into Luke instead. Then I would've been the one stuck here all week." Drew grimaced. "Sorry. That didn't come out right. But you know what I mean. It must be rough."

He was the first person to empathize with me. I'd never considered the accident from his perspective. But it got me thinking. He was right. If only a slight change was made that night—a touch of the brakes, a bit more gas, or even another movie showing—life would have been so different for Josh. For me. For all of us. How much of our lives were altered by so many seemingly trivial decisions? But as fate would have it, Josh was left in a coma while Luke walked away.

We sat there, not saying much else until Drew had to leave with his brother.

Julia stopped by over the weekend too. After a brief visit with Josh—ninety seconds, tops—she whispered, "I've got to get out of here."

Ten minutes later, we were seated at a corner table

in the cafeteria. It was quiet since few people ate at this time of day. We bought two sodas and a huge chocolate chunk cookie to share. A sugar high would help me get through another long afternoon.

Julia broke the cookie in half and gave the bigger half to me. "I don't know how you do it. I'd go crazy here after a day."

"It's not exactly fun. But I can't imagine leaving the hospital right now."

"So tell me. How is he?"

Julia patiently listened while I filled her in on everything I knew about my brother's condition. She even hugged me when I broke down at one point. It was nice to feel close to her again.

"I'm thinking I might not return to Dickensen."

She sipped her soda. "Really? It's that bad?"

I shrugged. "I don't know. I'm thinking maybe I should stay here with my family, however it all turns out." It wouldn't be so terrible to transfer to Haller Lake. I'd miss my new friends, but we'd keep in touch—if that was allowed. And Ben, well, that would be even tougher. But we could always try the long distance thing, and I could see him on school vacations. Maybe I'd become close again with Julia. She was here now. That had to say something. And I'd have Drew. It was a huge school. I'd make new friends. Moving back home wouldn't be the end of the world...so long as Josh got better.

"I'm so sorry, Autumn. I'd love for you to transfer to Haller Lake. Not because you have to but because you want to."

I nodded. "So what's up with everyone these days?"

Some of Julia's usual enthusiasm came back. Obviously she was relieved to switch subjects. She recapped everything happening with our old friends. As it turned out, many of them had found new social circles in high school like Josh had foreseen.

After she left, I thought long and hard about my situation. My perspective on life had changed this week. My family was so important, despite the pressure they put on me to be someone I'm not. Maybe I wasn't cut out to be a dream-maker. And now that I was removed from it all, I could admit to myself I'd been living with fear of the unknown aspects of telepathy. Besides, I could hardly believe how stressed I'd become with each conveyance failure. After being in the hospital with Josh, I realized I hadn't known true stress before. The life I had at Dickensen now seemed frivolous—a life for someone naive who didn't realize it could all be taken away in an instant.

Chapter: 36

My voicemail was full of messages, and my phone had countless unanswered texts and emails. Everyone wanted to know how Josh was doing. So far, I hadn't responded. Not even to a text. Every time I tried, my fingers froze. And it felt wrong to check in on social media or post status updates about his condition.

On Sunday before I left for the hospital, our home phone rang.

What area code is that? I picked it up, expecting to take a quick message for Mom or Dad. "Hello?"

"Autumn!"

"Aditi?" A mixture of emotions ran through me. Part of me warmed I had a friend who hadn't given up on me, but I wasn't in the mood to talk. I'd barely been able to think about my Dickensen friends for more than a fleeting moment here and there.

"Yeah, it's me. I can't believe I finally got you. How's it going?"

"Uh, not that well." I walked upstairs to my bedroom for privacy. "Sorry I didn't return your calls. I haven't had the chance."

"It's okay, I get it. If something happened to my brother...well...anyway, I called most days, but only left a couple of messages. I figured there was no point leaving more."

"I haven't been home much. I'm practically living

at the hospital," I said as I paced my room.

"That must be rough."

I bit my lower lip and stared up at the ceiling. I noticed a pale gray watermark near the window. In the pre-coma era, Mom would've wanted to get that taken care of immediately. But now, it probably wouldn't even register if I mentioned it. "Yeah. But I feel like this is where I should be."

"Of course. How is he?"

I gave a five-minute spiel on my brother's condition. "Maybe you could pass that info along to everyone? I don't have it in me to keep repeating this stuff."

"Sure, I'll send a message. I'm in San Jose, for break."

"Oh, that's right." Spring break. It seemed like a million years ago I'd looked forward to this week.

"But you should at least reach out to Ben. He's freaking out you're ignoring his messages."

Guilt hit me. I pictured Ben calling and texting and emailing me, growing more and more frantic with each passing day. But I was having a hard enough time holding it together here in Seattle. Opening up to him might push me over the edge. Besides, what would I say? When I'd left Dickensen, things were so good—no, make that great—between us. And now, with Josh, it seemed wrong for me to have been so happy. I supposed I could send a short message about Josh and skip over the *us* part. If *us* still existed.

"You still there?" she asked.

"Uh, yeah. Sorry, Aditi. You're right. I'll call him or something."

"I was hoping you'd only been called home as a

precaution, and you'd be back soon. But when Mr. Robbins spoke to me about my sleeping arrangements, I knew it was bad."

"What'd he say?" I hadn't even considered how this would impact Aditi. I eased myself down at my desk and began doodling on a scrap of paper.

"Do you know Sarah Chen? She's a sophomore."

"Is she the one with the pink streaks in her hair?"

"Yeah. This year, there are an odd number of sophomore girls—someone must not have come back from last year—so Sarah was given a single because she didn't need a roommate. Apparently at the start of the school year, she could already convey across the hallways."

"Sounds kind of like Ben." I found I'd drawn several stick figures and took a pink highlighter and colored one figure's long hair.

"Yeah, he's trying. He keeps conveying his ski dream to me each Sunday, but nothing's coming through. I can tell he's frustrated. But hey, it's a sophomore skill."

I couldn't help but feel a bit relieved, even though it was my idea in the first place. The farther ahead he soared, the farther behind I fell. Jealous wasn't the right word for how it made me feel. More like inadequate, like I'd never be good enough for him. And now, maybe I'd never catch up or even become a dream-maker.

"Anyway, Mr. Robbins arranged for Sarah to sleep in your bed on my conveyance nights, beginning after spring break. On your nights, she'll convey to me from her room."

It probably wasn't the first time a student had to

leave for an emergency. I couldn't help but wonder if a standard protocol existed for dealing with students once the crisis passed. So far I hadn't heard anything from Dickensen faculty except homework assignments and *thinking of you* types of messages. I'm pretty sure I'd be welcomed back. But what would happen if I chose not to return? Would I be subject to the disciplinary committee? Or were exceptions made in cases like mine where I hadn't done anything wrong?

Aditi's voice lifted. "The good news is the room will stay open for when you return."

"Well that's good...I guess." I wasn't sure if I should say anything. "But don't count on me coming back."

"You never know. Josh might get better. You said the doctors don't know."

"True." But what I didn't say was the longer I remained at home, the more convinced I was I belonged in Seattle with my family regardless of what happened with Josh. "Well, I better go. My grandma's here. She's going to drive me to the hospital soon. Say hello to everyone and remember to give them the update."

"Well, okay. I hope he wakes soon."

"Thanks."

Chapter: 37

Josh's new room could've passed for a flower shop. Colorful bouquets released their fragrant scents and masked the antiseptic smells. Helium balloons vibrated in the airflow from the vents. I sat on the vinyl chair, alone, next to his bed and took it all in. This was so much better.

Only yesterday Josh had been in the Neuro-ICU, and I was present when the nurses unplugged some of the monitors—the doctors had gradually decreased his medications all week to the point where he was breathing on his own. When they unplugged the ventilator, I swear I could hear the silence. The ventilator had been so loud. Scary too, with its measured intake and outtake of air. Now it was easier to believe he was sleeping peacefully.

He was still in a coma, and the doctors made no assurances that he'd ever wake up. Josh was in a coma when he arrived at the hospital, so removing the coma-inducing drugs didn't guarantee he'd wake even after they worked their way out of his system. Nevertheless, my parents hovered more, constantly checking his monitors and speaking to him, clearly looking for indications he was coming out of it.

More than ever, Mom wanted to ensure Josh wasn't left alone, which was why I was here with him now. She told me when he woke up, she wanted someone to be with him. I wasn't sure if she truly believed he'd wake or if she'd said that for my sake. She was on the phone, as usual. Probably speaking with an insurance company about Josh's medical treatment or the car accident. Or maybe calling into her practice to discuss her own patients' care.

I leaned toward his bed and began to tell him a story, inside my head, about his upcoming graduation— I was too embarrassed to speak out loud, in case somebody entered his room.

You'll wear a heavy, green silk robe over your shirt and tie, like all the other guys. The girls will wear gold ones with their fancy new heels peeking out.

I'll be in the bleachers, halfway up, squished between Mom and Dad. Grandma and Grandpa Clarke, Aunt Kelly, and Uncle Michael will be there too. Uncle Greg will drive over for the weekend to join us, and he'll bring his girlfriend. Even Grandma Mattison will fly out to watch you graduate.

The band will play "Pomp and Circumstance" as the graduates file into the gymnasium. You'll be a valedictorian. When it's your turn to give a speech, you'll talk about the accident and how it changed your life and inspired you to be the best person you could be. Our family will listen with tears rolling down our faces, even Dad.

When the ceremony is over, you'll exit with the graduates, and we'll find you in front of the high school in a sea of green and gold. Afterward, we'll take photos on the steps. It'll be a beautiful, sunny June day.

Finally, we'll all drive home. Grandma Mattison will sit up front with Dad while Mom will ride back with us. The rest of our family will follow in their own cars. Afterward, we'll have a party in our backyard.

But remember, you need to wake up and return to school for it to all play out.

****

Every day, often several times, I went through this exercise. With each rendition, my story grew more elaborate. After a few days, I converted it to the dream format. Why not? It was worth a chance. Maybe I could somehow reach him.

As soon as I switched to telepathy, it was as if the cell reception had gone from *no signal* to *five bars*, and I was speaking to the real Josh rather than to his unconscious form laying in front of me. I immersed myself into my dreams, losing all track of time. I swear he could hear me, although of course, he couldn't talk back—his side was on mute.

****

More days passed, and Josh simply lay there. Dr. Johnston would periodically check in on him. He'd sail into the room, perform a few tests, review my brother's chart, and scribble some notes. If Mom or Dad were there, he'd speak with them for a few minutes before leaving.

My parents' faces were covered with deep lines of worry, as if they'd aged five years in the span of two weeks. They spoke optimistically, but the fear in their eyes made me question if it were all an act. They encouraged me to talk to Josh. I wanted to tell them I already was, telepathically. But they would look at me with pity, believing all the trauma of the past couple weeks had pushed me over the edge to madness. And perhaps they'd be right. What did I know about conveying? My perception that Josh was latching on to my mind might have been my imagination, something to keep my spirits up. But until he woke—or died—I wasn't going to stop. This might be my last chance to communicate with my brother.

****

Each time Mom, Dad, or the medical personnel stepped out of Josh's hospital room, the tension left my body. I'd begin to convey to him, not only the story about his graduation but a new one. I told Josh how he'd attend medical school after graduating from UW. For his residency he would choose neurosurgery because of his ordeal at Harborview. Besides, he'd always wished to be a surgeon like Dad.

Again, like with the graduation story, it became more elaborate with each retelling. I explained how he did so well in med school he would attend a top program for his residency. Other times I'd add in details about how Josh would compare surgeries with Dad. Josh would talk about the intricacies of the brain, while Dad would discuss the complexities of the heart.

But never did I add anything about the medical field I might choose. I didn't feel in my heart I wanted to become a physician, and I had to truly believe my story to communicate it to Josh. With him laying before me in a coma, it didn't feel right to lie.

****

Mom pulled on her coat, then picked up her purse from the table in my brother's room. "Are you sure you want to stay here, Autumn? I could drop you off at Julia's on the way to the house."

"No, I'm good here. Go home. Do your things. You'll feel better. You'll smell better too." Mom's hygiene was fine, but I'd say anything to get her to

283

crack a smile these days.

She rewarded me with a little smirk. "Okay. I won't be much more than an hour." She leaned down and pecked Josh on the cheek.

Once she was gone, I pulled a chair alongside Josh's hospital bed. I didn't even need to meditate to get into the right mode. I simply focused on his cerebral cortex and began the conveyance steps. I envisioned us in our twenties sitting next to the fireplace in our parents' house having a conversation. I could feel the heat on my back and see my brother at my side with the flicker of orange light dancing across his body.

"Remember ten years ago when I went off to boarding school?"

"Yeah," you'd say.

"What if I told you they were hiding a big secret? They were teaching the students to become dream-makers, and we'd use telepathy to send dreams to our roommates. I could never make it work. But I received all these elaborate dreams from my teachers."

Then I went on to describe Dream Management, including the academic dreams.

You'd listen patiently like you did when we were kids. As a neurosurgeon, I'd expect you to tell me it was my imagination and might even use some medical terminology to explain why it wasn't real. But instead, a moment of clarity would come over your face, and you'd explain the possible mechanics...

After I finished the conversation, I snapped out of my trance and my breath hitched. I was only in a hospital conveying a dream to Josh. I wasn't foretelling the future.

Chapter: 38

I hunched over the Formica table, alone in the near-empty hospital cafeteria, my homework splayed out in front of me. I reread the same line in my history textbook over and over. My eyes grew heavy even though it was only mid-afternoon.

Beep!

I jumped in my seat. A text. From Mom.

Come quick!

I gathered my papers, jammed them into my messenger bag, and heaved it across my shoulder. Then I raced up six flights of stairs, two steps at a time, and burst into my brother's room huffing and puffing. Mom sat on Josh's bed, holding his hand, tears streaming down her face.

My heart made one decisive beat, sending waves through my body. Then it stopped.

It hit me: Josh had died.

I grabbed the doorframe for support.

There he was, lying in front of me, white and motionless.

Mom looked up at me. "He's waking up."

I couldn't answer at first. I was still out of breath and my heart wasn't beating right. I had an overwhelming urge to hit her. "I...I thought he was dying," I finally spat out.

"Sorry." She smiled through her tears. "I didn't

mean to scare you."

"Mom! How could you text me like that?"

I had to take a moment to calm down. I looked around the room and again at my brother. A nurse stood off to one side. Nothing out of the ordinary.

Mom patted the bed. "Why don't you come over here?"

Still a bit shaky, I eased down on the opposite side of his bed, took his right hand in mine, and watched. Relief gradually replaced my anger as my heart rate slowed.

"Your dad's on his way."

I nodded, grateful Dad wasn't mid-surgery. He wouldn't want to miss this.

I didn't know what to expect, something like in the movies perhaps. Maybe he'd open his eyes, look at us, and say, "Hi." But in reality, it was more like watching a slug cross wet pavement.

"Be patient. Before I texted you, he was flailing his arms. He even moved his head—slightly, but still." Mom pointed to the monitors. "His stats have changed. His EEG indicates his brain is active and his heart rate has sped up."

We each held one of his hands and spoke to him. The nurse remained in the back of the room, giving us the illusion of privacy. Every time I glanced over, she had her gaze glued to his monitors. After what seemed like an eternity, Josh squeezed my hand lightly. Was it my imagination? I squeezed back. He squeezed again. He must've done the same on his left side too because Mom gasped.

His eyelids started to quiver, like he was struggling to wake up. The nurse dimmed the lights. It took a moment for my eyes to adjust; however, sunlight coming through a slit in the curtains lit up half the room while the monitors glowed on the other side.

His eyes fluttered open briefly.

Will he be able to talk? Will he know me? Will he still be Josh? I hadn't been told much about what might happen.

At first he stared off into space, but after a short while, he focused on Mom.

She leaned down close. "Josh. I love you. I'm here. Your sister too."

Then his gaze traveled slowly to me. I read recognition and confusion.

"Josh. It's me, Autumn."

After a few seconds, his eyes glazed over.

Mom placed her hand on his forehead. "You're okay. You're in the hospital. They gave you medicine to keep you asleep."

He nodded ever so faintly and closed his eyes.

"You sleep," Mom said. "We'll be here when you wake up."

He nodded again without reopening his eyes.

The nurse stepped forward. "I'll notify the doctor again."

Minutes later, Dr. Johnston strode in. He performed a few brief tests and jotted down more notes. "His behavior is encouraging. The act of waking is tiring. It may take him a few tries."

We stayed silent or spoke softly while we waited. We were now in a room with a sleeping boy— literally—whereas before, we had wanted him to wake, and so we'd spoken in our regular voices.

Soon Dad arrived and had a whispered

conversation with us. We sat vigil for hours. It was like waiting for the birthday guest to arrive at a surprise party. I wanted to sing and dance and talk with all my friends. But instead, I remained quiet.

At last, Josh rewarded our efforts with a faint twitch. He was waking. The nurse had kept the room dim to make it less traumatic for him to open his eyes.

This time Dad took his hand and spoke. "Josh. It's Dad. I love you."

Josh opened his eyes a slit. Again he stared off into space but eventually focused on Dad. His mouth moved slightly, like he was struggling to talk. I could've sworn he said, "Dad." Then he gazed around the room, his green eyes wide. No idea what he could be thinking.

The nurse adjusted his bed to bring his head higher.

"Wh-wh-what happened?" His voice was raspy and difficult to make out.

Mom gave the *CliffsNotes* version of the accident and his hospital stay. Josh struggled to say more than a few words at a time, but he seemed to follow the conversation and listed the names of his three friends, as if he wanted to know they were okay. He also kept asking the date, which was April third. He worried he'd slept away two and a half weeks. Our parents assured him it didn't matter. The important thing was to get better.

I sat there savoring the love, the relief, and the excitement. A flashing ticker tape with the words *My Brother is Awake* scrolled across my vision. Although deep down, I'd always believed he would eventually wake up, I was unprepared for the flood of emotions now flowing through me.

While Josh was still awake, Dr. Johnston returned.

He shined a light in his pupils and asked him some basic questions such as, "What is your name?" and "How old are you?" The doctor smiled as Josh answered each one correctly. "It's nice to finally meet you, Josh." Before Dr. Johnston left, he pulled my parents aside.

I leaned toward them, straining to hear. He explained he was cautiously optimistic based on how coherent Josh was. Often patients had much more confusion after being in a coma for so long. I nearly pumped my arm in the air and yelled, "Yes!" If the conservative doctor was happy with his prognosis, then Josh was bound to get better.

Soon Josh grew drowsy, and the nurse explained he needed rest. She suggested we take a break too. Mom refused, of course, but as soon as he fell back to sleep, I went home with Dad.

The car couldn't go fast enough. I was anxious to tell the world my brother was awake. Time to finally return all those calls and texts and emails. The entire drive, Dad explained how Josh's short conversation allayed many of the fears he'd kept to himself. Josh's memory was intact, he could see and hear, and he was capable of a brief conversation. Some of his speaking limitations could be for trivial reasons, such as being parched or tired, rather than an indication of permanent brain damage.

I grew dizzy and overwhelmed as he described potential scenarios of what might lie ahead: seizures, difficulty concentrating, blurry vision, headaches, dizziness, changes in personality, depression, and the need to relearn some basic activities. But as I listened, I took cues from Dad and remained upbeat. He was almost giddy rather than his usual controlled manner. It was a new side of him—the wall between us thinner than usual. Obviously he was beyond relieved that, so far, Josh had passed the tests. But he made it clear my brother had a challenging road ahead. And although neither of us said it, we both knew Josh's dreams were far greater than simply living.

Chapter: 39

Days later, I sat beside Josh on his hospital bed and fed him dinner while our parents looked on. It reminded me of when I used to feed Skylar baby food. Josh was now capable of full-on conversations, so each evening after Dad arrived from work, we would spend hours around his bedside. We had even started playing board games as a family—Dad had always been too busy before, but when Dr. Johnston noted games were beneficial for Josh's rehabilitation, Dad participated with gusto.

"Here comes the airplane," I joked. My brother made a face but ate it anyway. He'd fed himself earlier today, but the high dose of pain medication for his headache made him dizzy, and he'd made a mess of himself.

"I just want to get moving," he complained. "I've gotta get out of here and back to school. Graduation's coming up."

My spine tingled. This wasn't the first time he'd mentioned something like this in the past few days. I'd been conveying a similar line while he was in a coma. A coincidence? Maybe. Of course he'd want to return to school and graduate. That's what all high school seniors fixated on, and Josh had talked of almost nothing else the last few months.

"You need to go slow," Dad said. "Simply eating

the mush your sister is feeding you is a huge undertaking for your body. You've been on IV fluids for nearly three weeks."

I chuckled. "Be glad that humongous cast is on your left arm, or I'd be feeding you for another month or two."

Josh blew out his breath in frustration but then opened his mouth for more.

Mom leaned over. "Be patient. The doctor said he's going to arrange for physical and occupational therapy soon."

A couple hours later, as Dad and I prepared to head home—Mom still slept at the hospital—Josh said, "Wait. One more thing."

He seemed to be addressing Dad, so I slumped in my chair to scroll through my phone and wait for what was sure to be another request to bring some random items from home.

Soon the tone of the voices changed. My ears perked up.

"It's okay, Josh. You can tell us," Mom soothed.

He took a deep breath and looked at each of us before focusing on the white bed sheets. "We were driving to the movie theater. I don't remember what we were talking about. But the music was loud, and we had to shout. Then my phone vibrated in my pocket. I know I shouldn't have tried to get it out. But a few girls were planning to meet us at the theater." His voice broke. "And I just wanted to read the text."

Dad's mouth pressed closed as if clamped in a vice. He reached out and grabbed Mom's hand, which turned white. My body went cold and rigid.

Josh was now full-on crying and choking on his

words, but my parents didn't interrupt. "I kind of had to struggle to get the phone out of my pocket. I was looking down, trying to see the message. Then I heard a scream…Kellan, I think. Never even saw the red light."

A nurse popped her head into the room but ducked back out.

I held my breath. If only I could somehow exit the room without my parents noticing, like the nurse. Josh's friends had never mentioned the text or his phone in the police report, or with us. Could he still be charged for that? Texting while driving was illegal in Washington State.

Mom lay down on the hospital bed and wrapped Josh in her arms while Dad sat there like a statue. Perhaps he was thinking something like his golden child wasn't so golden anymore. Maybe more like bronze. Poor Josh. Disappointing Dad was going to be tough on him. Mom murmured something to my brother. I couldn't see her face, but she had to be as devastated as Dad. After all the warnings they'd given us about cell phone usage in the car, I couldn't believe this was the reason for the accident. So stupid. He could've killed his friends. And he nearly killed himself.

Dad jumped up and started pacing, flapping his jacket open and closed like it was a hundred degrees before he announced, "I need to get out of here." I took a deep breath, hoping he'd hold it together. A hospital was definitely not the right arena for one of his outbursts. They were rare, but when they came, I stayed away.

My body was sticky with sweat by the time I climbed into the car with Dad. I slumped, motionless, in the front seat like an animal hoping to remain invisible before a predator. His breathing was heavy. Mine rapid.

He muttered under his breath, "I can't believe it."

I waited for the inevitable explosion. An explosion that never came. I could only assume more cell phone restrictions would be put in place once Josh was able to drive again. And for me, if I ever got my license. Driving practice had already plunged to the bottom of my priority list weeks ago.

****

Thoughts of what might happen to my brother had been eating at me all night, but I wasn't about to ask Dad. After he dropped me off at Harborview the next morning, I took my chance with Mom when we went to the cafeteria for coffee. An aid was with Josh, cleaning him up. Now that he was coherent, he preferred privacy anytime something bordering on embarrassing was happening to him.

"Last night, after I went home, did you guys talk more about the accident?" I asked.

She nodded. "It was easier to have a rational discussion once your father left." She sighed, but her face remained expressionless. "It's good it's all in the open now. He needed to get that off his chest."

"Are you going to tell the police?"

She shook her head. "It's not up to us. Josh is eighteen and will soon be well enough to give a statement to our insurance company. But I don't think this will make much of a difference. They've already accepted liability based on everyone's statements and the police report. Not sure if he will need to speak with the police or not."

"Oh." After a few more moments, I asked, "Is he

going to be punished?" I hoped not. I knew my brother. He had to be racked with guilt.

She turned and gave me a sad smile. "I don't know. They don't have parenting rulebooks for situations like this. Part of me thinks he's already been punished enough. He'll have to live with this for the rest of his life. He knows he was lucky to survive. I'm pretty confident he's not going to even touch a cell phone in the car from now on." She sipped her coffee. "I suppose your father and I'll have to work out some sort of punishment. But with everything going on, that's the least of our concerns right now."

Poor Mom. She had the weight of the world on her shoulders. And I thought I was stressed.

****

I was struggling with an algebra problem at the minuscule table in Josh's room when I overheard him tell Mom about a dream he had about his upcoming graduation. "Oh, and Aunt Kelly's family and Uncle Greg were there. Even Grandma Mattison."

I stared at the quadratic equation in front of me, but the numbers blurred. My attention was on my brother.

"That sounds nice," Mom said. "But don't count on your grandmother. You know she doesn't like to fly."

"And it was a gorgeous day. Wow. Wouldn't sunshine be something? We'll be lucky if it doesn't rain."

No way! That's the exact dream I conveyed. Although I thought I'd been getting through to him, I didn't truly know what it felt like. Besides, I didn't believe he'd comprehend the dream, let alone remember it, being in a coma and all. I wanted to jump up and down right then and there. But of course, I couldn't.

Mom took a deep breath. "Let's not worry about the weather quite yet. I'm just hoping to get you home soon."

Similar incidences happened over the next few days. When he returned from physical therapy stinking of sweat, he told us he couldn't give up. He referred to his dream and insisted he'd be there, walking on graduation day. My heart swelled with pride. I'd always known he had a can-do personality but was thrilled he kept latching on to the dream. I must've conveyed it successfully, at least in part, and prayed I hadn't created false hope.

One day he seemed down and frustrated, so I re-conveyed the dream, which seemed to invigorate him the following day. I was shocked. It was working.

Josh was also obsessed with Dr. Johnston. He asked him all kinds of questions as the doctor completed his evaluations. Josh said he'd always planned to go to medical school but had never known which field to pursue. He'd thought perhaps cardiothoracic surgery, like our dad, but now was considering studying the brain. Dr. Johnston liked his enthusiasm and offered to tour him around his department for a day this summer. Maybe even arrange a volunteer position in neurosurgery during college if Josh became serious about it.

Could I have conveyed the dream about the neurosurgery residency as well, or was Josh's behavior a side effect of Dr. Johnston being so influential in his recovery? My dream must've played a part. Although I was overjoyed, my success was bittersweet. What dumb luck to finally learn how to do it after leaving

Dickensen. Once I officially withdrew, I assumed the skill would be taken from me along with the rest of my Dream Management knowledge.

****

I'd been dying to talk to Josh about his dreams but hadn't known how to go about it. Besides, he was never alone for long. I had to know if after all these months of failure I'd actually conveyed to Josh, a person more adult than child. Or was it wishful thinking?

But today, Dad was at his hospital, and Mom was at her own clinic where she worked part-time. She planned to take a leave of absence but wanted to organize everything there to make it easier for the physicians who would take over her patients.

I had to take advantage of this opportunity.

"So you've had some dreams about graduation…sounds like they were pretty amazing." I tried not to be too obvious, but over the course of fifteen minutes, I managed to ask several detailed questions. My heart beat faster and faster as he answered each one accurately. I confirmed I did convey both dreams, multiple times, and—just as impressive— they'd stuck with him.

Eventually he asked, "What's with all the questions, sis?"

"Just curious. I rarely remember my dreams, but you've been talking about yours nonstop." Then I steered the conversation to safer topics, summer and UW.

I returned to my homework when an orderly arrived to help him into a wheelchair and take him to physical therapy.

When Josh returned and the medical personnel left,

Josh caught my eye. "I believe you somehow made me dream those dreams."

My stomach somersaulted. I did my best to play dumb. "What? How could I do that?"

"No idea. But I can't get them out of my mind. While I was in the coma, I had this recurrent dream about graduation. Then I had another about becoming a neurosurgeon. I was thinking perhaps being in a coma made my dreams more intense, but I dreamed about my graduation this week too."

I kept a poker face as I listened. *I can do this.*

"So today I replayed them in my mind during physical therapy since you asked me all those questions beforehand." He snorted. "And PT is so boring. I recalled seeing you in one of them. You were talking about Dickensen Academy and how they were teaching students to be…dream-makers?"

I averted my eyes but could feel my cheeks flush. *Uh-oh. Now what?* Never in a million years would I have put those words into a dream if I thought he might receive it *and* remember it.

"I knew it!" he cried, grinning ear to ear. "Part of me thought it was some crazy result of my brain injury."

I leaned over his bed and caught his eye. "You can't tell anyone! I'll get in so much trouble…they'd expel me or send me nightmares." Then something worse came to mind. "Or maybe send you nightmares."

"Calm down. I'd never tell. Who'd believe me anyway?"

I took a deep breath and gazed toward the ceiling for a moment. "You're right. But getting expelled doesn't matter anyway. I'm not going back."

"Why not?"

I snapped my head back to face him. "Why not? Are you kidding? I've been sitting by your bedside for over three weeks! I thought you might die. I'm not leaving now. I'm going to stay home with you. With Mom and Dad."

He smirked. "But I didn't die. I'm going to be fine...well, one day. Besides, if you return there, you'll be home in two months. You'll be here for my graduation." He winked. "I saw it in my dream."

"But the dream wasn't real. I made it up and conveyed it to you." He scrunched up his face and tilted his head, so I explained, "I created a perfect graduation day dream because that's how I believed and hoped it'd be."

"Well then, that's how it'll be." He sat there smiling, all cheerful and confident, like his old self. "That dream pulled me out of my coma. Every time I had it, I experienced this overwhelming urge to wake up, so I could return to school. I think my mind somehow forced me to wake up once my body was healthy enough."

"Really? I didn't know it could do that."

"It did for me. You have to go back so you can learn more."

I shrugged. "Well, I wasn't good at it. Until now, I've never been able to send a dream. I didn't think I could. And then there was Dad's voice in my head telling me it was impossible."

"I'm telling you that you did it."

I stared at him, unable to one hundred percent trust what he said was true.

"Many times."

I jumped up and paced the room. "I'm way behind in Creative Core. I'm not sure if I can catch up. At least not well enough to earn an A. Dad was furious when I got a B minus in it last semester."

"Leave Dad to me." Then Josh looked out the window and his voice lost some of his enthusiasm. "Never mind. I don't think he trusts my judgment these days." He took a deep breath and turned back to me. "Maybe you can do better this time?"

"Maybe. But not until you're out of this hospital."

"Fine."

"Fine."

We stared stubbornly at each other until I almost burst out laughing at the silliness of it, but Josh caved first. "In the meantime, tell me more about this dream-making."

I'd already spilled the secret, so what could it hurt to tell him everything since he promised never to repeat a word? I sat down on the edge of his bed and began with the dream I received last summer before my appointment at the testing center.

My brother listened, only interrupting to ask me to clarify a point here and there. He didn't think it was silly or childish. He thought dream-making was remarkable and could be an asset to my future in ways I couldn't yet imagine.

He was right. Telepathy was much more powerful than they'd told us. I'd never thought beyond education and entertainment and the occasional nightmare, but it had genuine real-world benefits. I could no longer focus on my fears.

I went on to explain about the academic dreams, including the language immersion ones. Josh paused his interrogation long enough to ask me a couple questions in Spanish—he'd been taking Level Four at Haller Lake. He was blown away when I spoke almost as well as him, yet with a flawless accent. He pointed out that even if I didn't do anything with the dreams, the education alone was worth attending for three more years.

****

Back home, as I got ready for bed, I examined myself in the mirror. I had a fresh round of zits and my cheeks had hollowed—a weird combo. I twisted around. My pants no longer fit right; they were practically falling down. I didn't realize how much stress I'd been under the past month. Maybe it was time to focus a little on myself.

I went to my desk and pulled down my wall calendar. I'd been gone almost four weeks, although one was spring break. My missed midterms would be a challenge, but I'd manage them somehow. Fortunately, I'd kept up with all the homework and continued to receive academic dreams. Dad had even taken over the role of algebra tutor when I got stuck. I sighed. It'd be nice to get back to my school tutor—he had a sense of humor and made math somewhat fun—not to mention my study sessions with Ben. But I had to admit, Dad no longer dropped remarks that made me feel stupid like he had over winter break. In fact, he admitted a few days ago he was sorry Josh's injury was taking such a toll on me.

The one class that might cause trouble was Creative Core. I needed to not only pass Dream Management but to pull up my grade significantly. Yes, I'd conveyed to Josh several times, but I doubted either of those dreams would count for the course. I'd already received approval for four of the six required dreams. With over two months of the semester left, I'd have plenty of time to develop the remaining two. The only question: could I get through all the required conveyances?

Chapter: 40

Our family was gathered around Josh's hospital bed, eating pizza, when Dad turned to me. "I think it's about time we get you back to school."

I blinked then glanced at my brother. "Can't it wait 'til he gets home?" I didn't want to say it in front of Josh, but I'd hate to return to Dickensen Academy only to be whisked back home again. The possibility of seizures still existed, which could cause a setback. He'd only had a minor one this past week, but still.

Mom exchanged a look with Dad, then turned to me and took a deep breath. "We've been discussing enrolling you at Haller Lake."

My chest tightened. That's what I'd been afraid of.

"Then you can visit after school each day," Mom explained.

Josh gave me an encouraging nod, which helped steel my resolve.

"Once Josh gets out of here, I want to go back to Dickensen."

"Really?" Mom's voice was pitched high with surprise. "I thought you'd want to stay in Seattle. I mean, after all this, Josh is just starting to get better." He had continued to make both neurological and physical improvements, but although the doctors were calling his recovery miraculous, he still struggled with retaining new information and couldn't walk more than three feet without assistance.

My gaze darted between Mom and Dad. Not long ago I wouldn't have even considered negotiating, but now I had to try. "I think it'd be easier to return there than transfer to a new high school so late in the year. You know, they might cover topics at separate times, and I'd have to get used to new teachers and everything." I swallowed hard. "It's only two more months. I'm not saying I'll go back next year. But at least for now."

My words hung in the air.

Dad licked his lips, and Mom rubbed her hands together.

"Besides," I continued, "we're only talking about waiting a few more days. Aren't the doctors hoping to discharge him within the week?"

Dad turned to Mom. "Liz, she has a point."

Did I hear him right? My pulse quickened. Had *Dad* supported me for a change? I kept the momentum going. "I'm almost caught up with my homework, and my teachers said they'd work with me on rescheduling my midterms."

Dad turned up his mouth a bit. "Looks like someone did her research."

I smiled and tore at the pizza crust in my hands. Compliments from him were rare.

Mom dropped her head and closed her eyes for a moment. "But…it's been so nice having you home."

Josh gulped down a bite of pizza. "She should go back. Unlike me, Autumn has a chance of catching up in her classes. But you know, without her around, I might be able to focus better." When my parents weren't looking, Josh winked at me.

Mom sighed and studied the three of us. "Looks like I'm outnumbered."

Bursting with joy, I leaned closer to give her a big hug. "Thanks, Mom!"

****

Before I returned to Dickensen, I needed to make more progress with Dream Management and confirm conveying to Josh hadn't been a fluke. The last thing I wanted was to return only to fail.

The next evening, I offered my aunt and uncle a date night, insisting a night with the kids would be good for me. After my cousins were asleep, I kneeled on the floor next to Alex—based on the disastrous dream review with Skylar at Christmas, an eight-year-old now seemed a better choice.

This past week, I'd analyzed what I'd done differently with Josh compared to Aditi, Hannah, Skylar, and Brady. Concentrating on each individual conveyance step had been tripping me up. It had been the wrong mindset. I hadn't done that with Josh, and I wasn't about to do it now. Confidence took over my mind as I immersed myself into the story rather than focusing on transferring exact words into my cousin's brain. Then I let the conveyance run its course.

The following morning, Alex woke up jabbering about opening presents under the Christmas tree. Uncle Michael thought it was an unusual dream to have in April, but I simply listened to my cousin rave while a flood of joy ran through my body.

In the afternoon, I phoned Alex. She was ecstatic someone had called for her. I was careful to talk about a variety of activities we did the previous night but interspersed questions from the *Dream Review*

Checklist. It was clear: Alex remembered.

The next night, Josh agreed to be a participant, so I conveyed a more complicated version of *Dream Two*. I hadn't told him any specifics about the dream, so although he knew it was coming, he was unprepared for how giddy he'd feel, almost like attending a Seahawks home game.

I was finally ready.

Chapter: 41

Wednesday morning, I lay in bed, staring at the ceiling. Still dark. I rolled onto my side and hugged my pillow but couldn't fall back to sleep. I was wide-awake, full of anticipation. Today I was returning to Dickensen.

Josh had been discharged yesterday. He'd slept in the guest room on the main floor last night so he wouldn't have to struggle with the stairs. Mom had probably stayed there too, to make sure he was still breathing and everything.

Footsteps passed outside my bedroom door. The stairs creaked. My alarm clock displayed 6:08. May as well get up too. The house was chilly, so I threw on my bathrobe and plodded down the stairs.

I found Dad in the kitchen filling his travel mug with coffee while Zoey chowed down her morning kibble from her bowl on the floor. No sign of Mom or Josh yet. Although with the meds Josh took, he might sleep 'til noon.

"Hey, you're up," Dad said.

"Couldn't sleep."

He nodded. "Big day." He twisted the lid onto the mug and returned the creamer to the fridge. "It's going to be tough. Just do your best."

I waited for something more, but then he gave me a quick hug goodbye and disappeared out the garage door.

I sat at the table, my body somewhat numb and in shock. He still hadn't said a word about my grades. Not that I expected a lecture as he rushed off to work, but it was like a new person had invaded Dad's body ever since the night of the accident. He hadn't even drilled me about school since I'd been home; he simply offered legitimate help. Probably the stress. But with Josh back home and our lives gradually returning to normal, his controlling side would likely reappear in no time, and he'd demand those As.

Hours later the doorbell rang, interrupting me as I was double-checking the contents of my messenger bag one last time. In the past month I'd managed to leave texts and notebooks in practically every room of the house.

I inhaled sharply—Mrs. Humphrey stood on our front porch. I don't know who I expected to bring me back to school, but definitely not her. In my mind, she only existed at Dickensen. But after my initial shock, I changed my face into a grin. I couldn't imagine another faculty member I'd prefer to ride with.

Mom shuffled into the entryway with Josh in his wheelchair. No school for him yet. He didn't have the stamina to get through a seven-hour day. And of course, they had to consider the chair. Haller Lake was a three-story building. Rumor had it an elevator existed somewhere, but no one ever used it.

"Mrs. Humphrey, good to see you. Care to join us for a late breakfast?" Mom asked.

"So kind of you, but we better get a move on. I need to get back before school lets out."

I gave Mom a quick hug. Saying goodbye to Josh

was harder. Tears threatened to fall, and I sniffled as I clung to him longer than usual.

He pulled away. "Hey, don't go worrying about me. My social calendar is packed. Let's see, I'm off to physical therapy at one. Then we have to race back to meet my new tutor. Oh, and if I'm lucky, Luke might come by with some work packets from my teachers." He grinned. "Fun times ahead."

I laughed.

He put his fingers to his temple. "Let's see, tomorrow I've got counseling at eleven and then…"

Josh's humor was exactly what I needed in my worry-filled state.

I waved goodbye, grabbed my bags, and followed Mrs. Humphrey to her—my jaw fell open—fire engine red Camaro. My eyes widened, taking it in. I staggered to the back of the car. She opened the trunk and I tossed in my things. I'd seen the car in the lot at Dickensen, but never did I imagine the sports car was my RA's.

"Is this really yours?"

She simply nodded, but her twinkling eyes betrayed her excitement. "Yes, dear. But I only drive it when the roads are clear of snow. I like to keep it looking nice."

Once I folded myself inside, the scent of leather tickled my nose. She turned the key and the engine purred to life. She turned the stereo on, filling the car with Elvis Presley's melodious voice. I had to laugh, guessing the sexy musician was the subject of Mrs. Humphrey's dreams when she was my age.

At a traffic light, I sank back into the passenger seat, happy and relieved to do something other than hang in the hospital all day. My RA chatted up a storm about my friends and teachers as we whizzed through the city, past the suburbs, and up the mountain pass.

When we reached campus, it had transformed from how it had looked in mid-March. The snow was gone except where it had been piled up. And the deciduous trees had tiny green leaves while others were covered in pink blossoms. Red tulips, yellow daffodils, and purple hyacinths had popped up everywhere. The brilliant colors contrasted with the surrounding dark evergreens. Even the air smelled sweet. Although the day was overcast, it was warm enough I could get away without my winter coat.

As we traipsed across the quad, the lightness I'd experienced during the car ride began to be replaced by my previous concerns. Had I made the right decision returning here? Would I be able to convey to Aditi? Did I seriously stand a chance at earning an A in Creative Core?

I took in the dorm in front of me, memorizing the bottom stone layer and the cream-colored structure rising from it with its rows of narrow windows and intricate designs. What if I failed and my memories of everything around me were erased? I'd hate to forget this beautiful campus and all my friends and teachers. Would Ben miss me? I bit my lip as I walked through the entry door Mrs. Humphrey held open. How was I going to study for my missed midterms on top of everything else? By the time the elevator opened on the second floor of O'Reilly, I had worked myself into a frenzy and felt I weighed an extra fifty pounds.

As we hauled my bags to my room, I breathed in and out and focused on the familiar brown carpet and door-lined hallway. I had changed since I last walked this corridor. I needed to remember that.

I unlocked the door to my room. *Oops, wrong room.* I began to close the door but hesitated and took another look. Aditi had used her month alone to clean and organize my side. Poor Aditi. She had never complained, but our perpetually disorganized room must've stressed her out more than she'd let on. I swallowed. I'd try harder.

****

Aditi eyes widened when she found me in our room after school. "Autumn!" She dropped her backpack and gave me an I-can't-breathe hug before she even removed her fleece jacket.

Her over-the-top greeting broke a protective shell around my heart, and I almost started to cry. I hadn't admitted to myself how much I missed my friends at Dickensen. I'd been in my own world back at home. There'd been a possibility I might not return, so it'd been safer to deny my true feelings. I had to blink hard to hold the tears back when she let go.

As she unloaded her backpack, I asked, "So how is everything?"

"I have so much to tell you. But Hannah and Grace will kill me if we get talking without them. I promised we'd meet up downstairs the second you arrived."

I grinned. "Okay. But I have to ask, is Hannah still having issues with Caitlyn?"

She shook her head. "Caitlyn's left her alone. But she's super tight with Tessa now. And Tessa's become just like her."

I raised my eyebrows and forced a smile. "Great. Just what we need. Two Caitlyns."

When we entered the dining hall, a group of boys

311

caught my eye. Ben was among them.

Aditi nodded to another table. "I'll be over there."

As I approached the boys' table, Ben looked up. So many emotions flashed across his face before he leaped out of his chair to embrace me in a bear hug. *Okay. He's definitely thrilled to have me back.*

After I said quick hellos to everyone at the table, Ben leaned over and whispered, "Do you want to study together this afternoon?"

His warm breath hit my neck and tingles spread out from there. "I think I'll be studying twenty-four seven for the next two months," I whispered back.

He laughed. "I'll meet you at four fifteen by the elevators."

I returned to Aditi's table where she'd saved me a spot with Hannah and Grace.

"So are you going to the library with Ben?" Grace asked.

"Yeah, he just asked me." I took a spoonful of my yogurt.

"He's been talking about you every day since you left," Aditi said. "He was beyond relieved when he found out you were coming back today."

I grinned. First the hug and now this. Ben missed me. A lot.

"I was worried you might not come back," Hannah said.

"You and me both. Josh helped me convince my parents to let me return. He believes Dickensen is a good fit for me. He always has."

I filled them in on my brother's progress, leaving out the part where I'd spilled the secret. Best if no one knew. In fact, I didn't even tell them I'd learned to convey. I wanted it to be a surprise for Aditi. I was fairly confident I could do it, but no need to jinx myself.

****

When I stepped off the elevator, Ben stood, shifting his weight side to side, staring at a mountain landscape oil painting on the wall.

I tapped him on the shoulder.

He spun around, grinned, and then started moving toward the exit.

"The library, right?" I nodded to his backpack over by the wall.

He turned a little pink before retrieving it from the floor.

As we exited O'Reilly, he asked, "Maybe we can take the long way?"

"Sure." I smiled, relieved to have some alone time to get over the awkwardness of our separation. I hadn't spoken to him all month and had only responded to a couple of his emails and texts.

"How's everything at home?"

I gave a short recap of the latest news, finishing with, "Make sure to thank your parents for the flowers. It was so nice of them."

He nodded. "We thought about visiting when I was home for break." He shrugged. "But I kind of assumed you guys wanted privacy."

"I'd have liked to have seen you. But you're right. When Josh was in the coma, visitors seemed uncomfortable. No one knew what to say."

"Well, I'm so glad he's getting better and you're back. It wasn't the same around here."

A breathless feeling filled my body. It was one

thing to hear it from Aditi, yet another to hear it directly from Ben.

He reached out and took my hand.

At that moment, with the sun shining down on us and a fresh breeze blowing, making me feel so alive and happy, I decided I wanted him to be the first to hear my news. "So I've figured out how to convey."

He twisted toward me, his eyes wide. "Really? I'd have thought you'd have taken a break from all that."

"So did I. When I got home, dream-making was the furthest thing from my mind. But then in the hospital, I'd tell Josh these stories about his recovery. At first, I think I was doing it more for myself than for him. It helped me stay positive. Then I converted my stories into the dream conveyance protocol and tried telepathy. Suddenly it was like he could hear me." I continued on with the details, leaving out the part about revealing the Dickensen secret.

"I always knew you could do it."

His comment was so sincere, I had to turn toward the forest so he wouldn't see me blushing.

"I have some news too. You know the ski dream I was trying to send Aditi?"

I nodded.

"After break, I got it through to her."

My eyes popped wide. "Through the walls?"

"Yeah. From my room. And I've done it every Sunday since."

"That's terrific!"

Ben let go of my hand and opened the library door for us. "But, Autumn—conveying wasn't the most amazing thing. It was Aditi. Your theory was right. Last weekend, we went skiing. And for the first time since

January, she begged to come."

"She did?"

"Yes! And she can ski." He let the door swing shut behind us. "She's still a beginner, no doubt, but she understands what she's supposed to do, *and* she's excited to learn."

A flush of adrenaline spread through me. Dream telepathy really did have its powers.

Chapter: 42

The halls were crammed with students rushing between classes. Loud voices called to one another. Metal lockers clanged shut. Such a change from the eerie silence of Harborview. After so much time isolated with my family and the solemn medical personnel at the hospital, diving back in among my boisterous peers was unsettling. The knots in my stomach were nearly as tight as on the first day of school.

"Hey, Autumn, you're back!" A guy from my Spanish class grinned as we passed each other in the hallway.

I swiveled my neck toward a girl's voice. "Heard your brother's finally home. Great news."

Everyone seemed to go out of their way to welcome me back. Even Principal Locke had found me earlier and told me how relieved he was to hear Josh was recovering.

As I traded a thick history book for a marginally lighter science book at my locker, a familiar voice rose above the hallway chatter.

"I thought we'd gotten rid of her."

I spun around. Caitlyn and Tessa both glanced back over their shoulders, as if to make sure I'd heard. Tessa hadn't spoken a word, but she was giggling.

My chest clenched and I scowled. "That's low,

Caitlyn. Even for you."

Not sure if they even heard me because they kept on walking.

I shook my head to push away the comment and held my shoulders high. I wasn't going to let it get to me.

****

At the end of the day, I met with Mr. Robbins to go through everything I'd missed. As the class cleared out, we talked about Josh. But the second the large room was empty, I blurted, "I learned to convey."

His eyes stretched wide in astonishment.

"I know I'm months and months behind, but I'm hoping we can work something out. I'm guessing my dad still wants to see an A."

He tipped his chair back so far it creaked. "So tell me. How'd this all happen?"

"It all kind of clicked like you said it would."

He kept nodding as I relayed the details. I skipped over the part about telling Josh about the dreams. Instead I mentioned I'd asked him unobtrusive questions to confirm key facts.

"Well, I hate that your family had to go through such a scare with your brother, but it looks like there was a silver lining for you. The two conveyances of *Dream Two* will count as completed. I wish I could give you full credit for the other dreams you sent to your brother, but they don't satisfy the freshman requirements." He grinned and wrote something in his notebook. "However, I can give you some extra credit. More importantly, I want to emphasize your experience conveying those dreams should help you master the required skills more easily."

I wrinkled my nose and tilted my head. "How so?"

"For example, you applied higher-level skills in the neurosurgeon dream where you had a two-way conversation with your brother. Even though you removed many of the variables in the dialogue by providing his words, it's still exceptional for an early conveyance."

A floating sensation came over my body.

"It'll still be a struggle to satisfy all the criteria to achieve an A between now and mid-June. I wish I could simply give it to you, but you were failing Dream Management before you left. Your biggest obstacle will be the lack of time."

He pulled out his calendar and studied it. "Hmm, eight weeks of school remaining. That gives you sixteen opportunities to convey to Aditi." He mumbled, "Not enough." He turned to his computer and opened the *Dream Calendar App*. "Looks like Ben Coleman has Aditi's next two Sunday nights. But other than those, her Sundays are available." He started typing. "I'm reassigning Ben's Sundays to you. This is a higher priority than his experiment. That'll give you eight more slots."

I rubbed my hands together. I was pretty sure Ben would be fine with it but felt a little guilty I was taking over his time.

After a few minutes, my teacher turned back to me. "Let me warn you, just because you've conveyed successfully doesn't mean there won't be setbacks. Don't count on perfection each night. Even our best dream-makers often get stuck learning new skills, and this tight schedule doesn't leave much room for error."

"Okay."

"Also, you're missing several art projects. I'll waive the ones you missed that weren't tied to any dreams. But if you're shooting for an A, you'll need to complete the rest, considering you can't convey the dreams without them."

I smiled. Skipping a few would help.

He pulled out a sticky note and wrote something down. "Give me a few days to decide the best way to catch you up in Visual Arts. I'll give you some rudimentary instructions for the lessons you've missed, but I'm sure some students could help you perfect the techniques. I'll get back to you with suggestions."

"Thanks. I won't let you down."

"Don't worry about me. It sounds like it's your father you don't want to let down."

"Right. I guess that's what I meant." Funny, but although the A would get Dad off my back, perfecting my Dream Management skills was what now motivated me most. I wanted to be as good as Ben someday.

****

I had a difficult time falling asleep because my pulse was beating like I'd downed a sixteen-ounce mocha with a double shot of espresso. I was going to convey to Aditi at one o'clock for the first time in over a month, and she still had no idea about my past successes. I couldn't wait to see her face in the morning.

As I sat in the dark, I smiled down at my roommate, my best friend. I wanted this to work. It had to work, or I'd have to leave this place. I took a deep breath and let my new confidence push aside the pressure already forming in my thoughts.

I immersed myself into the script and went through

the dream in detail: the rustle of the fallen leaves, the warm afternoon sun on my face, the fresh earthy smell, and the outdated spiel about my favorite musicians—I didn't dare change them from my October list.

Then Aditi latched on.

Or so it seemed.

The next morning, I woke before our alarm. The spring sunshine streamed through the windows. I felt different. I felt relaxed and at peace.

I rolled to my side. When I saw Aditi, my stomach went nauseous. She didn't look any different than any other morning. Her eyes were closed, and her arm clutched a lavender pillow. I was positive I'd conveyed successfully. But what if I was wrong? I'd been wrong before. I swallowed hard and stared at the clock as it worked its way toward seven.

The alarm blared and I slapped it off.

When I turned to Aditi, she was already resting on her elbows in bed, grinning ear to ear. "You did it!"

My heart skipped a beat.

"How?"

I swiped my notebook from my desk. "I'll tell you all about it at breakfast, but I need to get through the *Initial Dream Checklist* first. I can't afford to miss a single one."

Chapter: 43

The snow at Stevens Pass was soft and the sun bright. It was a relief to give myself a break after ten days of nonstop studying. My plan had been to stick to my self-imposed, rigorous schedule weekdays and weekends. School was out in less than seven weeks, and I had to make the most of every minute. But I'd given in to pressure from my friends to go skiing today in exchange for Aditi's and Hannah's help tomorrow in the art studio. We were carving animal figures out of clay in Creative Core, which relied on the sculpting techniques they'd learned during my absence. They would've helped me regardless, but it was their way of convincing me to come. Besides, as Aditi pointed out, the concept of teaching her to ski through dreams was originally my idea.

The rhythmic swooshing of my skis cutting through the shaved-ice-like snow was the only sound I could hear until I tucked and the noise changed to a soft whistle as my speed increased. I inhaled the crisp mountain air. Cool but far from freezing. It felt so good to exercise my legs after a month of inactivity. While skiing, Hannah was able to keep up with Ben and me, as long as we avoided the *For Experts Only* signs. Although her form could improve, she made up for it with her natural balance and athleticism.

We skied a few runs with Aditi after her lesson.

The exhilaration in her eyes as she glided down the hill was infectious. Back in January, they were full of fear. Yes, it was still the bunny hill, but this time she was in control and didn't fall. Looked like my theory was correct. Too bad the ski resort would close soon.

"Ben, you did it! I'm so impressed," I said.

He smiled. "Thanks. But don't forget your part in this." Then he leaned close and gave me a kiss on my near-frozen lips. I'd forgotten how such a gentle action could affect my entire body—it'd been forever since our last one. Unfortunately, I had to pull away too soon, painfully aware Aditi and Hannah were about six feet away—PDA was so not my thing.

****

Sunday night, I called home from one of the phone booths. Josh picked up. He jabbered about how his cast had finally come off, so he'd get to return to school tomorrow. As I listened, I leaned back on the wooden bench built into the wall and placed my feet high up on the opposite one, making the most of the tight space. I'd spoken with my brother almost daily this past month. We kept each other motivated. He was also on an aggressive plan, with his own set of activities: physical therapy, memory exercises, doctor's appointments, and sessions with a psychologist. Not to mention his tutoring and homework. Even after dropping a couple of classes, he was still far behind. Some days he was pretty down, but today he was in high spirits. I'd have loved to keep talking, but after a few minutes, I told him I needed to speak with Dad.

I'd been rehearsing the conversation in my head all day. Being back on campus the past week and a half was long enough to know I wanted to graduate from

Dickensen Academy more than anything in the world. And it wasn't only about becoming a dream-maker. Or even Ben. I belonged here. The school's culture seemed made for people like me. I was becoming who I was supposed to be because I didn't have to hide my true self.

"Hey, Autumn. Ready to review science? You have a test coming up this week, right?"

Dad couldn't see me, but I still planted my feet back on the ground and sat straight. "Yeah. I mean, no. I do have a test on Wednesday, but I don't want to review it right now."

"You know weeknights are tough. This is really the best time for me."

I took a deep breath. If I was going to remain at Dickensen, I needed to keep standing up for myself. "I mean, I don't want to review science with you at all."

"What?"

"I can do it on my own. I've been doing fine this year. I'd rather use my study time on Sundays the way I want to."

Silence.

I braced for the inevitable blow and softened my tone. "I appreciate everything you've done. I know it's taken a lot of time."

"You haven't even completed all your midterms."

"I know. But I'm fifteen years old, and I don't need so much help."

He paused again. "Okay. You might be right."

That's it? He didn't even sound angry. Maybe he was too busy dealing with Josh. Or maybe, just maybe, he trusted me.

"So...how was skiing yesterday?"

****

To my delight, Ben asked me to take another walk in the woods for a study break. It had only been a few days since the kiss on the slopes, and I could hardly keep my mind off him, especially after yesterday's make-out session along the trails. When he reached for my hand, I held on tight. This is what I'd longed for since September.

The forest was greener than it'd been in months. Although most of the trees were conifers, the undergrowth was full of bushes sporting shiny new leaves. The birds, back after their winter's absence, filled the woods with their melodies. As we strolled by one low hanging branch, a squirrel chittered at us in a fevered pitch until we were past. I had to laugh.

Once we were out of sight of campus, Ben spun me toward him. As my heart rate accelerated, I silently thanked myself for brushing my teeth after class.

Ben wrapped his arms around my shoulders and leaned down to kiss me. His lips were so soft and my body warmed. Soon, his fingers traveled slowly down my back. Although I wore a long-sleeve T-shirt, my body jolted at the new sensation.

I pushed back. "I don't think I can do this."

His eyes filled with remorse. "I'm sorry. Too much?"

He had nothing to be sorry about, so I leaned back in. It had felt amazing. We continued to kiss, but I could no longer let go and enjoy it. Ben's hands remained on my shoulders. He must've thought his wandering hands were the issue.

After a couple of minutes, I pulled away again.

"What's the problem?" His voice held a mixture of

confusion and annoyance.

I focused on the trees for a moment while my body returned to normal.

When I turned back toward him, I said, "It's nothing. But…"

Ben looked back and forth down the trail. "I don't get it. We're alone."

"It's…it's…can we walk?" I couldn't face him any longer.

He nodded. "Is it your brother? I tried to give you space your first week back. I know it was a big adjustment, coming back and all."

"No. It's not that." I took a deep breath. "I'm scared this is a big mistake. At least for now. Last night when I sat down to convey, I couldn't get my mind off you. And kissing you."

He grinned. "Is that so bad?"

"Ugh!" I shook my head. "This is so hard. It's just… I had a tough time blocking all that out."

"Uh-huh."

"I was awake half the night wondering if the conveyance was successful."

"Was it?" he asked with genuine concern.

I nodded. "I didn't tell you, but the week before the dance, I was starting to get some images across to Aditi. Finally. But then the following week, you know, when we started to come out here, well, the little progress I'd made disappeared. And now, I'm afraid it might happen again."

Ben didn't say anything but only stared into the forest, so I kept going. "It's still all so new for me. And I'm not like you. This year hasn't been easy."

He frowned as if he were trying to understand.

"And I've been thinking, it's not just that. But if, you know, we became a thing, it'll be that much harder for me to leave this place. And you aren't even going to be around Seattle most of the summer."

He took a deep breath and ran his fingers from his forehead back through his blond hair.

Tears formed in the corners of my eyes. "Believe me, I know I might be throwing away the best six weeks of my life for nothing. But I don't want them to be our last. I have to do everything I can to return here in the fall. And getting good grades is one of them."

Ben took a deep breath and let it out in a deliberate stream. "So that's it?" He looked around at everything besides me.

"I'm so sorry. I'm going to work on my parents. I'm pretty sure I've got them convinced to let me come back if I improve my Creative Core grade. And I promise I'm going to stand up to them no matter what. But for now, maybe we can slow down a bit? Kind of put things on hold?"

He closed his eyes and nodded slightly.

I reached for his hand. Although he allowed me to take it, it remained limp in my own. And he didn't say anything more as we walked back to campus. My mind became a turmoil of emotions and unanswered questions. I wanted to pull him back through the woods and tell him I'd made a terrible mistake. What was he thinking? Where exactly did I leave us? I hoped more than anything I'd made the right decision.

****

As the weather warmed, spring fever became contagious. Everyone seemed anxious for summer break. But not me. I wanted more time. I *needed* more time. Every once in a while, I'd catch a piercing glance from Caitlyn or Tessa, but I ignored them. After everything I'd been through with Josh, I was above petty schoolgirl conflicts.

Most of my nights were spent at the library. After about a week of avoiding me, Ben became my study partner again, but the focus was schoolwork. We hadn't talked about *us* once since that walk in the woods, and a thick wall of tension had emerged between us. I poured out my heart to Aditi and Hannah about Ben, and they assured me I was doing the right thing, although Aditi admitted she wasn't sure if she'd be strong enough if she were me. They said Ben was hurt, but he'd come around. It's not like I was choosing another guy over him; I was choosing to focus on school and Dream Management, for now. I hoped my friends were right and he'd still have feelings for me if I managed to come back next year.

I kept the grueling pace I'd set for myself when I returned. I grew so tired as the weeks passed by that once I actually fell asleep during dinner. Aditi suggested black tea—her caffeinated beverage of choice. It was disgusting, even with a ton of sugar. Nothing like the herbal tea Mrs. Humphrey served. So I stuck with diet cola.

My hard work was paying off. I'd caught up in all my classes except Creative Core, but I was making steady progress there. I continued to improve, seldom having trouble with each new skill or variation I added to my dreams. Being exhausted during the conveyances seemed to help keep my mind from racing. I was too darn tired to concentrate on multiple thoughts at a time. Thoughts of Ben now rarely snuck in.

Aditi enjoyed playing catch-up three nights a week as my dream recipient. She was glad to be a part of my excitement and relief, and she loved the increasing creativity of my dreams. She promised to do her best to avoid any boundary exploration. I didn't want her to get kicked out of a dream prematurely, which would require me to resend it and thus waste a precious night.

Before long, finals were upon us. I sat at my desk, struggling to finish my history exam while other students turned in their tests one by one. I took a deep breath, trying not to panic that my test paper was only three-fourths complete. I continued to meticulously match up dates of various wars occurring over the last few centuries. Thanks to all the cramming, I knew this stuff. Good thing because these detailed facts weren't covered in any of the academic dreams.

At last, the second semester was officially over. I went straight to bed after my final exam, and Aditi couldn't even wake me for dinner. I'd given it my best, and now it was out of my control. I wouldn't get my grades for another week. Even if they weren't perfect, Dad had to cut me some slack since I'd missed so much school.

****

I spent the morning packing and saying goodbye to my friends. We all promised to keep in touch over the summer. I kept my farewells light and upbeat, holding back my fear these might be permanent goodbyes.

Mom arrived in the afternoon. I was riding alone with her since I had so much stuff to take home. Students had the option to store their belongings over the summer, but I might not return. With our huge vehicle, we could've driven someone else, but a packed

328

car was a good excuse; I wasn't in the mood to talk with anyone for the long ride home…especially Ben.

Before we pulled out of the parking lot, I told Mom I'd forgotten one thing. I hoped Aditi was still in our room. I wanted a private goodbye.

I found her packing, humming a playful tune. The sight reminded me for the millionth time how lucky I was to be given the gift of such a wonderful roommate. How many times had her cheer gotten me out of a funk this past year?

My eyes became moist as I gave her a tight squeeze. "I'm going to miss you so much."

After a few moments, Aditi pulled away, held me by the shoulders, and looked me in the eyes. "Stay positive. All your studying had to boost your grades. And your dreams have been incredible. You'll be back."

"Hope so."

She grinned. "You could always resort to begging."

I gave a hint of a smile. "Maybe." I'd been developing a strategy if my parents tried to make me transfer. Although I had asserted myself more during the past two months, I hoped my resolve wouldn't crumble when I moved back home.

I jogged to the car where Mom waited.

As we drove away, I faced backward until the buildings were out of sight. "I'm going to miss this place."

"We have all summer to decide."

Chapter: 44

The moment our SUV stopped in the garage, I jumped out and raced into the house. Mom said Josh would be home. As I burst into the kitchen, Zoey started hopping on her hind legs, blocking my path. As I stooped to scratch behind her ears, I did a double take.

"Grandma?"

Grandma Mattison sat hunched over the table beside Josh in the kitchen nook, the sunlight from the window lighting her silver hair. She studied me through her wire-framed glasses. "Autumn, is that you? My, you've grown so big."

I dashed over to her, with Zoey stuck to my side, and wrapped my arms around her bony body. Joy spread throughout me. I couldn't remember the last time she'd flown in from Albany. "I didn't know you were coming!"

"Well, I had to when your father told me all about those fancy graduation dreams your brother had where I showed up at his ceremony."

"Pretty cool, huh?" Josh said.

I walked around the table and gave him a big hug. It was a relief to see him looking more like his old self. He'd gained some weight, and color had returned to his cheeks.

"Look at your hair!" I touched it gently. "It's so long."

Josh ran his fingers through it and turned his head side to side. One-inch, light brown strands covered the shaved patch, although the incision line was still visible. "Might grow it a little longer and see what it's like." He shrugged. "But I don't know. I'm also considering cutting it short again to show off the scar. It's badass."

Grandma's hand flew to her mouth. But it looked as if she were covering laughter rather than shock.

He checked himself. "Sorry, Grandma."

I shook my head. *Silly brother.* "Let me see your arm."

He lifted it up. The scar near his elbow had already faded to pink.

"Much better." Looked like this spring had been good for him too.

****

Josh's high school graduation was set for late afternoon on Saturday. Surprisingly, the weather cooperated. June could often be overcast and rainy, but today the temperature hovered around eighty degrees without a cloud in sight, so Mom and Dad were already moving tables and chairs into the backyard for his party. When Mom commented on the gorgeous weather, Josh said, "I knew it'd be this way. I heard a pretty accurate forecast." He winked at me.

Josh had been selected as one of the valedictorians. Since only a few grades from this past quarter were calculated into his GPA, he maintained the 4.0 he'd held back in March. Although his final GPA might fall when he completed his most challenging courses—calculus and physics—during summer school, there wasn't a teacher or administrator at Haller Lake who didn't believe he deserved to be one of the valedictorians and participate in the ceremony. He'd been busy writing and practicing his speech over the last couple of days but was frustrated at having to rely on his notes. He was still having a tough time with memorization.

"You should've been more specific in my dreams instead of summarizing," Josh teased. "Then I wouldn't have had to develop this speech from scratch."

I laughed nervously and glanced about, as if the walls could hear. Being able to put the exact words in his mouth by conveying a dream was not something I wanted advertised. "Be careful when you say stuff like that."

He acted like the Dickensen secret was our inside joke, although it was no joke. I was going to have to have a serious talk with him, *and soon*, to make sure he understood the danger.

Josh grinned. "Don't worry."

****

"Pomp and Circumstance" played, and the graduates in their green and gold silk robes marched into the huge gymnasium.

"There's Josh." I pointed him out to Mom. "In front of Luke."

She didn't say anything.

I turned to my side. Her eyes were moist. Perhaps the music and the typical emotions shared by many parents at seeing a child graduate were to blame. More likely, it was because not long ago she'd thought this day might never arrive. In truth, only when I was actively conveying that dream over and over did I wholeheartedly believe Josh would graduate with his class.

Partway through the ceremony, Josh approached the stage for his valedictorian speech. Although it was a huge school and he'd always been popular, by the decibels of the cheers, news of his accident and miraculous recovery had obviously spread far beyond the student body.

Josh shuffled his notes and adjusted the microphone. "Good afternoon." When the gym fell silent, he continued, "I would like to welcome you to our high school graduation. I am here today, thanks to...thanks to..." He glanced down at his notes. "I am here today thanks to many of you. As you may know, I almost didn't make it because of a terrible car accident back in March."

My heart ached for him. Josh had to be disappointed he had to read his speech, but everyone outside of our family probably chalked it up to nerves instead of his brain injury. Hopefully his memory problems would improve soon.

After several minutes of encouraging words, his gaze glued to his notes for the most part, he ended with, "My accident changed my perspective. I was lucky to learn at such a young age how priceless life can be. It inspired me to become a better person because I now realize I only have one chance to live my life. Don't live in the past, live today...and remember to dream." Just then, he looked directly at me. "If you work hard, your dreams will become your reality."

My heart skipped a beat. That line hadn't been in the speech he'd practiced in front of me. I glanced over at Drew's Uncle Tom—likely the solitary dream-maker in the entire audience besides me—who sat with Luke's family off to our right. He looked like he'd swallowed an insect. I took a deep breath and clasped my shaking hands. Lots of graduation speeches were full of stuff about dreams. His uncle couldn't possibly tie them to me. Maybe it was my imagination that he looked so uncomfortable.

I gulped as I refocused on the stage.

Josh left the podium and everyone burst into applause. His fellow graduates on the gym floor stood and cheered. Soon everyone in the bleachers joined the standing ovation. Through my tear-filled eyes, I saw even Dad's eyes glistened as he clapped enthusiastically.

****

Our family gathered on the steps in front of the school to take photos. The weather was so bright I had to squint, and the pictures would surely have dark shadows, but Josh swore he wouldn't have it any other way.

When we arrived home, Julia and our cousins, Alex and Skylar, were waiting out front. The little kids dragged my brother out of the car and toward the house. Inside green and yellow helium balloons covered the ceiling, and a huge sheet cake with a tiny, green, plastic graduation cap and diploma sat on the dining room table. Even Zoey wore a mini graduation hat. Someone had been hard at work setting up for the party. As it turned out, it was Lisa, Uncle Greg's girlfriend, who was arranging appetizers on the table outside. I hadn't even known she'd come to town. But maybe I should have. I'd put her in Josh's dream.

Guests came and went throughout the evening. A feeling of warmth wrapped around me. I was home, surrounded by family and friends. I wouldn't have been as excited about a graduation if not for the accident. I'd assumed high school graduation was a given for both of us. Josh's accident made me appreciate everything more. However, part of me felt more like an observer, and I couldn't fully immerse myself into the celebration. In the back of my mind, I was worried about Dickensen and my report card and was already missing my other friends. I pushed those thoughts from my mind as best I could.

The doorbell rang, and Zoey began barking.

Josh was nowhere in sight, so I ran to answer it. It was probably Drew. He'd promised to stop by when he could step away from his own brother's celebration taking place across the street. What if he came with his uncle? My body tensed. Until Josh's speech I'd been eager to talk Dream Management with him in private. But now I wasn't so sure.

I opened the door and froze.

It was Ben.

He held up a package wrapped in silver and blue foil paper. His eyes met mine for the first time in nearly two months, and they held only happiness. The anger and hurt were gone. "I wanted to stop by and give this to Josh."

I bit down on the smile, which was probably lighting up my entire face. Then I held out my hand.

Chapter: 45

Four days later, I received an email from Dickensen Academy. It could only be one thing: my report card.

As I stared at my inbox, I wiped my sweaty palms on my cotton shorts. These grades could impact the trajectory of my entire life. I held my breath and clicked it open.

****

June 19 at 2:08 p.m.
Subject: Semester 2 Grades—Dickensen Academy
Joan Rothchild, Dean of Students
To: Autumn Mattison

~*~

Autumn K. Mattison
Year 1—Semester 2
History: A-
Science: A-
Physical Education: A
Spanish 1: A
Algebra 1: B
Language Arts: A
Creative Core: A-
****

The third time I read the screen, the heaviness that had been weighing me down for so long vanished. I'd proven I was more capable than either Dad or I had ever thought possible. And I'd done it on my own. I grabbed my notebook and opened it to the page which read *Reasons to Allow Autumn to Return to Dickensen Academy*. My handwriting already covered three-fourths of the sheet. I grabbed my ballpoint pen and at the very top, under the title, squeezed in the simple word: *grades*.

A word about the author...

Dickensen Academy is Christine's debut young adult novel. After graduating from the University of Washington, she earned her MBA at the University at Albany. She honed her technical writing skills in marketing and consulting but attributes the creative part of the process to her passion for reading.

When she isn't reading or writing, Christine can often be found running, skiing, or hiking. She lives in Newcastle, Washington, with her supportive husband, two avid teen readers, and their energetic wheaten terriers.

Connect with Christine online at:

http://christinegrabowski.com

Facebook: christinegrabowskiauthor
Goodreads: Christine Grabowski
Instagram: @christinegrabo
Twitter: @christinegrabo

CPSIA information can be obtained
at www.ICGtesting.com
Printed in the USA
LVHW080138031218
599034LV00009B/154/P

9 781509 221233